THE DECLARATION

A Novel

WILLIAM
HIRSCH

ISBN 978-0-9884149-1-4

First Edition 2012
Second Edition 2016

For information regarding special discounts for bulk purchases, please contact Echo Lake Books, 1131 7 LKS N, West End, NC 27376 or bhirsch@williamhirsch.com

What Readers Are Saying about *The Declaration*

"I thoroughly enjoyed this book - once started I didn't want to put it down. If there is anybody who doesn't understand "absolute power corrupts absolutely" - this book spells it out."

"Texas governor Brewster Steele thinks he's found the answer to turn his state's fortunes around and begins to implement his plan… The plan? To exercise their state's rights to the letter of the US Constitution, and as some believe, even beyond. Is the stage set for a second Civil War?"

"*The Declaration* is a novel, full of today's current events wrapped in a story that will hold your interest and make you think."

"A thought-provoking book full of what-ifs, why-nots, and could-happens. It's also a very chilling political thriller that provides page-turning entertainment even if you don't wish to be drawn into its brand of political thought and possibilities."

"If you are looking for a quick read, that holds your interest and makes you say 'HMMMMMMM, I wonder if we CAN do that,' read this. More importantly it encourages you to say, 'If I don't take politics seriously, shame on me.' I thought it was thought-provoking."

"The split between the political parties gets wider and the states want the burden of Federal mandates without attached funding lifted. President Sanchez will do whatever he needs to do to maintain power. Governor Brewster Steele needs to pull Texas out of its downward spiral."

ACKNOWLEDGMENTS

It takes a special person to put up with a writer who is wrestling with a story. And my lovely wife, Maureen, is just that special person. I must thank my friends who listened to me bounce story ideas off of them and several of whom read drafts and offered encouragement. And I would like to extend a special thanks to Michael Levin, my writing coach, advisor, and editor. His expertise and support were terrific.

"Timid men prefer the calm of despotism
to the tempestuous sea of Liberty."

- Thomas Jefferson -

Declaration of Interdependence

THIS STORY IS EITHER a warning or a prediction. But it might be the solution. That's for you and every other American to decide. This story is fiction, but it reflects the truth. My hope is enough people will read this and do something to stop the inevitable.

America is a country of individuals who have always enjoyed the freedom to make their own way in life. Our freedom is unique, and it is fragile. It can erode quickly. We can easily take it for granted and let it slip through our fingers. It can also be used against us, as we see happening every day. America's success in making our lives safe and comfortable has bred complacency in our society. Now we sit at a tipping point where those who get from the government outnumber those who give to the government. This is unsustainable. Sooner rather than later, the payers into the system will be overwhelmed by the demands from those who get from the government. Our monstrous debt will crush us. The system will collapse.

I often wonder how this can be reversed or if it can. If we truly want to save America as it was founded and as we have known it, we must rely on ourselves and on each other. Do we have the courage of our founders to risk everything to preserve the "Idea of America"? Are we willing to give up our comfortable status quo to renew freedom for our children and grandchildren? We are the generation with the opportunity and obligation to preserve this "Last Best Hope on Earth." And we must rally together or it will be lost.

I thank you in advance for reading this story. Please tell your friends. The more people who read this, the more chance we have to set this country back on the path of greatness.

William Hirsch

Part 1

The Campaign

CHAPTER 1

*"All men having power ought to be
distrusted to a certain degree."*

- James Madison -

WITH NINE DAYS until the election, she still trailed by twelve points even in the most sycophantic polls. Florida was crucial, as always. It was time for the Hail Mary speech. She needed to deliver a message that would galvanize her supporters. Four years ago, she had watched President Carlos Sanchez manage to rally large numbers of unlikely voters to come out and carry him to an equally unlikely re-election victory. She watched how Sanchez had created an irrational fear of his opponent in the minds of enough voters to eke out a second term. It worked for him. And she desperately needed it to work for her now.

Vice President Theresa Goodwin Lewis stood tall and struck her signature pose. She was so close to being the first female president, she could practically smell the flowers in the Rose Garden. But the roses were wilting along with her poll numbers.

"That Oval Office should be mine," she muttered through a forced broad smile.

With her chin slightly raised, she appeared to rise above the bonds of earth as if in direct communication with the heavens. Or so she hoped. She'd learned the pose and its magical effects on audiences by watching Sanchez for the past eight years. But somehow it never seemed to work for her as it had worked for him. Usually the media would call her aloof each time she used it.

"What to those bastards know?" she thought as she stiffened her back and gave it all she had.

Theresa Lewis was supposed to be President Sanchez's unofficial third term. They were supposed to be creating an American dynasty of elite liberal presidents. One after another who could straighten out everything. Lewis despised the fact that the Constitution required her to go through the agony of an election just to gain the office she rightly deserved.

With a regal nod, she acknowledged the energetic applause and pointed toward a group of public service union members who, under the orders of their union leaders, had taken one of their fifteen annual personal days to come hold placards in the warm October sun. Each poster held a three-quarter silhouette of Lewis from the shoulders up, striking the pose and framed with her election year mantra: "Dreams Can Be...Reality." As if on cue, the chant began. "Dreams Can Be...Reality!" "Dreams Can Be...Reality!"

Lewis smiled and waved to the rest of the crowd. Beyond the throng, she saw Secret Service sharpshooters patrolling the nearby rooftops. Her eyes drifted to the second floor windows of the Miami Freight and Shipping building, but she quickly looked back out to the crowd.

Gesturing for silence, she took her place at the podium. Behind her, four majestic Corinthian columns, along with a dozen American flags, defined the speaker's platform. Another campaign feature borrowed from President Sanchez's campaign playbook. She had opposed Sanchez in the primaries eight years ago, but faded before they ever got to South Carolina. Sanchez waltzed into the White House from there. But Lewis knew that her chance would come. When Sanchez suggested she join his ticket as the vice presidential candidate to coalesce their combined support, she jumped at the opportunity. That decision led to eight years of agony sitting in the backseat of the Sanchez administration. But it was all worth it to get to this moment as the Democratic nominee.

Over his terms, Sanchez had doubled Federal spending. Lots of goodies went back to states and districts who supported him. Lewis was confident that she could claim credit for most of those projects and reap the votes that would come with the pork barrel spending since she was usually sent to represent the administration whenever a new bridge or federal building was opened. Unfortunately, based on the polls, the gratitude did not turn into electoral support.

The governor of Florida, also trailing in his re-election bid, was noticeably absent. Governor Chalmers had formally sent his regrets along with the excuse he was urgently needed at a ribbon-cutting ceremony for a new wastewater plant in Clearwater — a project that cost three times the estimates, was paid for, in part, by the President's, and by extension Secretary Lewis', highly touted Economic Jumpstart program, and failed to create a single job. In reality, Chalmers, in keeping with his often-used campaign strategy of not being seen with losers, welcomed the excuse to keep his distance from the politically toxic presidential candidate.

At the Lewis's right, Miami Mayor Al Rivera sat grinning. He had already assured his own reelection through strategic handouts of taxpayer money and could risk an association with Lewis. And on the off chance Lewis won the White House, Rivera would be repaid for his loyalty many times over with pork from federal taxpayers directed his way by her administration. He had nothing to lose and a possible windfall to gain. The Sanchez administration had been outspoken critics of the favorable treatment Cuban exiles got once they hit the shores of Florida, while Mexicans were being deported and turned away at the border. The irony of a Cuban and a Mexican supporting each

15

other seemed to prove the rule that politics makes strange bedfellows.

"Thank you, Florida!" Lewis called out.

The crowd erupted once more. Scattered among the audience, "facilitators," as they were called, rallied enthusiasm like cheerleaders. The chant of "Dreams Can Be...Reality" began again. Lewis tried to speak, only to be drowned out. She smiled and motioned for the cheering to stop. But the facilitators spurred on the uproar by holding up signs reading "Dreams" for half of the audience and "Reality" for the other half. The chant got tossed back and forth from side to side.

"Dreams," came the cheers from the right. "Reality," came the cheers from the left.

After a minute, the Lewis spoke and the facilitators hushed the crowd.

"Dreams can become reality," she said. "And we're halfway there!"

The roar began again, intensified with recorded cheering piped through the PA system. News cameras panned the audience, recording the event for the evening news.

Beyond the crowd, Special Agent Hank Samson left his post. He gave a quick glance toward the other agents, who were busy scanning the crowd. Unseen, he slipped into the Miami Freight and Shipping building and closed the door behind him. Samson climbed the steel spiral stairs to a catwalk above the massive loading dock doors and found the dispatcher's loft. The shipping company had declared bankruptcy a year after exhausting the last of their chunk of the federal Economic Jumpstart money Mayor Rivera had dished out four years earlier in a grandstand effort to aid his last re-election bid. That bit of federal largesse saved Rivera, but not Miami Freight and Shipping.

Samson slipped on thin rubber gloves embossed with another man's fingerprints. He reached under the dispatcher's console and plucked a semi-automatic rifle from the magnetic bracket he had installed while sweeping the building that morning. The gun was where it was supposed to be. Romeo Costa, the chief of Lewis's Secret Service security detail, had come through as promised. It was all going down according to plan.

When he had been approached by Costa a month ago, Samson expected to be fired. He had foolishly voiced his negative opinion of the President several times and he knew his days were numbered. He had grown to despise the man he was sworn to protect. Samson had his reasons. But had Romeo Costa, the President's closest ally, the man who had been with him since his earliest days as an activist in Southern California, also turned on the President? Was that the reason Costa was recently assigned to Vice President Lewis and away from the White House. Certainly Sanchez had broken most of his many idealistic campaign promises. Samson was convinced Costa had turned when Costa spun the story of his family in the Gulf. Costa told him how their lives had been damaged by the oil spill and ruined by the President's edict banning off-shore drilling. The latest presidential order to curtail all shipping of petroleum products through the Gulf of Mexico wiped out what few oil industry jobs remained.

The federal relief Sanchez promised never materialized. Despite the tough talk and soaring rhetoric, the President's boot seemed to slip quickly from the neck of Big Oil when the campaign coffers needed refilling. Now rumors of illegal campaign contributions coming from Mexico were spreading through the Washington grapevine. The money was purportedly quid pro quo for blocking competition from American oil companies and giving Mexico unfettered access to some of the richest oil reserves in North America. Near tears, Costa told Samson how his personal plea to the President met deaf ears and even mockery.

Costa's story was fiction. His family made their living in real estate in Chicago. But Samson bought it hook, line, and sinker.

"The man's out of control," Costa insisted. "The President's been bought and paid for by corporate America and rich, foreign investors. He doesn't give a shit about the real people who work hard to take care of their families. It's all campaign bullshit. He secretly hates America and is doing everything he can to tear it apart one brick at a time. His presidency's illegal. He was born in Mexico and brought here as a baby when his parents crossed the Arizona border."

Samson had read the stories. When he heard how soldiers, some of them men from his unit, died while frantically evacuating Afghanistan during a botched pull-out, he began to believe Sanchez was actually working against his own country. After Romeo Costa showed him secret documents proving that both President and Vice President had actively blocked the support the troops needed to make a safe exit from that war-torn country, he knew the man and his puppet successor had to be stopped. Today, Samson would help make Sanchez and Lewis pay for their betrayal. They had another man who would take out the president almost simultaneously with him popping Lewis. Somebody even further inside the White House. Samson didn't let himself speculate about who it might be. Probably someone he'd worked with for years. Certainly another patriot like him.

Costa told Samson that wealthy and powerful men wanted Sanchez and Lewis dead at any cost. The money had been deposited in a Swiss account in Samson's name, as promised. His plane ticket was in his pocket, and his new identity in Costa Rica awaited him. They had rehearsed it. After the shots, Costa would be the first to enter the warehouse. Together, Samson and Costa would race out of the building, in apparent pursuit of the assassin. In the chaos that would surely follow, Samson would slip away.

Samson adjusted the stabilizing tripod, rested the gun on the dispatcher's desk, and aimed the muzzle through a corner of the window he had broken out during the morning sweep. Carefully, he centered the Vice President's head in the powerful scope. All of his training as an elite Army sharpshooter was about to save his country, he thought. He had done this a dozen times in the rugged wasteland of Afghanistan. One shot was all he would need. But this felt different. He had an American in his sights, not some Taliban raghead. And not just any American: he was centering the crosshairs on possibly the first woman President of the United States.

Samson took a deep breath and slowed his heartbeat. He pulled back from his emotions and let his training take over.

"It takes more than eight short years to do a job this big. Let's push on and finish what President Sanchez started," Lewis called out to the crowd. "I'm asking for your support. I'm asking you to send me back to Washington to get the job done. Will you finish the job with me?"

"Yes, we will! Yes, we will!" the crowd yelled, again bolstered by a recording blaring through the loudspeakers.

"Then join me next week and show the world what America can be. Corporations have exploited American workers and oppressed this country for far too long," Lewis said, continuing the outrageous rhetoric that had become the mantra of her campaign.

Her campaign staff had warned her that continuing Sanchez's vilification of corporations and making faceless business entities the villains and oppressors of the lower class would never work. But Lewis disagreed. Her instincts were right. Her characterization of large corporations as essentially the second coming of Hitler worked like a charm. She knew people needed someone other than themselves to blame for their troubles. And corporate America was an easy target. The tactic had helped close the gap in the polls. The question now was whether she could motivate her followers to actually come out and vote.

"We need every vote to end the slavery of the American people. We will not be victimized by Wall Street power brokers."

Lewis did not have Sanchez's public speaking skills. He would instinctively time each pause perfectly. Her cadence was usually stilted and forced.

"We have done much. But there is much more still to be done. When the President was elected, this country was in turmoil. Never had the economy been worse, worse than even the Great Depression. From the moment of my swearing in as vice president, I have worked tirelessly with the President to repair the damage left behind by the previous administration. We saved the nation from falling into the abyss of financial ruin. But two years ago, with the help of greedy special interest groups, the Republicans ruthlessly seized control of Congress. There are those who claimed the elections were illegitimate. There were those who felt they were disenfranchised. Legal challenges were thrown out by Republican appointed judges. Now, I don't know the truth of any of these charges. But I do know we cannot dwell on the past. Our future lies ahead. We must move forward!"

Another round of "Dreams Can Be...Reality" arose. Lewis raised her hands to quiet the crowd.

"On election day, you have a chance to right all wrongs. You have a chance to control your future, to write your own destiny and save this great democracy. If you vote for me, I will focus like a laser beam on the powerful forces that oppress the citizens of this great land," Lewis said as she involuntarily glanced at the freight warehouse.

"Focus this, you bitch," Samson thought as he squeezed off a round.

The pop of the rifle could barely be heard above the chanting crowd. The side of a Corinthian column exploded behind Lewis. Samson looked through the scope in disbelief. He never missed. How could this be? Costa was supposed to calibrate the scope. He was supposed to test fire the rifle and make sure the crosshairs were precisely on target. Costa was an expert marksman himself. How could he have overlooked such an important detail?

Samson had no time to ponder the question. In a split second, he gauged the miss and made a mental calculation. This time he would go for the body shot. More room for error. He aimed low and to the left to compensate for the faulty scope. He squeezed and half of the "Theresa for President" emblem fronting the podium shattered like a window pane.

At the first shot, Secret Service Agent Kowalski's instincts took over. From his position at the edge of the stage he dove to shield the candidate. The second bullet hit just as Kowalski caught the side of Lewis's knee. They tumbled to the safety of the floor behind the bulletproof podium. Lewis's head smashed one of the teleprompters, and she heard a sickening snap come from her left knee. Kowalski heard it, too, and knew exactly what it was. He'd snapped enough ACLs while playing linebacker at Ohio State to know the damage he'd inflicted. But the candidate was alive and safe beneath him.

On cue, Romeo Costa ran through the door of the freight warehouse, gun in hand, and scrambled up the spiral stairs. Samson turned.

"The scope was screwed up," Samson said. "I missed."

"Right," Costa answered, with the coolness of an executioner.

"But I…"

Samson never got a chance to finish the sentence. Costa raised his gun and squeezed the trigger. The bullet tore through Samson's head, jerking him backward. He was dead before he hit the floor. Costa peeled off the dead man's gloves and pocketed them. He carefully reached into Samson's black suit jacket and prodded Samson's handgun from his shoulder holster with a pen. The gun fell free. The only fingerprints on it were Samson's. Costa kicked the gun to Samson's left, the dead man's dominant side, and waited for the swarm of agents that would follow the shots like moths to a light on a moonless night.

CHAPTER 2

"The citizens of the U.S. are responsible for the greatest trust ever confided to a political society."

- James Madison -

"YOU'VE GOT NO BULLET HOLES. The guy must have been a bad shot," Doctor Fernandez told Lewis with the straight-forward candor of the old-school doctor he was. Secretly, Fernandez wished he could ask Vice President Lewis if she had just experienced actual Islamic extremist terrorism or if this was just some workplace violence. But that was a discussion for another day. Today, his job was to see to it the possible future leader of the free world would live.

"You're in good medical condition, albeit a bit banged up," Fernandez said. "You have a head laceration that we stitched up nice and neat. And your knee is a bit of a mess. But neither of those things will kill you."

That was the final diagnosis that ended nearly two hours of controlled chaos in the emergency room of Sacred Heart Hospital.

Lewis was moved to not just a private room, but a private floor. Every patient on the crowded top floor had been relocated within an hour of her arrival in the emergency room. Security was as tight as the days immediately following 9/11. Gunshots aimed at a presidential candidate could only mean one thing: there was a serious hole in the safety net that was the Secret Service and no one knew where the hole was yet.

Secret Service agents prowled the corridors of every floor and patrolled the rooftop. Across the street, any building with a clear view of the Lewis's hospital room window was evacuated and locked tight. Only Lewis's personal physician and three thoroughly screened staff nurses occupied the nurses' station. All other staff had been moved to other floors. An agent manned each elevator and the top floor stop was reprogrammed to be key-access-only.

The door to the Lewis's room was locked and guarded by two agents. Lewis's husband was on a business trip to the Bahamas with his long-legged blond personal assistant. Lewis had given strict orders to keep them there. The last thing she wanted was her publicity hound husband stealing her air time. Her only visitor, Romeo Costa, sat in the chair next to the bed tapping on his encrypted smartphone. From her hospital bed, Lewis turned up the volume on the aging television to hear Warren Tufts, the GQ slick anchorman for KBS News, describe the day's top story.

"Today, at one-thirty-seven, on a sunny October afternoon, shots rang out in an apparent attempt to assassinate Vice President Theresa Goodwin Lewis at a campaign rally in Miami," Tufts said with genuine concern. "Details remain sketchy. Here's what we know at this moment. Witnesses reported hearing four shots come from two different directions. Separate shooters are suspected. The initial shots were followed by several more reportedly coming from a vacant warehouse. These accounts of the event are, as yet, unconfirmed. The extent of the Vice President's injuries has not been disclosed. Her campaign has issued a statement saying that the she is alive and undergoing emergency treatment."

A video showing a chaotic scene filled the screen as Tufts spoke. Images of people running in all directions alternated with pictures of the damaged podium. The video switched to an obscured view of Lewis being lifted onto a stretcher, blood streaming down her face. The video ended as a Secret Service agent shoved the camera to the ground. The clip looped endlessly. A Chyron graphic dubbed the event, "Mayhem in Miami."

"I repeat," Tufts continued, "we do not have confirmation of the extent of the Vice President's injuries. It appears one of the shots may have hit her somewhere in the head. Initial reports are that she was conscious but unable to walk."

"Always good to hear news reports that you're not dead," Lewis said.

"It's the same report on all the channels," Costa said. "They all have their medical experts diagnosing your injuries from those videos. You want me to straighten out the facts?"

"Let them go nuts until the West Coast news hour. It'll hold the audience," Lewis said. "What did Sanchez have to say?"

"The President said this was clearly a case of a rogue gunman who is upset that the planet is dying," Costa answered.

"Very funny. Did he mention terrorism?"

"Yeah, right," Costa said. "He doesn't know how to pronounce the word. But he did say something about gun control. I wasn't paying that much attention."

"Damn, I just thought of something," Lewis said suddenly. "The shooter wasn't Muslim, was he?"

"Uh, I didn't check."

"I hope to hell not," Lewis said. "That could flip the whole narrative. That's Roberson's top campaign issue."

"I'll check," Costa promised.

"Is Roberson getting any airtime?"

"Just a fifteen-second bite that they haven't bothered to repeat, yet. He expressed his sympathies and is praying for you," Costa said.

"That's touching," Lewis said. "I'll bet he's pissed. Less than two weeks until the election and now the *Post* won't print his name until the Style section."

Senator Wes Roberson was the junior senator from Arizona, a former border town sheriff, and the Republican presidential nominee. In less than two years, the brash and outspoken Roberson galvanized his conservative following by digging his heels in on the explosive immigration issue and embracing the Tea Party movement. He came to national prominence by sponsoring bills to repeal President Sanchez's federalizing of health care and the recent controversial Personal Identity Protection Act, government's answer to the growing problem of identity theft. Opponents of the bill warned that the PIP Act, as it was known, would give a brand new government agency access to and control of the personal information of every American. Critics claimed the program was ripe for abuse, but Sanchez argued that everyone, not just the rich, were entitled to identity protection and it was as much a constitutionally guaranteed right as life, liberty, and the pursuit of happiness.

Efforts to repeal both of the bills died quickly beneath the President's veto pen, but the effort and notoriety of Roberson's crusade against the bills pushed Roberson ahead of his rivals. He easily defeated billionaire New York Mayor Jonathan Potter. Potter had been strongly backed by the party establishment, but damaged his chances when he backed a controversial mosque near the World Trade Center site. Roberson, and a majority of voters, had no trouble painting Potter as a Muslim sympathizer who failed to see a problem in allowing a mosque to be built where 2,606 innocent people died at the hands of terrorists dedicated to the Muslim faith.

"Damn, my ass is sore and my leg's killing me," Lewis complained as she tried to adjust herself. "What the hell did Kowalski think he was doing? Dumb jock. I never saw him coming."

"He was known for hitting low in college ball. I guess old habits are hard to break," Costa said.

"The docs want to operate. They say my ACL's torn. The surgery has to wait a few weeks for the swelling to go down. But they're making me wear a fucking brace," Lewis moaned.

"How's the head? You on anything?"

"Sore on the outside, but clear on the inside. I told them to go light on the painkillers. The teleprompter took a chunk out of my forehead. Four stitches. Bled like a sonofabitch. One good thing. Kowalski gave us a terrific visual. There's always a silver lining. I'll bet it looked like half my head got blown off. You get some close-up stills for the media?" Lewis asked, still in campaign mode.

"They're getting sent out as we speak. They ought to make the evening news hour, although the timing's moot since they run news nonstop even when our beloved future Commander in Chief isn't on her deathbed. And we got some great video footage of you going down. The shots hitting the podium and the column behind you are clear as day. It's the Zapruder film on steroids," Costa said, referring to the famous home movie of the Kennedy assassination.

"Let them run the photos without any explanation so the rumors can get ramped up. I still want the media time. Save the video for my statement. Never let a disaster go to waste." Lewis grinned then grimaced when she tried to move her injured leg.

"Nine-thirty Eastern," Costa said. "That will give the West Coast news shows thirty minutes to babble but still catch most of the country in prime time. It'll be past bedtime for the Florida seniors, but they'll catch it on The Morning Show."

"We'll be interrupting Sunday Night Football."

"It should be halftime about then," Costa said. "They agreed to delay the start of the second half until you're off the air. And we've agreed to stall your start time if the first half runs long. At this point, they don't know it will be you. All they know is that there will be an official statement. We can add the teaser that you'll be addressing the nation just before you come on, just like if you were already the president. That'll hold the audience."

"Perfect. Can't mess with football. Guns, religion, and football. The three pillars of middle class America. We can regulate guns and vilify religion, but football is the heroin of the people. It's even more powerful than us."

Lewis winced when she laughed.

"Damn it. I need a cigarette. What about the shooter?"

"He's dead, Ma'am."

"The gun?" Lewis asked.

"Lost in the chaos. A cold trail. The FBI will suffer a lot of crap over that screw-up."

"Christ, you didn't lose the damn gun, did you?"

"Hell, no," Costa said with a touch of resentment. "I did some recycling to save the planet. That's why the FBI can't find it. Right now that gun's a plug of scrap metal. Soon it will start its new life as a hood on a Honda. You could call it my witness protection program for illegal weapons."

"I didn't mean to doubt you," Lewis said. "And how's our mole doing?"

"He said he'll have everything set within twenty-four hours."

CHAPTER 3

"The natural progress of things is for liberty to yield, and government to gain ground."

- Thomas Jefferson -

ROBBIE TREXELL HUNCHED OVER his keyboard typing strings of code in furious bursts. He paused, popped a fresh piece of Juicy Fruit into his mouth, and took a gulp of his supersized McDonald's coffee. The big cup had been sitting next to his keyboard for nearly half an hour and by now was only slightly warmer than room temperature, but Robbie didn't care.

It was late on a Sunday afternoon and the headquarters of the Bureau of Identity Protection was like a morgue. On a typical Sunday, a couple of the young and zealous staffers would drop in to catch up on work, a practice usually frowned upon by veteran federal employees. Stay with the flow and don't make waves. That was the strategy for rising in pay grade and avoiding a transfer to another department.

But this wasn't a typical Sunday afternoon. Someone had shot a presidential candidate and that meant no one even thought

29

about work — except Trexell. He had an important job to do. He thought of himself as a sort of techno minuteman. His country needed him, and he would answer the call 24/7.

It was taking him longer to crack the database than he had expected. Trexell was a geek's geek. He dreamed in computer code. He even named his dog "Byte." For him, hacking was better than sex. And it paid well. Considering his string bean build, a face ravaged by teen acne that still blossomed from time to time, and his total lack of social skills, opportunities for sex were nonexistent for Trexell. But in the world of computer espionage, he was a regular Fabio. Today, he was servicing the hottest and richest horny housewife of them all. Today, he was the President's, and by extension the presidential candidate's, gigolo. Trexell couldn't care less whether his clients were from red states or blue states. His only interest was in green, the kind of green with pictures of Ben Franklin.

In the name of protecting the identities of millions of Americans, President Sanchez's signature legislation, the Personal Identity Protection Act had consolidated every piece of private information on every citizen and most non-citizens into one enormous database. The PIP Act proponents promised the greatest safeguards ever seen. The President himself said that he would personally guarantee the safety of private information. He said it was the most important piece of legislation ever passed and was a cornerstone of his legislative agenda. It would launch the United States as the leader in identity protection and create, or save, a million jobs. He pointed out how billions of dollars are lost each year to cyber-pirates, and those dollars often went overseas, thus depleting the struggling economy. By the time he was done making his argument, the President had called identity theft the greatest threat to the security of the United States, impugned his predecessor, ridiculed the Republicans, and blamed a lack of government regulation of the technology industry for causing the problem, and said the only solution was his three-thousand-page bill that Congress needed to pass immediately or risk catastrophe.

The details of what was in the legislation would be clarified later, but America would love it once they saw its benefits.

This was known in the White House inner circle as the Sanchez Triple Play, or the STP for short. Call the problem the worst ever seen, blame your opponents for creating the problem, and declare that only more government could solve the problem, and only if we act fast. Even the President himself continued to be amazed at how well it worked and how hard it was for the Republicans to defend against the tactic.

The PIP Act got pushed through Congress in early December almost two years ago following the now famous Great November Massacre. The midterm elections had been devastating for the incumbent Democrats. The economy was in the toilet, jobs continued to be lost despite the administration's claims to the contrary, and several colossal bills were rammed through Congress despite overwhelming opposition from the voters. Voter outrage was at an historic high.

Leading the pack of unpopular bills was the universal health care act, known officially as the Wellness Security Act but disparagingly called the Washington Socialist Act. The WSA never enjoyed popular support. Democrats blamed the biased media and the usual Republicans for the negative public reaction and said their message had been suppressed and distorted. They claimed the Republicans were racists for opposing the bill, saying that opponents were afraid of the growing numbers of minority voters and wanted to shorten their life expectancy by denying them proper health care. But the majority of voters did not buy it. Lawsuits followed from many states, and the polls took a dramatic turn against the sitting Congress. The November midterm election flipped a Democrat super-majority to a slim Republican majority.

But the majority was tenuous and was a majority only if the nascent Tea Party members were included as Republican votes. Democrat leaders sought revenge for what they characterized as a "seizing of Congress." Before the January swearing in of the new

Congress, the lame duck session, with its super-majority, rammed through much of the President's remaining legislation, legislation they dared not pass prior to the election. Now they had nothing to lose and had a chance to get in their last licks.

The controversial Marriage Equality and Family Rights Act, MEFRA, overruled state laws banning gay marriage. The Wireless Information Neutrality Act, WINA, placed all web-based commerce under the control of the FCC, opening the floodgates for claims for equal time. The Madsen GRA Act eliminated private retirement accounts, seized all existing accounts, and brought all pensions under federal control. And the Federal Roadway Consolidation Act, FROCA, placed control of all toll roads and bridges under the Department of Transportation. Toll revenues now went to Washington despite the fact that the bulk of the operating and maintenance costs were the responsibility of the states. Dozens of lawsuits challenging all of these bills were still stuck in the courts. And the ones that did not get tossed out by liberal judges along the way were destined to eventually land in the Supreme Court.

Over the objections of his outspoken atheist wife, President Sanchez signed the stack in a Hollywood-style ceremony on Christmas Eve in front of the Nativity scene at the National Cathedral, calling it, "The greatest nondenominational holiday present the nation had ever received." The metaphor of the three Wise Men bearing gifts dripped with irony.

"The salvation of America is born," Sanchez had crowed in a transparent ploy to link his policies to Christianity's most sacred holiday. "This is the most important legislation of the modern era. Prior to this historic occasion, the gap between the rich and the poor, the haves and have-nots, the privileged and the forgotten has grown to be the largest in history. For years, no administration has taken stronger action to correct this basic human inequity. In fact, the previous administration caused this gap to widen. The Republicans sought to block this important legislation. Now, with quick action by the Democratic Congress, America is poised to lead the new age of human rights. Millions of people will be saved from the oppression of years past. I thank Congress for moving swiftly and giving the nation this important gift."

The speech was another Sanchez Triple Play. In reality, the pile of legislation constituted the largest takeover of the rights and powers of the individual states by the federal government since the New Deal. The Constitution was being interpreted in ways unimaginable, and the legal battle lines had formed.

At the top of the pile was Sanchez's crown jewel, the Equitable Immigration Act. The vote on the EIA was extremely close. It was opposed by every Republican and even a handful of outgoing Democrats who feared for their safety and the safety of their families if they supported it. The President threatened several corporations with the choice of losing plum government contracts or offering lucrative, post-election lobbying jobs to selected outgoing senators and representatives who would support the bill. The behind-the-scenes dealing, the characterization of the bill as reform, and a launching of repeated claims of racial discrimination by the bill's opponents managed to let the EIA squeak through. The deciding vote came from a disgruntled Republican who had lost to a Tea Party candidate in the primaries. He voted for the immigration bill in a final fit of spite before emptying his desk. Death threats followed, and he never returned to his home state. Throughout the process of passing the immigration bill, the President postured as a savior of the oppressed and a leader in a heroic crusade. For two years, Democrats were successful in stalling the legal challenges to the EIA, keeping them out of the Supreme Court until after the presidential election.

Red state outrage overwhelmed the President and he spent most of his second term below a forty percent approval rating. Meanwhile, Wes Roberson's popularity skyrocketed. The tough talk, his appeal to the sovereignty of the individual, and his advocacy of states' rights were so effective he claimed his party's nomination without a serious challenge. He was the voice of what he called the American "country class," the people outside of Washington, the people outside of government, who work hard every day to better themselves and their families. He railed against what he called the "ruling class," the people in the government, from both parties, elected and appointed, who thought they knew better how every American should live, making rules and regulations that they often exempted themselves from.

And Wes Roberson was squeaky clean: a family man with three grandchildren, a church-going Baptist with a warm word for all, and an engaging smile that softened his tough guy image. His unyielding stance on illegal immigration and his challenges to the authority of Washington earned him the mocking nickname of "Clint" Roberson by his opponents. As a gun-toting Arizonan, the mockery was actually seen as a compliment by his followers, and signs bearing the message, "Go ahead, make my day," became fixtures at every Roberson rally.

Robbie Trexell raised his arms in triumph as Wes Roberson's identity file popped up on his computer screen. He was in. He scrolled through Roberson's bank accounts and added several entries. He tweaked his credit rating. He grinned when he added a bankruptcy fifteen years ago. That wasn't on the list. It was Trexell's personal contribution to the cause.

He tapped the keyboard and found Roberson's police record. It was blank. The man had never even been stopped for speeding. Trexell popped a fresh stick of gum in his mouth, took a gulp of his now room temperature cold coffee, and started typing.

CHAPTER 4

*"If the American people ever allow private banks to
control the issue of currency, first by inflation,
then by deflation, the banks and corporations that will grow up
around them will deprive the people of all property until their
children wake up homeless on the continent their fathers
conquered."*

- Thomas Jefferson -

A N AMERICAN FLAG ON the right and a Florida flag on the left framed the speaker's chair. On the television monitor, the Cardinals were trailing the Bears and Joe Hawkins, fresh out of retirement for the third time, was leading another frantic drive to take the lead going into halftime.

"There's no way I'm stepping in front of that," Theresa Lewis said. "Hawkins has a higher Q score than me."

Lewis was making her way from a wheelchair to the desk in the hospital media room. She'd never been much of an athlete, although in a moment of ego fantasy at a campaign stop she had claimed to have tried out for her high school football team. Coordinating the crutches was next to impossible for her.

"You're gonna have to get better with those, Ma'am. You look about as awkward as when you threw out the first pitch for the Nationals," Costa said.

Lewis glared. She'd heard way too much about her twenty-foot moon ball. The blooper had been replayed on late night television for a week. Conan said the radar gun clocked Lewis's pitch speed at five miles per hour less than rush hour traffic on the Washington Beltway.

Lewis settled behind the desk and checked the teleprompter. She wore a blue bathrobe with a floral collar. A fresh bandage covered the stitches on her forehead framed by perfectly hair-sprayed hair. She smiled and winked at the female technician as she adjusted the lighting. The young woman would have given Lewis the finger if jobs weren't so hard to come by. But with her husband laid off for over a year, she forced a polite smile.

"The half's over, Ma'am. We'll hold a couple more minutes so they can run their commercials and give a brief intro," Costa said.

"Did Hawkins do something miraculous as time ran out?" Lewis asked.

"He threw a twenty-five-yard pass to the corner of the end zone," Costa answered.

"Well, that will bring joy to St. Louis," Lewis said with a "Who cares?" tone. "Good thing we're ahead there since half our audience will have their heads in the refrigerator looking for another can of beer."

Costa did not bother pointing out to the candidate that the Cardinals had moved to Arizona years ago. The "ready" light came on. Lewis took a deep breath and exhaled through tight lips. None of this came easy for Lewis like it did for President Sanchez. The technician cued her in.

"Good evening, my fellow Americans. Today, in a futile act of desperation, the powerful forces that oppose change in America attempted to alter the course of history and end my campaign and our historic revitalization of America. An attempt was made on my life. Fortunately, our mission to improve the lives of millions of Americans and set this country on a path toward total equality and justice could not be stopped by a would-be assassin's bullets.

"Thanks to the heroic action of the Secret Service, I was not hit. The injuries I sustained were a byproduct of the quick and effective response by those who bravely stand by my side.

"I want to thank all of you for your prayers. My injuries, while painful, are not life threatening. At no point was I incapacitated."

Lewis imagined great cheering inside the Washington Beltline with that reassuring news since that was about the only part of the country where she enjoyed a substantial lead. Hopefully the day's events and those that were soon to come would pull many more key districts around the country into her camp. Sympathy is a powerful emotion, she hoped.

"I remained conscious and in control throughout the ordeal. The good people here at Miami General Hospital have been extremely kind to me and I thank them for all of their efforts. Tomorrow, I will be returning to the campaign trail and resuming my mission to continue what President Sanchez has begun. I will continue to repair the damage to America that was caused by earlier Republican presidents and influential lobbyists.

"What we witnessed today demonstrates the lengths to which our opponents will go to stop what is right and just. My administration will work tirelessly to move the control of power in this country away from massive corporations, Wall Street fat cats, and rich special interests. We have moved to protect every individual, no matter their race, ethnicity, or personal lifestyle. Clearly, this threatens the powers-that-be. Clearly, they will resort to anything to maintain the oppressive status quo. Clearly, today's events are a culmination of their fears that a new American way of life is dawning. But an assassin's bullet cannot stop what destiny has preordained.

"You elected President Sanchez and myself eight years ago to carry out a mission. We have made significant progress on that mission, but the job is not yet complete. The Republican administration that preceded us and their destructive policies left enormous damage, much more than could be repaired in eight short years. We began our mission to rescue America with vigor. But two years ago rich special interests seized Congress, and our efforts were stalled. The Republican Congress has blocked each and every attempt we've made to continue with our mission of putting this great country back on track. They have openly wished for our failure and lied about issue after issue. They have placed countless roadblocks in our way. Because of the irresponsible actions of this Congress, progress has slowed. There is much more to be done.

"Today, destiny spared my life. I believe that happened for a reason. I believe I was spared so I could complete our mission of setting America on the proper path. I have a dream of a better America, an America where every individual, no matter race, religion, or place of birth, can have a safe home, proper health care, enough food to eat, and safety from poverty. That dream can be reality.

"Today's events are a vivid reminder of how powerful the forces against us are and to what extents they will go to preserve their stranglehold over the citizens of this great land. In eight days, you will have the opportunity to right the wrongs of the past. You will have the opportunity to put the errors of this nation's past to rest. You will have the opportunity to prevent what one misguided individual and the evil forces that sent him on his mission were trying to do. Do not think your vote is unimportant. Every vote counts. Your vote is more powerful than any assassin's bullet. Your vote can keep me on my mission. You can keep this country moving forward.

"Thank you for your prayers and your support. Good night."

The technician signaled they were off the air, and the klieg lights dimmed.

"What'd you think?" Lewis asked.

"Perfect," Costa answered. "The Republicans will be pissed. They'll claim it was a campaign speech and demand equal time."

"Fine. They can have it. But they'll be up against America's favorite quarterback."

Costa's cell phone rang. It was their campaign manager. Costa handed it to Lewis.

"We've got the social media metrics in, Theresa," Tony announced.

"I'm fine, Tony. And how are you?" Lewis asked.

Social skills were foreign to Delgado, but Lewis didn't care. She hired Delgado for his ruthless campaign strategies and complete focus.

"You're only five points back now. That shooter took you down, but he gave you a big bounce in the polls. A "#Theresashooting" hash tag went up on Twitter before they even got you in the ambulance. The Tweets are flying. And they're coming heavily from your base. That's good news. It means they're getting energized. And more importantly, people who admitted they probably wouldn't bother to vote are now determined to come out and support you. It's unbelievable."

"There are silver linings everywhere, Tony," Lewis said with a grin. "We're within striking distance."

"That was just the first barrel from our double-barreled shotgun," Delgado said. "In a couple of days, we'll pull the other trigger."

CHAPTER 5

"There are risks and costs to action. But they are far less than the long range risks of comfortable inaction."

- John F. Kennedy -

AS THERESA LEWIS AND her team debriefed, a thousand miles west of Miami, at the southern edge of Texas, a high-tech stealth Shallow Water Interceptor gunboat cruised quietly across Falcon Reservoir, beneath the glittering celestial blanket of the Milky Way. Texas governor Brewster Steele adjusted his life jacket over his bulletproof vest and watched their wake dissolve into the darkness.

"You sure you want to do this, Governor?" Ensign Harper asked. "Never know what's out there."

"This ain't my first rodeo, Ensign." Steele said. "I need to see what you're up against here. I can't just sit in Austin and read reports about our border problems. And it's a lot more persuasive when I can say I've seen the problem with my own eyes. It validates the severity of the issue when I press the legislature for funding."

This was not an election year for him, but Steele was so popular at home, there would be little need for him to campaign when the time came for another term. His record of turning the state's finances around, guiding it through the Great Recession, standing firm for a tight border with Mexico, his recent confrontations with federal regulators, and an unyielding stand against accepting Syrian refugees into Texas gained him folk hero status in his home state. Brewster Steele was a Texan's Texan who always stood his ground. He had a reputation for living by a strict code of conduct and expecting others to do the same — just one of the things that made him so despised by the left. And part of his code of conduct was seeing things for himself.

"The wind's freshening. We'll be fighting this chop all the way," Harper said. "But that's good news. The waves will hide our wake. We're gonna run our patrol upwind, working our way north, so the wind'll mask our sound. We'll go by the flooded city of Old Guerrero where those honeymooners said they were attacked."

Only a soft grumble of the heavily muffled engines gave any hint of their presence.

"How do you know when you're in Texas or in Mexico?" Steele asked.

"We don't always know, Governor. The reservoir straddles the Texas-Mexico border making the location of the line fuzzy at best. And the GPS is not dependable when it comes to finding that line"

The long Southwestern drought had finally broken, and the Rio Grande was slowly refilling the lake. The shoreline was back near the tree line, and the numerous coves were navigable again.

"You like your new toy, Ensign?" Steele asked.

"It's sweet, sir," Harper said with a grin. "Normal radar can't see it, it's armored, and we got plenty of top shelf electronics. What's not to like? And it'll outrun anything the drug lords got, except maybe a cigarette boat. But they won't use those on the reservoir. Too noisy and too hard to hide. They're usually in tricked-up fishing boats, trying to look innocent. Sometimes they like camo Zodiacs for a fast jump. We can run those things down all night long."

"And the Feds still don't know we've got this?" the governor asked.

"No, sir. They don't know much about what goes on here. Last year they promised us a hundred new agents. They all took desk jobs, or they sometimes ride the shore on daylight patrol. Once in a while a Fed boat goes out. But chances are that's a lone wolf working both sides. Meanwhile, we've got citizens vanishing and Mexican police chiefs losing their heads."

"The Anderson case," Steele said. "That couple on their honeymoon who went missing. Mexico said they'd crossed the border, but there was no proof of that. President Sanchez publicly demanded justice, but Mexico's impotent against the cartels."

"The Gulf Cartel used to control this area," Harper explained. "Now Los Zetas has pretty much pushed them out, but the Gulf hasn't given up yet. The Andersons must have ridden their jet skis where they shouldn't have. My guess is they got between the two sides and simply got caught in the crossfire.

"Not too long ago the Mexican government actually hired the Los Zetas Cartel to run the Gulf Cartel out of the area. They were a sort of mercenary army for the government. Juan Esparrosa, the Los Zetas boss, is the Mexican president's cousin, so you can figure out how that went down. Things were fairly calm for a while. Now it's heating up again."

"Our sources say the cartel is trying to establish a strong-hold on our side of the border," Steele said.

"That's what we hear, too. The police fear for their lives, so they have no choice but to go along with Los Zetas. The Feds say they're working on the problem and told us to stay out of it. They tell us it's under their jurisdiction because it's a U.S. border issue," Harper said.

"Well, Ensign, the state of Texas has no plans to sit back and watch its territory being invaded a bite at a time," the governor said.

"I hate to say it, sir, but the drug cartels have more money and bigger weapons than we do. They've got a damn rocket launching helicopter, for Christ's sake."

"Son, Texas Rangers always stand their ground."

"I hear you, sir. But even when the federal agents show up with their nice shiny badges, they aren't much help."

"We don't need no stinking badges, Ensign," Steele said. "We need manpower and firepower."

Harper caught the reference to the classic line from *Blazing Saddles* and laughed.

A gunshot echoed across the water.

"You got anything on the radar, Scotty," Harper asked the first mate.

"No, sir. Not yet. There doesn't seem to be anything out on the lake. Probably came from the shore."

Harper scanned the horizon through night vision goggles.

"You can see gunfire two miles away with these, Governor," Harper said, handing him a pair. "Shots make a bright flash you can't miss."

"Boat movement ahead to starboard, sir. Coming out of Arroyo Leon Cove. They're moving slow. It might be a patrol."

"Let's head over there and see what's cooking," Harper said. "Can you identify the craft?"

"Looks like the Feds," Scotty said. "That's strange. It's almost two in the morning. We never see them out at night."

"I've got visual," Harper said. "Gunfire."

A second later the sound of three single shots arrived.

"I've got a second boat on the screen, sir. Looks like a fishing boat."

Governor Steele watched green silhouettes and a couple of flashlight beams through the goggles. The faster boat was circling the fishing boat. He heard a garble of shouts.

"Those Feds are fools," Ensign Harper muttered. "They've got a twenty-eight foot inboard with no protection, and they waltz right in there thinking their badges will protect them."

"Which boat is the Feds?" Steele asked.

"The low slung one," Harper answered. "See how they're circling in. Right now they're asking for identification. The druggies will have all that. Papers are real easy to get."

Steele watched the two boats merge. Harper kept sliding his boat quietly closer. The outlines of the men were easy to pick out. Suddenly arms started swinging and shouts rose up in Spanish.

"I only see one man on the Fed boat," Steele said.

"Then he really is a complete idiot. Here's where the trouble starts," Harper said. "He's in deep shit now, and he still doesn't realize it. Either the Mexicans' papers didn't fool anyone or there was some sort of deal going down and now it's gone bad. Only one Fed? I'm betting on the second option."

"What kind of deal?" Steele asked.

"Some of the federal agents work both sides," Harper answered. "I'll bet you this guy's been taking protection payments from one of the cartels and the rival cartel found him out. Now he's caught in a turf war."

Another shot and a splash. Someone gunned an engine and the federal boat took off. The fishing boat came to life with a roar and turned to chase it down.

"Looks like a fishing boat but runs like a jet boat, Governor. I told you the druggies had all kinds of toys."

Harper leaned into the throttle. The stern dug in, lifting the bow. In seconds, they were clearly gaining on the fishing boat that by now was nearly on top of the Fed's. Through the night vision goggles Steele saw green flashes come from both boats. The Fed carved a quick figure eight, desperately trying to swing behind the Mexicans and gain a strategic edge. But the Mexican boat was too agile. The maneuver only let the Mexicans gain a full broadside on the Fed.

"What now?" Steele asked.

"Thanks to you, Governor, we have a few toys of our own," Harper answered. "Scotty, give them a little fireworks show."

The first mate lifted a shoulder-fired grenade launcher. A flash lit the night sky and an instant later the engine exploded on the Mexican fishing boat, splitting the stern like firewood. Two men leapt into the reservoir.

"These are only baby grenades, sir. But heat seeking. They run right up the exhaust pipes. Those folks probably aren't dead, just nicked up a bit and scared as hell. The druggies aren't so macho when we take away their guns."

The Fed boat reacted quickly, circling back to the wreckage and hauling the Mexicans out of Falcon Reservoir. Harper sidled alongside and saw a face he knew.

"Agent Harrison T. Perkins, I do declare. What brings you out on a night like this?" Harper asked.

"Ensign Harper," Agent Perkins sputtered.

"To the rescue. And don't get too attached to those two," Harper said with a nod to the Mexicans. "Those are my prisoners."

"You're out of your jurisdiction, Ensign Harper," Perkins barked. "And this is no concern of yours. Get the hell out of here before I drag you in for interfering with an agent of the United States government."

"And that's the thanks I get for saving your sorry ass?"

"You had nothing to do with it, Harper. I had this under control and then their engine blew."

"Correction. We made their engine blow. That was no asteroid that hit it. I got it on video in case you want to watch the rerun. I never knew you could run that fast. Did your deal go bad?"

"Watch what you're saying, Harper. You think the FBI will believe a Texas cop over a federal agent?"

Ensign Harper swung a leg over the gunwale and slapped handcuffs on the Mexicans. "Usted está bajo arresto," he told them. He pointed to Perkins.

"¿Sabe este hombre?"

No answer. He kicked the Mexican in the tailbone.

"¿Sabe este hombre? Do you know him?"

"Sí."

"Thought so. We can do more talking mañana," Harper said. "And you're going to need to join us, Agent Perkins. You have some explaining to do. I want to get it exactly right in my report."

"Hold it right there, Harper," Perkins said as he swung his gun up and aimed it at Harper's nose. The boats bobbed on the choppy lake and Perkins held his pistol with two hands to steady it.

"You want to settle this now?" Perkins asked. "Or maybe you'd like to get back on your boat and forget all of this ever happened. I don't offer a choice like this to everyone, Harper. But I like you and—"

In a spray of sparks, Perkins' gun and the tip of his thumb went hurtling through the dark sky and into the lake. Perkins crumpled in pain as blood soaked his sleeve.

"What the..." Harper said, looking back at the governor. A curl of blue smoke drifted up from Steele's gun.

"Like I told you, Ensign." Steele said, "This ain't my first rodeo."

CHAPTER

6

*"Democracy is two wolves and a lamb voting
on what to have for lunch.
Liberty is a well-armed lamb contesting the vote!"*
- Benjamin Franklin -

SHE HANDLED THE SIDEWALK, but going down the steps was a new challenge. Theresa Goodwin Lewis set the tips of her crutches at the edge of the top step, leaned forward, and attempted to step down. The crutches wedged into her armpits, acted like a vaulter's pole and launched her from the top of the steps. Kowalski saw it coming. He jumped in front of the Vice President, caught her, and steadied her, being careful not to injure her more than he already had the day before.

"These things are going to take some practice," Lewis said.

She looked around to check for cameras. Romeo Costa already had the lone videographer cornered and was removing the memory chip from the camera. The man tried to pull his camera back, but Costa had him by four inches and fifty pounds of muscle.

"That one won't make it to YouTube," Costa said. He handed the videographer a business card. "Call this number and you'll get this back after it's been erased."

"Hey, that's private property. You can't just take it," the cameraman objected.

"National security, hotshot. Keep bitching and you'll lose your press pass."

"But I've got other news footage on that."

"Not anymore," Costa said as he pocketed the chip and handed back the camera.

"First the crutches go down, and then your feet," Agent Kowalski coached.

"Takes a bit of coordination, doesn't it," Lewis said.

"Yes, Ma'am," Kowalski answered, discreetly keeping his thoughts to himself.

From the wings, Lewis listened to Congressman Martin prime the audience, denouncing the grass roots Tea Party movement that had placed his House seat at the top of their hit list. Martin recited a litany of government benefits his opponent was certainly going to take away from the blue collar workers of Ohio. The so-called Rust Belt continued to hemorrhage manufacturing jobs to China primarily due to the ever increasing taxes and onerous environmental and safety regulations Martin and the Sanchez administration kept adding to through EPA and OSHA directives. Enormous compliance and permitting fees were effectively additional taxes, but by characterizing them as fees, the administration had sidestepped Congress and shielded the de facto taxes from the public eye. With Martin's clever spin, these added costs, fees, and regulations were touted as critical protections for the workers. Martin was going strong and the hand-selected audience was cheering right on cue.

Martin got the nod from Romeo Costa and started to close his warm-up act. "When President Sanchez took office nearly eight years ago, change marched into Washington. But two years ago, a mid-term election fraught with scandal and voting irregularities..."

Martin paused and let the audience murmur and boo on cue. "Voting irregularities" had become the code words for a controversial Supreme Court decision allowing late absentee ballots from deployed military personnel to be counted in a pivotal election in Pennsylvania, giving one more Senate seat to the Republicans.

"...obstructed the President's efforts," Martin continued. "Now is the time to finish the job we started. Now is the time to make Theresa Lewis our next president. No would-be assassin's bullet can stop what is right and just. Ladies and gentlemen, I believe that our best hope for a better America was miraculously protected for a reason. Let's help her fulfill her destiny to become the greatest President this country has ever seen. A week from now, we are going to elect Theresa Goodwin Lewis as President of the United States."

Theresa Lewis hobbled out on stage looking like a wounded hero. The crowd roared. The TV cameras panned to strategically placed faces streaming with tears. Lewis waved, then placed a hand over her heart, acknowledging the emotion of the crowd. She looked up to heaven through eyes watering on cue. The audience saw her tears forming, and cheered even more wildly.

Lewis waited for the ovation to gradually die down, waving all the while. "You don't know how good it feels to be here," Lewis began, grinning from ear to ear. The crowd cheered again, as the TV cameras showed both men and women wiping their eyes and nodding their support.

"If you had doubts about how far our opponents will go to stop change, to oppose our efforts to return America to the people, then look no further than the events of the past two days for the truth. The extreme right is losing its grip on the workers of this country. They know the end is near. They know that my policy proposals of fairness for the American people will forcibly remove them from their positions of power and oppression."

The crowd roared again. Lewis beamed at the ovation. It was by far the best rally she'd had in over a month. And it almost seemed spontaneous, despite the careful orchestration by her campaign operatives. The scene would cover the network and cable news like wallpaper. The emotion of the crowd would be palpable in every living room in America that still bothered to watch the evening news. She could just picture voters' eyes welling with sympathetic tears at the sight of a wounded presidential candidate in her first address since an attempt on her life, calling out her opponents and implicitly accusing them of being behind the assassination attempt. Her opponents would cry foul and claim no connection with the shooter. But the idea would have already been planted. The claim would energize the occasional and usually apathetic voters and help them temporarily forget about her pending legal troubles that followed her like a hound. The poor and blue collar voters, the student voters, and the thousands of illegal immigrant voters Lewis and the Democrats gained voting privileges for would now have a compelling reason to come to the polls.

"The attempt on my life was an act of evil desperation," Lewis continued. "But each and every one of you has the chance to see that justice is done. You can show the world that America is still the land of opportunity for each and every man, woman, and child. Let's finish the job. Ted Martin and I will not rest until everyone shares in the American dream. Thank you for your support and God bless America."

A tall man with a dark moustache, sunglasses, and a Texas Rangers baseball cap stood in the middle of the cheering crowd. Brewster Steele had flown to Ohio with one purpose in mind: he wanted to follow Lewis and personally monitor the crowd reaction to her stump speeches. He needed to know just how likely it was that Lewis would win. He had a plan, but it was so drastic he had to be absolutely sure before he put it into action. If Lewis lost the election, the urgency in implementing the plan would be far less than if she somehow managed to pull out a win. If that happened, he knew he would have to act fast.

Steele moved slowly through the standing audience trying to judge the sincerity of the support, and relying on his fake moustache, sunglasses, and uncharacteristic slouch to disguise his recognizable features. Each section of the auditorium had been staffed with a campaign facilitator who knew each applause line and rallied the people around them on cue. The facilitators passed out pamphlets and buttons. An exuberant young woman approached Steele, pressing close and fingering his lapel. Steele stepped back.

"Don't worry, honey," she said. "I'm not hittin' on you. I just need you to wear one of my buttons. Everyone's got to have one. You never know when you'll be on camera and show up on the news."

She adjusted the pin and gave him a wink. "Actually, I mighta been hittin' on you. You here alone?"

"My wife just stepped out to the ladies room," he lied while trying to cover his Texas drawl.

"What a shame. I might be a bad girl when I want to be, but I'm no home wrecker," she cooed. "I could have made your dreams a reality, honey."

She blew him a kiss as she slipped between two burly auto workers union thugs who were zeroing in on Steele. The governor knew it was time to leave. He stepped behind a group of retired school teachers waving flags and ducked though a nearby exit. He had another lady waiting for him.

CHAPTER 7

"Every step we take towards making the State our Caretaker of our lives, by that much we move toward making the State our Master."

- Dwight D. Eisenhower -

B REWSTER STEELE WAS one-half of one of the most unlikely couples in politics. His wife, Mary Ketterling-Steele, was a United States congresswoman representing the first district of Pennsylvania, a leader in the Movement for Compassionate Governance, and a die-hard liberal.

Kettering-Steele was born and raised in Philadelphia, in the district she now represented. Her grandfather, Gardner Ketterling, founded Ketterling department stores in the 1920s. He started with a tiny newsstand in Center City Philadelphia. The story goes that every morning a Mr. Gillespie would buy a morning paper from Ketterling. He saw how Ketterling worked seven days a week and made sure to carry the magazines and papers his customers wanted. When the storefront behind Ketterling's newsstand went vacant, Gillespie offered to put up the money and partner with Ketterling to open the first Ketterling's News in 1923. When Gillespie died a year later of a sudden heart attack, he left his interest in the store to Ketterling.

Gardner Ketterling lived to ninety-five, and as the family's wealth grew, he always gave back by establishing and funding several foundations to assist the poor. Now, the Ketterling family was the wealthiest in Pennsylvania, with over two hundred department stores up and down the East Coast and hundreds more with other brand names, but under the Ketterling umbrella, throughout the country.

The Ketterling family was also one of the biggest Republican contributors, but Mary Ketterling-Steele had strayed from the family politics when she attended Sarah Lawrence. By the time she met Brewster Steele, she was as liberal as they come.

Steele sat unnoticed in the audience, watching as Ophelia Morgan, the most popular daytime talk show host in history, interviewed his wife. He never got tired of watching the immaculately groomed, dark-haired woman he married. He had been a widower when they met, with two children. Mary cared for those kids as though they were her own; the grandkids all called her "G-Mom." Steele couldn't help but smile just thinking about their two brand-new granddaughters doing the same.

"Have you always been a liberal?" Morgan was asking.

"I didn't really think in political terms when I was growing up," Ketterling-Steele said. "But when I went to Sarah Lawrence, my eyes were opened to the inequity in our country, and the corruption of 'good old boy' politics. I became troubled by the fact there is so much poverty in the richest nation on earth. The average person had no voice. Special interest groups funded by large corporations and the wealthy dictated government policy. Instead of taking a degree and slipping back into the very comfortable existence I enjoyed as a young girl, I made it my mission to do what I could to change things."

"And yet you married a rock-ribbed conservative," Morgan said. "Our staff was taken by Governor Steele's resemblance to your grandfather. Is that what attracted you to him?"

"No, no," Ketterling-Steele said, denying the question she was asked too often. "Brew is a Texas cowboy and Grampa was a Northeastern gentleman."

"But they do have similarities, don't they?" Morgan asked.

"Yes, I suppose," Ketterling-Steele said, admitting what she knew to be true. "I will say that they are both the kindest men I have ever known."

"Even if your husband is a conservative Republican?" Morgan asked, drawing a laugh from the audience.

"Even in spite of that," Ketterling-Steele said with a grin. "That is how our seemingly odd attraction happened. I didn't like Brew when I first saw him because he was introduced to me along with his political label. But after working with him on committees, I came to see who he really was. We care about the same things. We want to solve the same problems. We simply disagree on how to achieve the solution."

"Do you mind taking a few questions from the audience?"

"It would be my pleasure."

Hands went up. Morgan shielded her eyes from the klieg lights and peered out. She pointed to a woman in the front row.

"I understand that you and your husband have limited time together with you being in Washington and him being in Texas. Does that put a strain on your relationship?" the woman asked.

"Sometimes. I also keep an apartment in my district in Philadelphia to stay in touch with my constituents. That keeps us apart even more. But we try to rendezvous there or in Austin as often as possible."

"Does absence really make the heart grow fonder?" Morgan asked.

"I think that is true. Brew often says it lets us enjoy an endless honeymoon," Ketterling-Steele said, blushing slightly.

A giggle went through the audience. Morgan pointed to the next questioner.

"The gentleman in the second row," she said.

"Yes, Congresswoman," said Brewster Steele. "May I have the honor of your company for dinner this evening?"

CHAPTER 8

"Our constitution was made only for
a moral and religious people.
It is wholly inadequate to the government of any other."

- John Adams -

WELCOME TO THE KBS News Special Report, 'Mania in Miami.'" Warren Tufts sat across a thick glass desk and introduced the show and his guests. "This morning, we dig into the background of Hank Samson, the would-be assassin who allegedly shot at Vice President Lewis, the Democratic presidential nominee, at a Miami rally almost a week ago now. With me are Dr. Angelo Fernandez, a psychologist and columnist with the *Miami Journal*, Martina Pelle, a nationally known blogger, and former FBI special agent and private investigator Arthur Campbell. Thank you all for joining us.

"Doctor Fernandez, I'll start with you. How could someone who has gone through such rigorous training as an Army sharpshooter serving in Afghanistan, and who had been so meticulously screened to qualify for the Secret Service, take an action like this?"

"Well, Warren, we'll never really know what the trigger was," Fernandez said. "But I can assure you that a basic mental instability existed in Mr. Samson. However, Samson probably looked completely normal. To him, everything was rational. I'm almost certain Samson thought he was doing something heroic."

Tufts turned to Martina Pelle. "Martina, you wrote that this event was a direct result of American foreign policy. What did you mean when you wrote that?"

"Hank Samson's actions are a manifestation of PTSD, post-traumatic stress disorder," Pelle said. "Here we have a man who was trained to be a stealth killer by the United States military. He knew how to look through his rifle scope, stare into his victim's eyes, and squeeze the trigger. When our military trains killers, exposes them to the trauma of war, and then shoves them back into society, this is what you get."

Tufts paused a moment as if to collect himself after Pelle's sanctimonious statement effectively accusing the United States military of breeding mentally unstable assassins. He turned to his last guests.

"Mr. Campbell," Tufts said, turning to the former FBI special agent, "do we have a major problem with military personnel suffering from PTSD in our neighborhoods?"

"Absolutely not," Campbell answered. "With all due respect, Martina, you are grossly exaggerating the severity of the problem. Hank Samson was an exception. I believe the more important question is: what if Hank Samson was not unstable? When Samson served in Afghanistan, he had been attached to the Second Attack Reconnaissance Battalion — the last battalion to leave during the pullout. It was a disaster. They were promised air cover, but the President never authorized it. Sixty-three soldiers were lost. Samson was serving in the White House at the time and was close enough to possibly see what was going on behind the scenes. Theresa Lewis, as Vice President, was part of the decision-making team. Maybe he overheard something the

Vice President said. Maybe he saw the real reason his buddies were left to be slaughtered."

"That's pure speculation, Arthur," Tufts said. "We're here to discuss what we can prove, not what we imagine."

"What we can prove," Martina Pelle interrupted, "is that Hank Samson attended a Tea Party rally two weeks before the shooting. We have photographic evidence."

"And where did that photo come from?" Campbell asked.

"My sources are confidential," she answered. "But I will tell you it came from a government surveillance file."

"Would that government source happen to have Photoshop on their computer?" Campbell asked.

"Are you questioning my journalistic integrity, Mr. Campbell?" Pelle asked.

"When I have questions, Ms. Pelle," Campbell answered, "I find answers. And believe me, that's what I intend to do."

Wes Roberson picked up the remote and hit the mute button. Sipping his second cup of coffee, he turned back to his pile of notes. There were only three days to go until the election, and Roberson's bid for the presidency was still the media's day-old bread. The only face time he got was the time he bought. It was the attempted assassination of Theresa Lewis 24/7 on every channel, both network and cable.

Roberson had just a couple more appearances to make before the fateful day arrived. The faithful would show up, but Roberson had lost the momentum and the all-important media attention that propelled his rise in the polls.

Before the Miami incident, Roberson was the outsider. He was making waves. He made a habit of saying the things most Americans thought. His position on illegal immigrants, climate change, and particularly his opposition to accepting Syrian refugees made him a daily target for the media. But he never backed down. And the tactic placed his name and face on every newspaper, television news broadcast and talk radio show in the country. The media attention had smothered his primary opponents. Until now, it had kept him ahead of Lewis. The irony of it all was how easy it was. All he had to do was ignore the party line and say what he believed. And what he believed matched what most Americans believed but were too timid to say for fear of rebuke from the politically correct crowd.

Roberson believed that when you distilled it down, the country was divided not into two political parties, but into the people who are elected, appointed, and hired to governmental offices, and the rest of us. Roberson aligned himself with "the rest of us," making him a true conservative choice.

Thanks to this attitude, Roberson was favored to win the election, and that made news. But an attempted assassination of a sitting vice president and presidential candidate just days before the election, no matter how unpopular the candidate was, stole the headlines over everything except a Martian invasion. His staff, who used to be juggling media requests, was now begging that same media for coverage. The election, that looked like a laugher just a week ago, became a horse race, and the media could smell it. They had turned their cameras on Lewis, fomented sympathy for her, and had done what they could to close the gap in the polls. A tight contest would boost ratings, and the media's candidate just might be able to pull this one out of the fire.

Roberson's wife, Ginny, wandered out from the bedroom, still groggy but smiling.

"'Morning, honey," Roberson said as she leaned down to give him a kiss.

"Anything new on Theresa Lewis?" she asked.

"Just more and more speculation. The left is trying to blame it on military policy — can you believe that? I'm so tired of seeing her face plastered everywhere, I can barely stand to look at the news. I just want to work on my stump speech for the stretch run and leave it alone."

"We can't pretend it didn't happen. We need to stay on top of it," Ginny said as she picked up the remote.

She turned the sound back up on the hotel television. The guests had departed the show, and Tufts was announcing that KBS now had footage of Lewis moments after the assassination attempt, taken from closer range. The Chyron read, "A KBS News Exclusive," followed by warnings that the scenes were graphic and may be disturbing to children.

A clearer video, taken from a slightly different angle than the one released on the day of the shooting, showed the presidential candidate's face covered in blood. She appeared to be nearly unconscious as they strapped her to the stretcher. The video was jerky and broken up. Hands and arms waved in front of the camera in the confusion of the moment. The video was both compelling and disturbing. There was no doubt the person who shot the film had managed a handsome fee from KBS for the exclusive rights.

"The shots appear to have come from a nearby warehouse owned by the Miami Shipping and Freight Company. The building was shuttered last year in bankruptcy proceedings. The Miami Shipping and Freight Company was one of the largest importers of bauxite and other minerals, primarily from Caribbean countries, and was a non-union company. As of this moment, no link has been established between the company, or former executives of the company, and the shooter," Tufts said. The lingering implication hung in the air.

"They're reaching for an 'evil corporate America attempts assassination,' angle," Roberson said. "It's ideal for placing Lewis at the head of the 'valiant crusade' to save the oppressed. Good God, I'm getting tired of that word. Everyone including my Aunt Mabel is 'oppressed' these days."

Roberson took another big gulp of coffee and washed down a fistful of vitamins. The television switched to a view of the warehouse, cordoned off with police tape and surrounded by squad cars. The cameraman zoomed in on the broken window.

"When we come back," Tufts said, "we have shocking new reports of more suppressed personal information concerning

Republican presidential candidate, Arizona Senator Wes Roberson. Will it influence the election? More after this break."

"It's probably more lies about that supposed personal bankruptcy they came out with a couple days ago." Roberson took a sip of coffee and turned up the volume. "They just can't stand that I'm so successful."

Each day brought a new charge. The Vice President's people were relentless. It was as if they kept a team of fiction writers busy making up so-called "new facts" about Senator Roberson's financial and personal histories. Last week's edition claimed Roberson had filed for personal bankruptcy thirty years ago and buried the story. The story went that Roberson claimed $213,700 in assets and $732,000 in liabilities in the bankruptcy papers. His liabilities stemmed from bad investments and risky real estate speculation. Allegedly, Roberson used his position as sheriff of San Luis, Arizona to extend multiple lines of credit and secure several unsecured loans. They said they had documents showing Roberson had been given a minor interest in six failed land developments that left behind substantial liabilities. It also appeared that Senator Roberson failed to report over $100,000 of income over a five-year period, and the source of the income was still unknown.

"Okay, what's the negative side of this?" Roberson had asked his wife when they heard the bogus report. "Who's going to believe this? The diehard Lewis supporters and the Kool-Aid drinkers, the folks with their hands out to the government will believe it, of course. They'd never vote for me even if I could promise they'd win the lottery. As soon as I say the charges are bogus, my supporters will believe me. It's those swing voters, the undecided and the ones who have hopefully had enough of Lewis, that matter. And unfortunately, this week will be a week of damage control instead of the sprint to the finish we had hoped for."

Today's news would likely bring another false charge that would consume Roberson's precious time and campaign resources to refute. Lewis kept throwing this kind of trash in Roberson's path. These were the tactics of a thug politician who was in a fight for his political life. Roberson knew it was confirmation that he was winning, but he hated the ugly process. He would have ignored the claims, if he could, but silence would be seen as confirmation among the left-leaning media.

A wry grin crossed his face as he waited for Tufts to return with the new charge. "The bright side of this is the media will be talking about me again. Sometimes bad press is better than no press at all. This will take some of the airtime away from the Vice President and the assassination attempt."

"You're an incorrigible optimist," Ginny said as she wrapped her arms around her husband. "And that's what I love about you."

He kissed her, welcoming her touch. No matter how this election turned out, no matter what attacks he had to endure, he knew he always had the love of his family. They couldn't take that away.

Warren Tufts' face reappeared on the TV. "As damaging as last week's revelations might be," he said, "there's more startling news about Senator Roberson's past. KBS News has confirmed reports of a child pornography charge against him along with a subsequent cover-up dating back to 1995."

Ginny Roberson involuntarily pulled away from her husband.

"The report states that then-Sheriff Roberson was charged with distribution of pornographic material involving underage children." Tufts continued. "At the time of his arrest, several explicit videotapes were seized upon his arrest. Because of his position as sheriff of San Luis, Arizona, the arrest was made quietly at his office and the media was not informed at the time. He was immediately released on his own recognizance. A past coworker of Senator Roberson has told KBS News that she was instrumental in convincing Andrew Axelman, the Arizona attorney general when the arrest was made, to drop the charge and expunge the records. At the time of the arrest, Axelman was in the midst of his unsuccessful run for governor. Axelman and Roberson have been closely tied, politically, and Axelman currently serves as an advisor to the Roberson campaign. Neither Axelman or Roberson could be reached for comment."

Ginny Roberson stared at the television in disbelief. Roberson jumped to his feet and banged his coffee cup hard on the kitchen counter, snapping Ginny out of her trance.

"That can't be true, honey, can it?" she asked, hesitantly.

"Absolutely not," he shouted. "It's a last minute dirty trick of the lowest kind from the Lewis cesspool. It shows how desperate they are, the sons of ..."

Roberson had vowed to stop swearing when the children were born. Now, even thirty years later, there were still some days he had trouble living up to the challenge. He stretched up as he tried to collect himself, his knuckles scraping the hotel room's popcorn ceiling. He took in a couple of deep breaths and relaxed. He never made good decisions based on emotion, and there was too much at stake to forget that lesson now.

Tears ran down Ginny Roberson's face. "How will you ever deny something like this?" she asked, fully aware that the charge alone was just as damaging as if it was genuine.

"How in the hell did they manage this?" Roberson wondered, shaking his head. He knew he'd been tarred and feathered, and with only three days to the election, there was far too little time to even hope to remove the sticky stains.

CHAPTER 9

*"It is the duty of the patriot to protect his country
from its government."*

- Thomas Paine -

BREWSTER STEELE SWITCHED on the radio in his old pickup truck just in time to hear Tchaikovsky's *1812 Overture,* complete with cannon shots, cueing the intro to the Hornsby Show. He was halfway between Waco and Austin, heading south on I-35, and Whit Hornsby was always a good way to idle away the miles. As much as Steele appreciated the security provided by the couple Texas Rangers trailing him in their state-owned vehicle, he cherished the privacy of his beloved pickup, where he could be alone with his thoughts — or with Hornsby's, as the case may be.

"Welcome, my fellow Americans," came Hornsby's drill-sergeant bark as the music faded, "and all the nations of the world who are lucky enough to have Internet access to the wisdom we broadcast every single day. Our mission here at the Hornsby Show is to provide you with the most accurate news and information available from sea to shining sea. And believe me, you need some accurate news today."

Whit Hornsby boasted millions of listeners across the nation and around the world. A former Army general, Hornsby had become the voice of Middle America. Despite his tough and unsympathetic rhetoric, Hornsby knew how to express the opinions of people who had become disheartened and angry over the rapid dissolution of the traditional values they believed formed the foundation of the country. Frustrated and desperate to shout their opinions, Hornsby's listeners found a soapbox through his microphone. He was the target of vitriol and hatred from his opponents on the left — the very people who claimed to be tolerant and nonjudgmental. But their tolerance vanished and knee-jerk judgment blossomed when the name "Whit Hornsby," or anyone else who disagreed with them, came up.

Hornsby was a thorn in the side of the President, and try as he might, President Sanchez had been unable to silence him. Sanchez's supporters launched boycotts against the products of Hornsby's advertisers, but Hornsby's fans went out and bought more of the products in a counter-demonstration of solidarity. Sanchez blamed Hornsby for any act of social violence, but the mention of Hornsby's name only brought him more listeners, curious to see how a single talk show host could provoke the ire of a President of the United States. Democrats in Congress even tried pushing through new regulations that categorized Hornsby's show, and others like it, as news, thereby demanding equal time for opposing viewpoints. But every effort to develop a talk radio show with a liberal viewpoint counter to Hornsby flopped badly.

Steele was interested in what Hornsby would make of the events of the past week. It was sure to be something a little different than what the mainstream, left-leaning media was saying.

"Last week," Hornsby began, "we witnessed a cataclysmic historic event. One deranged individual took it upon himself to do what the rest of us are going to do in a nonviolent way on election day. One man tried to end the Sanchez-Lewis regime in a single-handed coup d'état. Fortunately, he failed. I say fortunately because violence in any form is not the way to settle political debates. We at the Hornsby Show, and all conservatives throughout the country, categorically condemn this assassination attempt. Despite what I may think of this Vice President, her destructive policies, and her outright hatred of America, I am sincerely glad to see her alive and recovering. I wish her the all the best and hope she gets back on her feet so she can enjoy her imminent retirement right after this election so we can get this country back on track.

"Before we get into analyzing the assassination attempt, I want to first talk about the Roberson story that broke today," Hornsby said. "Can you say, 'dirty trick'? Can you say, 'smear tactic'? This is all this is. Roberson got too close to toppling the house of cards. He was pulling the curtain back and exposing the wizard for the charlatan she is.

"Do you think for one minute that these charges are legitimate? Let me raise a few questions our mainstream media has failed to ask. Who released this information? KBS News broke the story, but where did they get it from? Who is this mystery source who, quote unquote, confirmed the child pornography charge? And where is the phantom coworker of Roberson's who supposedly witnessed the cover-up? It makes you wonder, doesn't it? And of course, there's the timing of all of this. Three days before the election. There's no time for Senator Roberson to adequately answer the charges. And that's exactly what Theresa Goodwin Lewis wants. It's all too transparent, if you know where to look. This is what I warned you about two years ago. Remember the PIP Act?"

Steele nodded to himself. He remembered all too well listening to Hornsby voice his own concerns about PIP and Hornsby's dire warnings about the Personal Identity Protection Act: that it would allow the President to seize control of every database of personal information about every citizen in the country. "This bill is akin to putting Bonnie and Clyde in charge of security at Fort Knox," Hornsby had quipped.

Now, Hornsby's predictions seemed to be coming true. "There is no doubt in my mind that this information has been planted by the Sanchez's and Lewis's people and none of it is true," Hornsby was saying.

Steele had to acknowledge that it made sense. It was a brilliant tactic, in a horrifically devious way. As soon as the phrase "child pornography" was uttered, it couldn't be erased, no matter how innocent the accused was. Wes Roberson could try all he liked to get the truth out, but the damage was done. Roberson's supports could put up with his habit of insulting his opponents, exaggerating facts in his overt bragging, and his sometimes obnoxious personality. Many of them seemed to like his way of telling it like it is. But not even the most rabid supporter could ignore the stigma of a child pornography charge.

"You might be asking, 'Whit, why would the media run a story like this without double and triple corroboration?'" Hornsby continued. "Because, my friends, the charge is too serious to wait for the facts. That's the stock answer from our liberal media when it comes to bogus charges against a conservative."

As the show cut to a commercial break, Steele considered what Hornsby was saying. He wished he could say that the notion of the Roberson charges being a set-up surprised him. Sadly, it made all too much sense. The question was, how far did the scheming go? His mind raced through several scenarios, each one more intricate and sinister than the one before until the radio show's bumper music snapped him back to the present.

"We're back," Hornsby said, "and none too soon. When this show's not on the air, all kinds of mayhem may ensue. We are the guiding light, the Sacajawea of America. Our job is to show you the way through the wilderness of the Sanchez-Lewis administration.

"There's going to be a lot of wild, uncontrolled speculation about the assassination attempt. Vice President Lewis herself is already pointing her finger at the 'vast right wing conspiracy.'

"My question is this: while she was being tackled by the Secret Service, when she was being strapped to the stretcher, what thoughts were running through her head? It's hard to imagine she wasn't scared out of her wits — after all, this may have been the first time our sitting Vice President has witnessed live fire, since she's never served in the military. Remember when she said she tried to join the Marines but they told her she was too old to join up? Another one of the Theresa Lewis whoppers.

"Do you really think maybe she's so totally programmed by now that as soon as the bullets hit, she thinks, 'Wow. What an opportunity. I can blame all of this on the Republicans? Did the thought come to her on the way to the hospital? She couldn't have timed it any better. The sympathy vote will roll out. The apathetic voters will rally behind their threatened hero. Combined with today's charges against Roberson, it's — there's no other word for it — it's perfect. I'm telling you, there's just something about this that doesn't add up. It's every bit as strange as the Sanchez-Lewis budget."

Steele switched off the radio. Ever since his reconnaissance mission at the Lewis stump speeches, he had a lot on his mind. Hornsby's doubts about the shooting and the Roberson charge only added to his suspicion about Lewis and where the election was heading. Steele knew he had to be ready. If Lewis won the White House, which now looked more and more likely, there would be no going back for Steele and the rest of Texas.

CHAPTER 10

"The Constitution is not an instrument for the government to restrain the people, it is an instrument for the people to restrain the government."

- Patrick Henry -

THE SLENDER BLONDE midday news anchor stood next to a mammoth touch sensitive computer display. With a sweep of her hand, the image on the screen changed from a head shot of a scowling Wes Roberson to a graph with two irregular red and blue lines. The blue line was clearly on the ascent while the red line that had once been tracking well above the blue line now dipped as low as it had been since the Democratic Party's convention when Theresa Lewis had enjoyed a meager bump in the polls.

"The latest KBS News tracking poll shows that the commanding lead once enjoyed by Senator Roberson in the presidential election has eroded quickly and significantly following this morning's revelation of an alleged child pornography charge in the senator's past," the anchor explained. "Senator Roberson now leads Vice President Lewis by only four points. With just three days until the election, the race is now too close to call."

She tapped the big screen bringing up a map of the United States. Each state held a number.

"This is a tidal change in the polls," she said. "The undecided states now account for over one hundred electoral votes. Neither candidate appears to have enough solid states to top the 270 votes needed for victory."

She tapped the screen again and another bar chart appeared.

"What makes this election even more difficult to forecast is this. The pool of so-called likely voters has exploded. The attempt on Vice President Lewis's life appears to have energized her base. On the other hand, the allegations against Senator Roberson have suppressed his support, even among those voters who voted for him in the primaries. A lower voter turnout among Republicans and a higher voter turnout among Democrats could have a significant impact on the balance of power in Congress. It is now conceivable that both houses of Congress will move to the Democrats."

Theresa Lewis hit the mute button. Things couldn't be going better. She looked across the table at Tony Delgado, her campaign manager.

"My, how things have changed," she said.

Lewis knew political history well. In 1960, the South was blue. Texas, Louisiana, and on through North Carolina were solid Democrat, even though they were ideologically very conservative. Now those Yellow Dog Democrats were conservative Republicans. What used to be a Democratic base was no longer there.

Lewis's base lived in the cities. As the population in the United States grew within the urban areas, the tide of city voters shifted from moderate to liberal. More unions, more government assistance programs, and more central planning added up to a huge block of voters that would consistently vote for the politicians who kept the handouts flowing. They would never vote to have their gravy train cut. The trick was to keep them from growing so apathetic they no longer had the motivation to trot out once every other year and cast a vote. The assassination attempt had done just that.

Delgado flipped open a stack of spreadsheets.

"Here are some figures you need to know," Delgado said. "During your time as vice president, we added fifteen million people to the food stamp program. Roberson is campaigning to cut those benefits and cut the duration of unemployment checks. You can depend on over three-quarters of those votes. They're counting on your promise to keep it going."

"But just like our pretty little newsgirl said, it's not about the popular vote," Lewis said. "It's about the electoral vote. Where do we stand in the swing states, now that the charge against Roberson has come out?"

Delgado tapped a couple of keys on his laptop.

"Looks like we're solid for two hundred and thirty votes. There are eighty-three votes in the toss-up states."

"Are those 'voter ID' states?" Lewis asked.

"Iowa, Nevada, and West Virginia are swing states that require no voter identification. And now Wisconsin overturned their new voter ID law, so that makes a fifth swing state. That adds up to forty-two electoral votes. We turn those and you're over the top."

"I trust you have boots on the ground where you need them," Lewis said.

"Yes, Ma'am. Our 'get out the vote' campaign is ramping up. Dimitri Borsky's group is spearheading that," Delgado answered. "But we could use some push in Wisconsin and West Virginia."

"Madison and Wheeling are two of my favorite places this time of year."

Delgado scrolled through his list of state organizers and fired off an email to the two in Wisconsin and West Virginia.

"Operation 'Free Lunch' is a go," was all it said.

CHAPTER 11

"(T)he foundation of our national policy will be laid in the pure and immutable principles of private morality;...the propitious smiles of Heaven can never be expected on a nation that disregards the eternal rules of order and right which Heaven itself has ordained..."

- George Washington -

WES ROBERSON STEPPED up to the podium, trying not to let the weight of recent events show. He had spent the past six hours, that should have been invested in campaigning, doing triage with his campaign staff and his family. Now he faced the daunting task of erasing the stain of a spurious allegation from people's memories within the next few days. Even his wife, who had trusted him for over thirty years, fell into the trap of doubt.

"I'm being tried in the court of public opinion," he lamented to her. "And now I'm trying to tell the jury to disregard the inadmissible comment."

The media was relentless with the story. Since KBS announced the charge that morning, not a single poll was analyzed without a reference to the allegation. Only conservative radio host Whit Hornsby seemed to be asking the questions

Roberson was pleading with the media to ask. How could something as volatile as this have been overlooked during the primaries? The press had gone after him aggressively during his primary campaign. They even found out he was a bed wetter until he was six. There was no way they could have missed this, and if they had found it, there was no way the media would have sat on it until now. Roberson knew that none of this existed in his identity file until this week. And he had a pretty good suspicion of who was behind the smear.

But when Roberson tried to ask these questions to prove his innocence, he was denied at every turn. When he claimed there was no evidence, he was shown a printout from the Department of Personal Identity Protection that said otherwise. The charge was there for all to see, spurious or not. And when he insisted that the charge must have been planted, his theory was shot down by the administration spokesperson. She asserted the PIP database was triple encrypted and required four levels of password entry to access any personal information records. That's what made the program so beneficial to the public.

"Security like this exists nowhere on the planet except in Washington," the Director of the Department of Personal Identity Protection had said. "This system is unhackable."

"And the Titanic was supposed to be unsinkable," thought Roberson when he heard that comment. The election that looked like a lock was now up for grabs. The charge had been made, and Roberson couldn't dispel it in time for the election. Worst of all, Lewis's hands were clean. A computer had done the slander for her. It was the dirtiest of political tricks.

It was time for Roberson's Hail Mary speech. It was time to come out swinging.

"Thank you, everyone," Roberson called out. The applause seemed tainted with desperation. Roberson waived his hands to quiet the crowd. The band took the lull as their cue to strike up the campaign theme song again, but Roberson signaled for an end after only a couple of bars.

"Thank you for the rousing welcome. But tonight we need to be serious. Tonight is not about fanfare, campaign signs, and noisemakers. Tonight is about the future of America. It might even be about the preservation of America as we know it.

"I thank you all for seeing through these false and slanderous stories about a past I never lived. The Internet and this age of information is the proverbial double-edged sword. Throughout history, inventions that we intended for the betterment of mankind often were later used as weapons against humanity. The Internet and databases like the Personal Identity Protection system can be turned into a personal assassination weapon."

As soon as the word "assassination" slipped past his lips, Roberson regretted it. Images of the sycophantic liberal media criticizing him for comparing his supposedly sordid past with an attempt on the life of a sitting Vice President flashed through his mind. Too late now. "Press on," he told himself.

"The Personal Identity Protection Act is nothing more than a way for the government to get Americans to voluntarily give up their constitutionally protected right to privacy, on the pretext of protecting the citizenry. It was a blow against liberty, just one of many the Sanchez administration has made, and now it has been turned into a weapon to prevent you, the people, from making a fair and honest decision in this election. We can't let these thug tactics stand in the way of freedom.

"Eight years ago, America rode a wave of optimism as President Sanchez was elected in a decisive victory. His promise of a better life for all, equality among classes, a cleaner planet, the end to corporate greed, and an end to racial discrimination was seductive. Four years later, we put up a weak, indecisive candidate against Sanchez and effectively handed him a second term. Since then, ISIS has invaded America while Sanchez is ignoring the threat and focusing on making your energy costs skyrocket in the name of preventing global warming that is not actually happening.

"I ask you this. Where are we now? Have any of President Sanchez's promises come true? Are you better off now than you were eight years ago? Is the environment cleaner? Are we closer to energy independence? Has the influence of money been lessened in Washington? Has the economy improved? Do you really want Vice President Lewis to step in and give us more of the same?

"The answer to all of these questions is 'No.' Unemployment is at record levels, inflation is raging. We spent trillions of dollars on a highly touted Economic Jumpstart package. It was supposed to fund millions of shovel-ready jobs. The President put Vice President Lewis in charge of the program. How did she do? Have you seen any of these shovel-ready jobs?

"Well, Vice President Lewis, I can help you out. I have found thousands of shovel-ready jobs. The entire Department of Education is shovel-ready. I propose we shovel it up and throw it out. Return control of education to the states and municipalities where it belongs."

There was light applause. Roberson stared at the empty seats in the back rows. It had been months since he failed to fill a hall.

"I propose we shovel up the Department of Energy, too," Roberson continued. "There are thousands more shovel-ready jobs there. Hundreds of years of natural gas, coal, and oil lie untapped within our boundaries. It's time we tapped those resources and stopped relying on foreign oil!"

The audience cheered again, but more politely than he hoped. Roberson took a sip of water. He was starting to feel like a comedian at a funeral.

"The EPA is on my list of shovel-ready jobs. If you wonder why our manufacturing has moved overseas, look no further than the volumes of regulations from the Environmental Protection Agency.

"And there is one more job that is shovel-ready: Vice President Lewis's job. Don't let the thug tactics of the Lewis campaign determine your future. It's time we shoveled up that stinking mess, and her entire administration, and pitched it into the dumpster."

That closing line should have brought thunderous applause and been the sound bite for the evening news. Tonight, the applause was there, and reasonably energetic, but it wasn't what it used to be. He only had two more days to take down the allegation against him and regain his standing. Roberson wondered what the half-life of an unfounded child pornography scandal might be. He had a bad feeling it was far longer than forty-eight hours.

CHAPTER 12

"From each according to his means.
To each according to his needs."

- Karl Marx -
communist philosopher

JUST HOURS AFTER Roberson's speech, the White House Press Room was full. Having grown weary of answering questions without preparation, and after the gaffe when he mispronounced the Marine Corps as the Marine Corpse, President Sanchez had not held a press conference in over six months. But tonight, he wanted the attention of the entire nation, and he knew he would have it — everybody would be anxiously watching to see if another nutcase would make an attempt on his vice president's life.

Couched as a statement on national security, Sanchez was able to get airtime on all the networks without using campaign funds or giving the Republicans access to equal time. They were going to scream foul, but the majority of the Fairness in Broadcasting Board consisted of Sanchez appointees. The Republican complaints about tonight's free airtime would be a waste of breath.

The klieg lights came on followed by the red indicator on top of the television camera. "My fellow Americans," President Sanchez began. "In recent days, our nation has seen an alarming increase in violence inducing rhetoric. Talk radio, street protest, and reactionary extremists are no longer content to merely voice their opinions. It is clear that hateful words and incendiary speech have ignited a tinderbox of violence against elected officials and ordinary citizens alike. Protection of the right to free speech requires me to take measures to protect the safety of those who participate in the political process.

"Because of the ongoing investigation into the violence against the Vice President in Florida last week, I cannot comment on the motives or backing of the alleged assassin. However, it is reasonable to expect that in these last days of the most critical election in a hundred years, others will attempt to imitate the actions of one deranged individual. Action must be taken to protect legal candidates running for all offices. In order to increase the safety of all citizens, by executive order, as of midnight tonight, I am banning the issuance of assembly permits nationwide through the remainder of the election season. Police departments across the country will be ordered to disperse any congregation of fifty or more people in the presence of a political candidate.

"I expect that Democrats, Republicans, and Independents alike will find other ways to get their messages out to the voters without the traditional rallies in the public squares. I encourage radio and television stations, as well as newspapers, to work with candidates to increase their access at reasonable rates. Web-based speeches would be a safer alternative to live speeches."

Sanchez could imagine the Roberson camp throwing things at the television screen about now. His executive order would effectively short circuit the late rally marathon Roberson surely had planned. This would mean a complete change in tactics in Roberson's last-minute attempt to clear his name and regain his advantage in time for the election. He could imagine Roberson's team frantically speed-dialing TV stations, trying to buy up any available time they could.

Sanchez continued his speech, promising that Theresa Lewis would continue to lift the downtrodden and exploited. He called out the Washington power brokers, saying that those who held the reins of power would not relinquish their stronghold on America easily. He blamed the rich and privileged for the suffering of the common man, for exploitation and oppression.

"Taking away their privilege is like taking a bone away from a pit bull," Sanchez said. "It can be dangerous, and we've seen the evidence of that. I have tried to work in a cooperative manner with the other party. It saddens me to say that discussions and negotiations no longer seem to be the choice of my opponents."

On cue, an image of the Vice President with her bandaged head came up behind him. He gestured to his own forehead. It was a blatant attempt to tie his political opponents to the would-be assassin, but it was too late for subtlety. His constituents needed bold clues to follow.

"What should be peaceful speeches and campaigning has now become violent. It saddens me to issue tonight's executive order. But I took a solemn oath to protect the people of the United States, and I intend to uphold that commitment," Sanchez said while looking deeply into the camera.

The questions from reporters were easy — he made sure only to call on people sure to toss him softballs. The only one that approached tough was asked by Arnold Sanger, the round little correspondent from the *Post*.

"Mr. President," Sanger had said, "it's been reported that the alleged assassin, Hank Samson, had ties to Thomas Perkins, the oil speculator who is backing the effort to drill on government owned lands, lands you recently asked the EPA to classify as environmentally sensitive. An unconfirmed report indicates that Mr. Samson was seen leaving a D.C. bar with Mr. Perkins just two weeks ago. Is there any truth to this rumor?"

Luckily, Sanchez was ready for this to be brought up. Tony Delgado, Lewis's campaign manager, had prepped him thoroughly, and Sanchez was a man who could worm his way out of unwanted conversation simply by relying on his charm and ease with words. "Mr. Sanger," Sanchez said with a sparkling smile, "you know I cannot comment of an active investigation. A lot of people go in and out of bars in Washington, D.C. every day. I'm sure it was merely a coincidence."

A few questions later, the press conference was done, the TV cameras were turned off, and President Sanchez was boarding Marine One.

The helicopter swung west and approached the presidential retreat, flying into the five knot breeze. The cluster of simple gable buildings nestled in the trees gave Camp David the look of a woodland Shangri-La, as Franklin Roosevelt had first named it. The chopper settled to earth as softly as an elevator. Yumi Narito, Sanchez's personal assistant, was waiting next to the landing pad holding her long black hair against the wash of air from the rotor.

"Mr. Cherkinov is waiting for you in the Truman cottage, Mr. President," Narito said as the President stepped out of Marine One.

Sanchez nodded and walked quickly across the lawn to a small building of grey clapboard siding and white trim. He pushed open the door to find Dimitri Borsky lounging on the sofa with a glass of wine. Sanchez plopped into the easy chair and picked up the glass Borsky had poured for him.

"Could you have picked a more idiotic name? Mr. Jerkin' Off?" Sanchez said.

"You don't like? Is a fine Russian name with proud heritage," Dimitri Borsky said with an accent he had been futilely trying to suppress. "No one have believed me if I was Mr. McDonald, would they? Besides, this name make me laugh. I never had much chance to laugh in Soviet Union. This is what I like in America. Is a happy place."

After the breakup of the Soviet Union, Borsky had much less trouble becoming a capitalist than he had losing his accent. As privatization came to Russian business, he quickly gained a monopoly on Siberian oil and natural gas. His KGB background taught him how to take ruthlessness to the highest level. Within a year, he also controlled the energy resources in Kazakhstan and Turkmenistan.

Borsky knew how to buy influence. When he brought those skills to the United States, it did not take him long to gain control of a stable of politicians at the state and federal level. He established Petro Energy Resources and registered it in Delaware to gain corporate legal advantages. When an explosion ripped apart a deep water drilling rig he owned and spilled thousands of gallons of crude into the Gulf of Mexico, his intricate web of holding companies made it impossible for the media to trace ownership back to him. His well-placed political contributions kept the government at bay. Borsky personally funded an investigation into the spill with a wave of media hype. The official conclusion was the spill was the fault of an independent contractor who set the blowout valve on the well head. The contractor never knew what hit him, and Borsky was praised for his passion for environmental protection.

Borsky parlayed his millions into billions through some dubious currency trades. By most accounts, he managed to trigger the Asian financial crisis in the late nineties when he shorted the Thai baht and made a half billion dollars in a single day. From that point, Borsky became known by the few people who actually knew him as a political kingmaker. His relative anonymity allowed him to work in the shadows and to guarantee his hedged bets always paid off.

"America will be an even happier place, Dimitri, if I win this election," Sanchez said.

"If you win?" Borsky questioned. "But you are not even running. Lewis is."

"What's the Russian word for 'puppet,' my friend? You Russians know all about puppet heads of state."

Borsky nodded.

"Our archaic Constitution blocks me from an official third term," Sanchez explained. "Vice President Lewis has been coveting the office since she was an acne-faced teenager with Coke bottle glasses. And the woman has no scruples. It was remarkably easy to strike a deal with her. She gets all the pomp and ceremony of the office. Her ego gets stroked big time. And I become the titular Chief of Staff and keep running the show. She's running from some serious legal problems. I'm the only reason she's not already in jail. If she doesn't keep up her end of the deal, she'll be trading her pantsuit for a jumpsuit.

"Actually, I think I'll like it better that way. She'll show up for the ceremonial events. I've had enough of that for a lifetime. This way, I can fit in more golf while making sure our reformation of capitalism doesn't run off the tracks."

"There are still many people who would want to see Lewis, and you, lose, Carlos. You are still behind in the polls. But do not worry. I come to your rescue."

"It's in your best interest if I win, Dimitri."

"No, my friend," Borsky said. "I will be winner if Roberson win or if you win. I know how to hedge. Is old Russian tradition, just like puppet government is. But I win bigger if you win. That's why I like you so much."

"The money's in place?" Sanchez asked.

Borsky took a contented sip of wine. "Money is power," he said. "Both are useless if you do not use them."

"No worries, my friend," Sanchez said. "We'll be putting your money to good use on election day."

CHAPTER 13

"Vote early and often."
attributed to Chicago Mayor
- Richard J. Daley -

IT WAS AN HOUR BEFORE noon and Bobby Barnes was looking for the white van. The organizers said to be ready anytime between eleven and noon, but Bobby's stomach was impatient. He had been dreaming about the feast for a week.

A woman in a light blue Prius lowered her window an inch and called out to him, breaking the trance. Bobby stumbled his way to the car, taking care to not look too able. He took the dollar bill she pushed through the gap at the top of the glass.

"God bless you, ma'am," Bobby said with a humble nod.

The woman smiled slightly and pressed the button to raise the window. Bobby saw her squirt a dollop of hand sanitizer in her palm and vigorously scrub away any contamination.

The Iowa winter chill was already blowing across the plains and Bobby was already shivering under his tattered Hawkeye basketball sweatshirt. He could see the white van two traffic lights away. A heater and a hot cup of coffee were waiting for him.

As the van got closer, Bobby could read the words "New Freedom People's Church" printed on a magnetic sign on the side door. The van barely paused at the curb before Bobby had loaded his lawn chair and himself on board. He didn't have to worry about protecting his corner from other panhandlers. He had claimed his spot three years before, and claim jumpers were dealt with harshly by the homeless community. Today was even safer than usual. It was election day, and virtually every other street person in town would be riding buses and vans to the polling places, just like him. In the business of homelessness, they called today "bonus day."

The Lewis campaign staffer drove the van into a shopping center parking lot. He turned to look at his riders. Six men and a woman. The driver sorted through a stack of envelopes and passed some out to the group along with jackets, clean shirts, hair brushes, and deodorant.

"How many of you have done this before?" he asked.

Every rider raised a hand.

"Can everyone read?"

Again, all hands went up.

"Great. All veterans. That's good. Go ahead and open your envelopes."

In each envelope was a slip of paper with a name and an address.

"It's best if you can remember the name. There's no need to memorize the address. Just read it a few times so it will sound familiar. Keep the paper with you or write the name in the palm of your hand, in case you get confused," the driver said. "If you do forget your name, just pick up the voting instruction flyer on the registration table like this and read the name you wrote on your hand."

The driver demonstrated several times.

"Take your time and they'll never guess what you're doing. Okay. Now tell me who you are."

He pointed to the riders one at a time.

"Tommy Garner," the first man said.

"Manuel Lopez," said the next.

Bobby Barnes wanted to take a peek at his paper, but worried about looking dumb. "Seen Summerfield," he said, finally remembering the name he had just read.

"That's pronounced 'Shawn' even though it's spelled S-E-A-N," the driver corrected.

"Hey, it's my name now. I can say it anyway I want," Bobby said with a sniff.

"Smart-asses don't get paid," the driver shot back. "Your choice, pal."

The rest of the passengers obediently recited their temporary aliases. Satisfied, the driver started the van and drove around the block to the elementary school housing the district polling place. His passengers filed out and took their places in line.

Bobby Barnes stepped up to the table with the big "QRST" sign. He smiled at the elderly poll volunteer and said, "Sean Summerfield," just as confidently as he could. The woman flipped through a thick accordion of computer printed pages.

"Is your address 4888 Willow Oak Road?" she asked.

"Yes, ma'am. Still there, and my wife and I love it."

Barnes could not resist the impulse to ad-lib. As soon as he mentioned his fictional wife, however, he worried whether the real Sean Summerfield had a wife and whether it would show in the voter record the woman was reading from. His anxiety was calmed when he saw her gently peel the label from the page and stick it on a 5"x9" card.

"Please sign here," she said, not bothering to call him by name.

Barnes scribbled out something that appeared to begin with an "S," but was otherwise illegible. The volunteer handed him a ballot and pointed him to a voting booth.

Bobby glanced over the ballot, not recognizing a single name. But the name Lewis did look a bit familiar, but fortunately he did not need to know the particular person he was supposed to vote for. He was voting "straight party." He found the line he was looking for and connected the black arrowhead with the black arrow tail with a thick felt tip marker next to the word "Democrat." Voting straight party made life easy. And Bobby was all about easy.

Bobby stuffed his ballot in the automatic vote counting machine. A red electronic "1131" lit up. The man next to the machine stuck an "I Voted" sticker on Bobby's new shirt.

When everyone was back in the van, the driver passed out more envelopes. These each contained thirty dollars in small, worn bills along with a coupon for lunch at the C&G Cafeteria. Bobby loved that cafeteria with its endless dessert bar.

"I'll be back in an hour," the driver said as he dropped off his voters. "Come right here to the curb and be on time. We have three more polls to hit this afternoon."

The driver knew his voters would be there. Four envelopes of cash, a free lunch, some new clothes, and the finale of a big dinner always guaranteed loyalty. They just had to remember their temporary names three more times.

CHAPTER 14

"It is not only his right, but his duty...to find the verdict according to his own best understanding, judgment and conscience, though in direct opposition to the direction of the court."

- John Adams -

IN THE LIBRARY OF THE governor's mansion, Brewster Steele tossed a cold can of Coors to Fred Cameron. The state attorney general snagged it with one hand, just like he'd done with a hundred and twelve passes from Steele when they played at A&M, including a thirty-two yarder to seal a win in the Fiesta Bowl.

"How about you, Stu? You want anything while I'm up?" Steele asked his campaign strategist. "It's going to be a long night."

Stu Timmerly was lost in the early returns on his laptop and only shook his head. The polls had closed on the East Coast less than an hour ago and already three Senate seats and seven spots in the House had swung to the Democrats. Three televisions stood at the end of the room on wheeled carts, the sound muted on two.

"KBS News can now call the state of New Jersey for Vice President Theresa Lewis," Warren Tufts said with authority from the third television.

"No surprise there," Timmerly said. "North Carolina, Iowa, and West Virginia are tight, really tight. Probably can't call those for a while."

"Congress is tipping blue," Steele noted.

"That's a pretty good indication that things are gonna tip to Lewis, I'd say," Cameron said. He took a long pull on the beer. He watched as KBS switched to a snowy scene in front of the Wisconsin capitol.

"Turn that up," Cameron called out.

"An early November snow could not suppress the turnout here," Jennifer Blaine said. Her face was framed in a fur-trimmed hood. The television lights lit up flakes as they swirled around her. "The past month has seen an intensifying of emotions, especially in the governor's race. But several precincts have reported demonstrators marching as a picket line and intimidating voters, particularly in traditionally Republican precincts."

"Jennifer, haven't the police been able to disperse the protesters?" Tufts asked.

"Actually, no, Warren. There is a one hundred foot 'no campaigning' zone, kind of a DMZ, if you will, here in Wisconsin. The protesters were out here early this morning with tape measures carefully measuring the legal distance. You see the cones behind me?" she asked, pointing. The camera swung to the left. "That's the line at this poll. We have reports that this same type of thing has occurred throughout the state. We've seen several cars pull up, often driven by elderly people, and slow down and look at the picket line and the piles of snow to each side, and then seemingly decide to not bother voting. They simply drive on."

"Is there that much snow?" Tufts asked. "It doesn't look like it's that heavy."

"We've only gotten a few inches, Warren. The plows have been busy keeping the roads and parking lots clear. But for some reason they decided to push the snow into the worst possible spot. They've ended up creating a narrow opening to the poll. And that has allowed the protesters to tighten their ranks. Voters have to funnel between the snow piles and squeeze past demonstrators carrying placards to get by. Some voters aren't that aggressive. And I'm sure the older voters worry about injury if they were to slip and fall."

"That's an unfortunate set of circumstances, Jennifer. Do you know who the protesters are?" Tufts asked.

"They don't call themselves protesters, Warren. 'Concerned citizens' is the term they use to describe themselves. Most of them are union members, many from the larger unions."

"'Concerned citizens' my ass," Timmerly said, still not looking up from his laptop computer. "They're union thugs. It's pure voter intimidation. Hey Brew, you got any guesses why those snow piles happened to end up where they did?"

Steele, a lifelong Texan, had only seen snow being plowed once in his life, and that was while changing planes in Chicago last year. He shook his head.

"The plow operators are all public employees. They're all union members," Timmerly said. "They could have pushed that snow anywhere. Instead, they made it into a box canyon, nature's ready-made corral. You Texans can appreciate how much easier it is to defend the narrow opening of a box canyon than trying to protect yourself out in the open. And is there a law stipulating where to pile the snow? I think not."

Steele hadn't really heard him. His attention was drawn to the TV tuned to ANN, the All News Network.

"There it is!" he said, pointing to the screen where an image of a blue-eyed brunette smiled above a checkmark. "They've called Mary's race. She's in for a sixth term." He raised his glass and toasted her victory.

From the television, anchorman Gordon Wexler's gravelly voice said, "We can call the race for the First U.S. Congressional District in Pennsylvania. The Pennsylvania congresswoman, Mary Ketterling Steele, an outspoken progressive, is half of America's oddest political couple. Her husband is the conservative Republican governor of Texas, Brewster Steele."

"Stranger than fiction, as far as the liberal media is concerned," Steele said. "They just can't believe a liberal would actually fall in love with and marry an evil conservative. And her constituents still love her. Hey, Wexler, you flipping idiot, look at her, she's beautiful, smart, and does what she pleases. That's why they still love her. She's not a party puppet."

"Cool down, Brew. We all love her," Cameron said.

Timmerly jumped in. "We've got a good one here. All three networks just declared Jerri Welsch has won re-election as governor. Glad there are still enough Arizonans left who believe in individual freedom to keep her in office."

Steele grinned. "There are more than you might think if you only judged by the vote count. I'll bet you half of the folks who voted Democrat really just want the government to keep out the bad guys and otherwise leave them alone to live the life they choose."

Steele turned up the sound as the TV cut to Welsch's location. Balloons and confetti danced through the air in the Phoenix Hyatt ballroom. A band blasted out the campaign theme song. Jerri Welsch had two speeches prepared for this moment. Had Wes Roberson won the presidency, she would have delivered an optimistic message of reconciliation with the federal government. She could burn that speech. The proverbial writing was on the wall. The charges against Roberson had destroyed not only his candidacy, but any chance that the Republicans could hang onto Congress. Once Florida fell to Vice President Lewis, it was all over.

Welsch's second speech, the one she nicknamed the "nuclear option," was the one she held in her hand. The time had come to plant a flag for states' sovereignty.

In CONGRESS. July 4, 1776.

The unanimous Declaration of the thirteen united States of America.

Part 2

Inauguration

IN CONGRESS. JULY 4, 1776.

The unanimous Declaration of the thirteen united States of America.

CHAPTER 15

"The liberties of a people never were, nor ever will be, secure, when the transactions of their rulers may be concealed from them."

- Patrick Henry -

A COLD, RAW DRIZZLE hung over Washington like the flu. President-elect Lewis looked out at the shivering crowd. Even though it was one of those January days when it seems as if the sun never rises, the stage shone in a ghoulish blue haze under hundreds of federally mandated compact fluorescent lights. Radiant heaters hidden behind the bunting-wrapped railing struggled to warm the President-elect and her entourage. Only the heavy-duty security detail seemed impervious to the cold. They stood stone-faced and menacing, and very, very visible — Lewis couldn't have the crowd fearing another attempt on her life.

As the Marine Band completed playing The Star-Spangled Banner, Catherine Begley, the president of Sarah Lawrence College, was delivering the opening inaugural remarks at President-elect Lewis's request. It wasn't so much a request as it was a peace offering. Lewis had flown into one of her famous purple rages when her soon-to-be chief of staff, outgoing President Sanchez, insisted she take the oath with her hand on a Bible. It was no secret that Lewis was a staunch atheist. Putting her hand on a bible was akin to her putting her hand on a hot griddle. But her advisors managed to convinced her she would lose significant support from the Bible Belt Democrats if he rejected the tradition, and she would end up spending the next two years, and plenty of costly pork legislation, trying to win them back. That pork would help them and not her. She needed all the federal funds she could garner to implement her own pet projects.

Begley concluded her remarks to some live, but mostly recorded, applause. Chief Justice Louis Weinstein and the President took their places at the podium. Vice President-elect Charles Stafford sat to the left. There would be no public swearing in for him. Lewis insisted on having the stage and spotlight to herself. Stafford, like the lapdog running mate he was, agreed and was sworn in by an Associate Justice in the White House that morning, thus remaining a footnote in history.

Chief Justice Weinstein took the podium.

"Ladies and gentlemen," Weinstein announced, "it is my distinct honor to preside as Vice President Theresa Goodwin Lewis takes the oath of office for the presidency of the United States."

Lewis placed a gloved hand on Weinstein's Bible and recited the oath.

"I do solemnly swear that I will faithfully execute the office of President of the United States, and will to the best of my ability, preserve, protect, and defend the Constitution of the United States."

"Congratulations, Ms. President," Weinstein said shaking her hand. Lewis had insisted on being called "Ms. President" saying the title "Madam President" sounded like she'd just been elected to the top job at a brothel.

A twenty-one-gun salute rang out above the cheers. The Marine Band played four ruffles and flourishes, then launched into "Hail to the Chief," while the freshly-minted President stood respectfully at the podium. A comforting wave of warmth rose from the heated mat beneath her feet. She slipped her hands from her thin leather gloves, turning the gloves inside out in the process, stuffed them into a pocket, and waved back at the enthusiastic applause. After less than a minute, as a concession to the weather, she signaled for silence and began the inaugural address she had rehearsed to near memorization.

"My fellow citizens," President Lewis began, "I stand before you humbled by the epic task before us, grateful for the trust you have bestowed upon me, and mindful of the promise of fairness and equality for all citizens of this great nation the founders created when framing the Constitution more than two centuries ago. We have made significant progress in realizing that promise. And on this momentous day, we can say the dream is becoming reality. Yet there still lies a long, arduous road ahead. The end of that road is in sight. I can see it. I can see an America where poverty has been abolished, the air is clean and fresh, and hunger is a distant memory. That will be our reward at the end of our struggle. My fellow citizens, I pledge to lead you to that reward."

Thirty frigid minutes later, Lewis had managed to claim fictional triumphs for the Sanchez-Lewis administration while laying blame for all the troubles that remained at the feet of their opponents. The sound bite that made the headlines came when she chastised the governors of Texas, Arizona, and Louisiana for attempting to block federal programs in their states and refusing to accept all immigrants and refugees, whether legal or not.

In Baton Rouge, Governor Marjorie LaPierre watched and listened as Lewis once again bashed her leadership of the state. This wasn't the first time Lewis had managed to raise LaPierre's blood pressure. Only a month ago the Vice President made a quick tour of New Orleans, ostensibly to monitor another Gulf oil spill cleanup, but in reality it was a fifteen-minute stopover for campaign images and free press coverage. It had been nearly twenty months since she set foot in Louisiana, despite her grandstand pledge to personally see to it that the oil companies cleaned every last grain of sand and scrubbed every gull and crab. On that earlier visit, she never actually saw the Gulf. Instead she stopped for a photo op at a federally subsidized wind turbine factory that, despite over two hundred million dollars from the Economic Jumpstart program, was teetering on the brink of bankruptcy.

According to the media, Governor LaPierre ambushed the Vice President as she stepped off Air Force Two, handed her a list of grievances, and got into a finger-wagging lecture. The governor acknowledged it was an emotional conversation, but she insisted the finger pointing came when she was emphasizing that President Sanchez was responsible for the lack of action on his pledges and did not have the strength of character to come to see the damage for himself.

"Instead, he hides behind the skirt of his Vice President," LaPierre was reported to have said.

Privately, she admitted telling the Vice President that she and the state of Louisiana wanted nothing to do with any federal money that came with piles of regulations and would terminate in a year, leaving the state with the cost of continuing the program.

The governor picked up the phone and tapped in the number for Brewster Steele's cell phone. Two rings later, a Texas drawl answered.

"Howdy, Marge. How's the sweetest Cajun on the bayou?" Steele asked.

"I forgot about caller ID, honey," LaPierre said. "I can't sneak up on you anymore."

"The way you light up a room, you never could, darlin'."

"You sure can make a girl blush, Brew. Mary's a lucky girl."

"Naw, I'm the lucky one, Marge. I don't deserve a girl like Mary, but she's always so busy in Washington or Philly, we have to arrange our play dates a month in advance," Steele said.

"Poor baby. If she ever leaves you, make sure I'm the first to know," LaPierre said.

Steele chuckled. "Right now Mary's sitting out in the rotten Washington winter listening to President Lewis explain how she'll save us all. I'm here keepin' my boots warm."

"Are you watching Lewis?"

"With one eye. Mary's sure to fill me in on every detail. I did agree to escort her to the inaugural ball tonight," Steele said. "I figured the inaugural address is what you were calling about. It just keeps getting worse. And you know as well as I do any state that went to Roberson is gonna get pounded for the next four years."

"I hear you, Brew. How long 'til we see those off-shore drilling permits?"

"You can kiss them good-bye. There's no way they'll get approved with Lewis in office. Plus, she's got a grudge against you since the tarmac lecture."

"I know, I know," LaPierre said. "I should have bitten my tongue. It just breaks my heart to see good men and women suffer with no jobs while the Chinese and Mexicans suck our oil out from under our feet."

"I was just kidding. I don't think that incident made any difference. She's acting the same way toward us. Course, I've poked her and Sanchez in the eye a few times, too."

"We've got plenty to decide when the Council meets next week. Have the other governors confirmed?"

"Mississippi and Alabama are in. Florida's out. Chalmers is getting cold feet."

"I suppose it's understandable," LaPierre said. "He's got a huge Democratic block in Miami he's got to worry about, especially after that stupid comment that it might be a good idea for elections to be suspended for a while so senators and congressmen could vote without fear of getting bounced from office. He's got some damage control to do."

"Chalmers was always a couple gallons short of a Stetson," Steele agreed. "I'm not sure he can even spell 'Constitution.'"

"You think the others will go along with our plan?" LaPierre asked.

"No idea," Steele answered. "It may end up being just you and me, darlin'."

CHAPTER 16

*"History does not long entrust the care of freedom
to the weak or the timid."*

- Dwight Eisenhower -

RED, WHITE, AND BLUE banners draped the Lafayette Hotel ballroom. Mary Ketterling-Steele dragged her reluctant husband by the hand, searching for their assigned table.

"It'll be in the back of the room," Brewster Steele said. "They can't risk having my mug caught in a photo op."

"Don't jump to conclusions, honey," Mary said. "I was on her re-election advisory committee in Pennsylvania. Remember?"

"All too well," Brewster answered with an undisguised grimace.

"None of that," she scolded. "Be a good boy or no nookie tonight."

"You've certainly learned Washington is all about power, darlin'," Steele said, pulling out a chair for her. "You sit right here and I'll run and get our drinks."

The room filled quickly and only two empty seats remained at their table when Steele returned. Three members of Mary's staff, all classmates of Mary's from Sarah Lawrence, and their spouses were now seated at their table. Brewster greeted each one cordially.

"Can I get drinks for anyone else?" Steele offered, seeing a chance to spend a few more minutes away from policy discussions. He took their orders and spent the next fifteen minutes ferrying chardonnay from the bar to the table. As expected, when he finally took his seat, the discussion about the next wave of the Sanchez-Lewis administration agenda was well underway.

"Of course, its fate all hangs on the decision of the Supreme Court," Malcolm Jones, Mary's chief of staff, said.

"Would that be the Washington Socialist Act you're discussing?" Brewster asked. He knew arguments for and against the WSA were expected to be heard by the court in June.

Mary shot him a glare.

"The Wellness Security Act is not socialist, Governor Steele," Jones sniffed. "Disparaging nicknames for critical legislation won't help forty-three million uninsured Americans get the health care they need. It's unfairness like this that needs to be stamped out."

"By robbing people through taxes?" Steele asked.

"Brew," Mary whispered to Steele, "you promised to not get into issues like this. Can't we just talk about sports?"

"I don't mind, Mary," Jones said. He wondered what Mary saw in this hayseed from Texas — other than the hard body Jones couldn't help but be attracted to. "Education is necessary to turn the tide against conservatism. They simply do not know what they do not know. Fear and hatred come from ignorance."

"I appreciate you helping me fill out my education, Malcolm," Steele chuckled. "So what is the forecast for the Supreme Court challenge?"

"Let's agree to table that discussion," Mary interrupted, glancing to her right at the elderly couple making their way slowly toward them.

"Chief Justice Weinstein," Steele said, rising and extending a hand. "You probably don't remember us from four years ago. I'm Brewster Steele, and this is my wife, Mary."

"Yes, Governor and Congresswoman, I remember you well. I haven't lost it, yet. We spent some time chatting at the last inaugural ball. And you remember my wife, Francis?" Introductions were made all around as the salads were served.

Seventy-three-year-old Chief Justice Louis Weinstein was either a pillar of the Supreme Court, or a relic who served beyond his time, depending on one's political point of view. Weinstein had outlasted six Presidents. When first appointed decades ago, the Democrats hardly raised an objection. It seemed a foregone conclusion that a Jewish judge would tilt to the liberal side. To the shock of all liberals, Weinstein was decidedly apolitical and took no sides in any election. He angered both parties equally. He took his job as an interpreter of constitutionality seriously and often wrote opinions condemning the trend towards reinterpreting the document that served as the foundation of the country.

"The framers of the Constitution had one goal in mind," he often said. "They considered all the powers governments had claimed, asserted, and often abused, throughout history and balanced them against the innate and natural rights of man. Only those powers of government that did not infringe upon the natural rights of man were allowed to remain with the government. All other powers not enumerated in the Constitution would remain with the people or the states. The key is the phrase 'not enumerated,'" he often emphasized.

Liberal wags called Weinstein the Supreme Blunder, regretting the fact that appointments to the Supreme Court are for life. Republicans sang from the conservative hymnal, but once elected, they were nearly as willing to expand government and its powers as Democrats, and they regretted how Weinstein had headed off many of their corporate welfare schemes.

To Mary Ketterling-Steele's relief, as Weinstein and his wife seated themselves, Weinstein's presence abruptly ended the discussion of the Supreme Court. As if reading her mind, Weinstein steered the conversation to the NFL playoffs.

"I'm hoping for another title for my Patriots," he said with a cough.

"I can join you on that, sir," Steele said, "now that the Cowboys got bounced out of the playoffs in the first round."

Weinstein coughed again and took a sip from his bourbon.

"Damn Washington weather," he cursed.

"I told you you'd catch something standing out there in the rain," Francis Weinstein said.

"I've never missed an inauguration or an inaugural ball since my appointment," Weinstein said. "It's an important courtesy to the President. This city needs to hang on to a few manners."

Weinstein coughed again and his cheeks flushed.

"I promise to stay indoors tomorrow, my dear," he said to his wife while patting her hand. "And we'll only stay here until the President has arrived. Hopefully that will be soon. I am feeling a bit feverish."

Francis Weinstein put a hand to her husband's forehead. The band began to play "Hail to the Chief" and the room lights dimmed. Senator Nate Cummings, the majority leader from California, took the podium. The audience rose in unison.

"Ladies and gentlemen," Cummings said.

Justice Weinstein wavered and caught himself, jangling his silverware and overturning a wine glass in the process. Brewster Steele reached for his arm to steady him.

"I'm fine," he whispered to Steele, refusing his hand.

Mary dropped a napkin on the spreading puddle of chardonnay.

"It is my distinct pleasure to present the President and First Gentleman of the United States, Theresa Goodwin Lewis and Michael..."

A crash and the sound of breaking glass stopped him short as Weinstein collapsed across the table. Secret Service agents closed ranks around the President, pushing her out of the room. Her armored limousine lingered with open doors under the hotel porte-cochère. In an instant, the President and her husband were inside the limo and speeding away.

Brewster Steele reached for Weinstein's carotid artery. There was no pulse. Steele rolled his tuxedo jacket around his arm and swept broken glass and shards of china from the table. He rolled Weinstein onto his back. Blood oozed from a dozen small cuts, but none appeared to be life threatening and none looked to be bullet holes. Steele plucked off Weinstein's clip-on bowtie and ripped open his shirt. Still no bullet holes, but the man wasn't breathing. Steele looked up at Malcolm Jones, who stood in frozen shock.

"Is he...?" Malcolm Jones asked.

"Shut up and call 911," Steele growled.

Mary stepped in front of Jones.

"I already did," she said, leaning over and loosening Weinstein's cummerbund. "They're on the way."

Steele started pumping Weinstein's chest hard and fast as he watched Weinstein's eyes roll back in his head. Steele felt a clammy chill creep into the man's flesh. He kept pumping even though he sensed it was too late.

CHAPTER 17

"Well, by the standards of a lot of countries, by Latin American standards, it [inflation] wasn't so bad."

- Paul Volcker -
former Chairman of the Federal Reserve

WARREN TUFTS, WHO had made a tradition of following each President from one inaugural ball to the next for the past seven inaugurations, looked shaken as he delivered his special report from a remote broadcast truck outside the hotel.

"The Chief Justice of the U.S. Supreme Court, Louis Weinstein, has died," Tufts said. "Chief Justice Weinstein collapsed while attending the inaugural ball just hours ago. Emergency personnel were unable to revive him. Weinstein was rushed to George Washington University Hospital where he was pronounced dead just minutes ago. Although rumors of another attack on President Lewis are completely false — I repeat, there has *not* been another attempt on the President's life — the remainder of the President's inaugural schedule for this evening has been cancelled as a security measure."

Brewster Steele sprawled across the sofa and took another swallow from his double scotch. He'd need more than a little aged alcohol running through his veins to neutralize the adrenaline and stop his brain from endlessly replaying the scene at the Lafayette. Almost worse than the tragedy of a good man suddenly dying were the political implications of Weinstein's unexpected death.

"Did you know Justice Weinstein ran the Marine Corps marathon just last year to celebrate his seventieth birthday?" he asked Mary. "He was in tremendous condition for a man of his age. His seat wasn't expected to be the appointment Lewis would have this term." Steele took another sip and cast a forlorn glance across his wife's Georgetown apartment, looking at nothing in particular. "Weinstein was the deciding vote on all the critical issues."

"Some people think it's about time the court came back from the far right and was receptive to the social reform we've been working for," Mary said.

"*You've* been working for, you mean. Not *we*. You and your people have been filling the courts with activist judges who have no qualms about legislating from the bench," Brewster said. "It's gone too far."

As soon as his mouth said the words, Steele's brain wished he hadn't. All he had wanted was a nice night with his wife, especially after the trauma of the inaugural ball. But now — well, he knew that look in her eye.

"What's gone too far?" Mary challenged. "School lunch programs? Do you want kids to go hungry? Health care for the needy? Do you want people to get sick and die? And guns, let's not even start that argument."

"Mary, honey," Brewster said, trying to put an arm around her and pull her close, to stop the storm before it started. She brushed his hand away.

"Weinstein had the Supreme Court anchored in the eighteenth century," she continued, her voice rising. "The

Constitution wasn't supposed to be frozen in time. It was supposed to change as society changed."

"We can agree on that," Brewster said, "we just can't agree on the method of change." Thinking about what Weinstein's death would mean, Brewster couldn't help but voice his disagreement, even though he didn't want an argument. "Every year a new stack of regulations come from unelected bureaucrats and crony appointees. The corruption is unbelievable. The only man who stood between 'The Party' and the people just keeled over in his hors d'oeuvre plate."

"Which party do you mean," Mary asked. "Democrats or Republicans?"

"Both," Brewster answered. "Anybody who works in Washington is a part of 'The Party' in some way or another."

"Are you saying I'm part of 'The Party?'"

Brewster paused a moment. What started out as an evening of marital bliss was turning sour fast. He didn't want to take this discussion further, but it was too late.

"Well, I suppose you are."

"That hurts, Brew," Mary said, taking another step away from him. "I didn't run for Congress to elevate myself. I came here with a mission. I'm trying to be part of the solution. Do you think corporations and the super-rich are going to make everything right? The only reason they do anything charitable is for the publicity it brings."

"That might be true for some, but not all." Steele countered. "Charity should be voluntary, not mandatory. Government has no business stepping in and forcibly taking money from people through taxes. It's robbery, plain and simple."

Mary glared at him. "So how's the voluntary scheme working out, Brew? The gap between rich and poor is larger than it's ever been. If charity is voluntary, how do you explain that?"

"I've got two answers for you, darlin'. First, that statement is totally false. The gap between the rich and poor is not the largest in history. Have you ever heard of John D. Rockefeller and his cronies? What do you think the income of the average worker was then compared to those robber barons? You liberals can repeat that line a million times, but it won't make it true. Second, even if you accepted that bunk about the gap between the rich and poor, where is the moral justification for taking money from one person and giving it to another? The government is not Robin Hood."

"I suppose you'd prefer to see people suffer?" Mary retorted.

"Your do-good programs have caused more suffering than they've relieved," Brewster shot back. "You've created generations of people who can do little to help themselves. You've stripped away their dignity and rendered them broken and useless. You've made them slaves to the government."

"God, you're such a racist," Mary said, shaking her head in disgust. "I can't believe you said that."

"No, ma'am. There's nothing racist about stating a fact. This has nothing to do with race. It's about freedom."

"These people needed help," Mary insisted.

"And your help is a time bomb," Brewster said.

"What do you mean by that?" Mary asked.

"How long do you think the taxpayers can keep up the pace? The only reason your form of socialism has been able to go on this long is because the American economy is so strong. It is the goose that lays golden eggs for your altruistic utopia. But you people just don't know when to stop. You don't realize that you're killing the goose and soon there will be no more golden eggs. If you think poor people suffer now, just wait until the dollar is worthless and the taxpayers lose their jobs. You'll see suffering you only see in third world nations. And I'm not about to sit by and watch it happen."

"If your prediction is right, and I'm not saying it is, what are you planning on doing to stop it?" Mary asked. "You lost the election. You've missed your chance."

"The fight's not over, darlin'. I plan to keep Texas from going over the edge."

"And you're blaming me for this problem?" Mary snapped.

"You and you friends let it happen. In fact, you encouraged it. When did you ever vote to slow down the spending? When did you ever vote against a tax increase? You just didn't know you were being duped. You didn't know they were exploiting your compassion for people. They used you."

Mary stormed to the bedroom and returned with a blanket and pillow. She threw them at him.

"You can sleep out here on your side of the aisle tonight, Mr. Republican."

In CONGRESS, July 4, 1776.

The unanimous Declaration of the thirteen united States of America.

CHAPTER 18

"And it proves, in the last place, that liberty can have nothing to fear from the judiciary alone, but would have everything to fear from its union with either of the other departments."

- Alexander Hamilton -

LIGHT FROM THE OVAL OFFICE spilled out across the rose garden. Inside, President Lewis kept the inaugural celebration going. Former President, now Chief of Staff, Carlos Sanchez scooped another bottle of Dom Perignon from the ice bucket, twisted off the wire collar, and sent the cork rocketing off the bas relief eagle carved onto the ceiling.

"Can't let that glass go dry, Mr. Speaker," Sanchez said as he poured another round for Representative Adrian Wilson. "We've got plenty of drivers to get you home."

"Not Mr. Speaker yet, Mr. President," Wilson said. "Is that still the proper way to address you, sir?"

"You'll be Mr. Speaker soon enough, Adrian. It's merely a formality now. And I'm not really sure what the hell's the proper title for a past President turned Chief of Staff might be. We'll have to make something up, right Ms. President?"

"How about we just call you 'Chief'?" Lewis answered.

"I like that," Sanchez agreed as he leaned over and topped off the glass held in the slender hand of Yumi Narito, his personal assistant. She was his fourth assistant in as many years, each one more beautiful than the last.

Tony Delgado stood and raised his glass. "I'd like to propose a toast. Here's to the ultimate Comeback Kid. Two weeks before the election, you were down double digits in the polls, Theresa. And now we sit here in the Oval Office once again. Here's to the greatest comeback in the history of presidential elections."

"Great job running my campaign, Tony." Lewis gave his campaign manager a Cheshire grin.

Romeo Costa gave the President a pat on the back and drained his glass. "It was merely a matter of closing out the game," he said. "We had a solid end game."

"I'll say," Vice President Charles Stafford piped in. "I thought we were dead meat. Lucky for us that Roberson turned out to be a pervert!"

"Lucky indeed," Lewis said, winking at Costa. She raised her glass, again. "Another toast, gentlemen. Here's to the luckiest damn politician who ever put his foot in his mouth, the man who'll say anything we ask him to, our Vice President, Chuck."

Stafford half grinned, not sure if he'd been praised or insulted.

"Both Houses, the Presidency, and now the Supreme Court," Sanchez said. "Let's drink to the repose of the cold, conservative soul of Chief Justice Weinstein, the last blockade between what this country was and what this country will be."

"We've got the short list of possible appointees ready for you, sir," Delgado said.

"Christ, his body's not even cold, yet, and you're already picking his replacement?" Nate Cummings said. "Have a shred of decency."

"You're right Nate," Sanchez agreed. "We'll give it another couple days before we make a formal announcement. We can leak it tomorrow to grease the chute for confirmation." Sanchez looked at his empty glass, frowned, and grabbed another bottle. He pressed the cork, bouncing this one off Jefferson's portrait.

"God, I love to do that," Sanchez laughed. "I ought to challenge that frickin' cowboy down in Texas to a champagne bottle duel at dawn. We'd see how tough he is when he's staring down the barrel of my magnum."

He snickered drunkenly. "You get that one, Cummings? You got any sense of humor?"

Sanchez reached out to put the bottle on the coffee table, missed, and dropped it on the rug. The bottle bounced and rolled, spurting champagne across the woven Presidential Seal.

"No harm," he said. "We're having that seal redesigned, anyway. That one's too military for my taste."

Romeo Costa tossed a couple of napkins on the wet carpet and pressed them down with his shoe.

"Actually, Tony," Sanchez said, "We won't need your short list. We're nominating Salvador Reyes. Right Theresa?"

"Right...Chief," Lewis answered looking like this was the first she had heard of it.

"Salvador Reyes from the Great American Boycott?" Cummings sputtered. "He's as radical as they come. I'll never get him confirmed. And it will be political suicide for me if I do."

"Nate, Salvador is my greatest friend. He's a lawyer. He's got legal credentials. And there are no actual qualification requirements for the Supreme Court. No hay problema, amigo," Sanchez said.

"The problem is three-quarters of my constituents see him as totally anti-American," Cummings whined. "Christ, he's been associated with groups that want to make California part of Mexico. I'm up for re-election in two years. You people might be bulletproof now, but I'm not. If you insist on Salvador, you'll be hanging me out to dry."

"It's actually quite simple, Senator," Sanchez said. "You either push his confirmation through and endure a rocky re-election campaign that we'll try to help you win, or you don't back him and we'll make sure you not only lose your re-election bid, but that you face charges of election fraud as well."

"I've never done anything that could be considered fraud," Cummings protested.

"Oh, come on, Senator. We all have, and you know it. It's just that in your case, the entire state of California will know what you did or might have done. And the details will be embellished enough to get the media salivating. Remember, it's not the facts that matter to them; it's the seriousness of the charge. There's no fair trial in the court of public opinion, Senator. Look what happened to Roberson."

Cummings knew the Roberson scandal ruined him, even though the allegations were never backed up. And he knew it could happen to him. Like it or not, he was going to have to march to the Sanchez drumbeat — at least on this matter. But he swore to himself that this would be the last time. He was going to take matters into his own hands.

Cummings stood up and looked the past President in the eye. "Fuck you, Sanchez," he said, and headed for the door.

"And a pleasant evening to you too, Senator," Sanchez mocked.

Romeo Costa tapped his double encrypted iPad and swiped his index finger across the personal identification app. A screen crowded with icons lit up. He touched the one named "Trexell" and a list appeared.

"Do we add Cummings to the action list or the pending list?" he asked.

Sanchez thought a moment.

"Pending," Sanchez said. "Let's see how he responds after he's had a night to sleep on it. He's been loyal for quite a while. He's more use to us in office than out. Plus, there's no need to break in a newbie, yet."

"Have you reviewed the action list?" Costa asked.

"I have. Go ahead and cue our man. It's best to put some time between the change in the identity records and when it hits the news. We can tip the media about the files when we need to persuade someone or take him out of the game."

Sanchez turned to his assistant.

"Yumi, do you know where Mrs. Sanchez is?"

"She said she had a headache and she's gone home to bed," Narito answered.

"Fine. I'll be staying here tonight." Sanchez said. "But first I need a good soak in the spa. Yumi, please ask the staff to set it up and be sure it's nice and hot. I need some steamy relaxation tonight."

Narito stood and walked out of the room as the men's eyes followed her slim, swaying hips longingly all the way to the door.

President Lewis looked puzzled.

"You're staying in the White House tonight?" she asked.

"Yes, Theresa. I've had the Lincoln bedroom set up as the 'Chief of Staff's' emergency quarters," he explained. "I need to be nearby in case you need my assistance and just to make sure things run smoothly. Besides, I've grown to like the amenities in the place. Don't worry. I won't bother you. The presidential apartment is all yours."

Sanchez turned and lifted his glass.

"One last toast, gentlemen," Sanchez said. "Here's to our new President and to 'our' America, the America of equality, and an America living under our leadership for a long, long time."

Ten minutes later, Sanchez dropped his robe and eased himself into the hot swirling water of the White House spa. Barry White sang softly in the background. Sanchez tapped the remote control and increased the volume, lifting White's seductive bass voice above the sound of the bubbling water. He leaned back, closed his eyes, and rested his head on the spa's cushioned rim.

A door opened and Sanchez heard muffled footsteps approach. He did not move. He inhaled the warm, moist air. A moment later, he felt a soft pressure against the outside of his thighs. Opening his eyes, he saw two perfect legs straddling his. His eyes involuntarily traced the sensuous lines of Yumi Narito's naked body. A trickle of perspiration drew a crooked line between her breasts. She held a bottle of champagne in one hand and two glasses in the other.

The new presidential Chief of Staff smiled.

"Yes, Yumi, I greatly value an assistant who willingly works overtime."

CHAPTER 19

"The only difference between death and taxes is that death doesn't get worse every time Congress meets."

- Will Rogers -

NATE CUMMINGS TOOK A deep breath. He knew what he was about to do was necessary, but he also knew it could destroy him. His mind went back to his confrontation with Sanchez in the Oval Office on inauguration night. He clenched his jaw. It was time to take a stand.

Cummings looked at the man seated across the desk from him. Former FBI special agent Arthur Campbell filled the chair, which seemed to strain to contain his bulk. Although it was still winter, Campbell's shirt showed splotches of perspiration.

"Let's get down to it, Mr. Campbell," Cummings said. "My people tell me you're the best private investigator in Washington. And I saw you on Warren Tufts' news show talking about what happened in Miami. You had a distinctly different take on things than the others."

"Okay," Campbell said.

"I have two jobs for you. As I'm sure you know, the President has nominated Salvador Reyes for the Supreme Court. You know who he is?"

"From the Great American Boycott," Campbell answered with a nod.

"My committee must confirm him. I need a full workup on his background. I like to run these things independent from the FBI. So that's where you come in. I'm retaining you for that job."

"You want all the dirt?" Campbell asked.

"No. There's no point to that," the senator said despondently. "It's a slam dunk with our majority in the Senate. He's the President's man so there's no way the Senate will turn against him. The background investigation is window dressing just so we can say we did it. We'll be the President's lapdogs."

"You don't sound very happy about it."

"The man has no business being on the Supreme Court. No experience and he's a relentless partisan."

"Then why not find the dirt and get him denied?" Campbell asked.

"Let's just say the President read me the political facts of life. I have no choice."

"Blackmail?"

Cummings said nothing.

"Bummer," Campbell said. "Life's a bitch. Okay, I'll do an independent background on Reyes for you. Now, what's the second job?"

"This conversation never happened. You understand?"

"I don't like talking much, anyway," Campbell said.

Cummings nodded, and cleared his throat. "When I heard you on television the other night talking about Hank Samson, you had an interesting angle on his motivation."

"When I was with the FBI," Campbell said, "they stressed the importance of looking beyond the obvious. Now I do it by instinct."

"I think you brought up some good points. And I don't think the whole episode is exactly what it seems, either. Essentially, I agree with your take on his motivation, but a couple of parts are missing in the storyline."

"How so?"

"It's all too pat," Cummings said. "An expert marksman misses from what for him is short range. The shooter is killed immediately. The weapon goes missing. The timing pushes up the sympathy quotient days before the election. That could be a simple coincidence, or it could mean Samson was feeling desperate, thinking that the new President might rotate him out of his White House assignment and he'd lose his opportunity. I really don't know what to think of it. But I need to find answers."

"You think Costa wanted the Vice President dead and he set up Samson to do it, but the guy missed the Veep so he had to off Samson himself. Is that what I'm hearing here?"

"Maybe," Cummings said. "But how'd he miss his shot? The guy's a trained sniper."

"Shit happens," Campbell philosophized. "I thought you and the Prez were tight."

"Things change quickly in politics," Cummings said. "Sometimes you're Caesar and sometimes you're Brutus."

"I'll need money, Brutus."

"You're always the wise ass, aren't you?"

"We all have our personality quirks," Campbell said with a shrug.

"I'll authorize the money in the morning," Cummings said. "It'll come out of the Reyes background check allocation."

Campbell nodded. Both men rose and shook hands. As the door closed behind Campbell, Cummings slumped back into his chair. He wasn't entirely sure what Campbell would uncover, but he had a feeling it might change the future of the country.

CHAPTER 20

"We must all hang together, or, assuredly,
we shall all hang separately."
- Benjamin Franklin -
at the signing of the
Declaration of Independence, July 4, 1776

"GOVERNORS," MARJORIE LaPierre said, "thank you for coming to the first meeting of the Gulf States Governors Council. This may be a watershed moment in history. Although I am the host, the true force behind this effort is Texas Governor Steele. This was his vision, and I would like to turn the meeting over to him."

"Thanks, Marjorie," Steele said, "but I can't take any credit for today. I simply speak what we are all thinking."

Steele looked around the table at his new partners in this radical plan. Sally Winston was in her second term in Mississippi and riding a wave of popularity for her firm stance against federal mandates in the shrimping industry. Charles Freeman II was named for his great, great grandfather, an Alabama slave who gained freedom after the Civil War and became a sharecropper.

Freeman carried on the family tradition of integrity, hard work, and independence. He had won the governorship on the strength of a simple campaign slogan: "Freedom means responsibility." "It's not my job to take care of you," Freeman often said, "and it's not the government's job to take care of you. It's your job to take care of yourself. It's my job and government's job to remove as many obstacles as we can. When you are responsible for yourself, you are truly free." This resonated with enough voters to elect him in a landslide.

"Marjorie," Steele said, turning to his earliest ally, "your state, more than any of ours, depends on oil production for a big chunk of your jobs and economic vitality."

LaPierre nodded. "The federal moratorium on new permits, and now these ridiculous new regulations, are strangling us," she said. "We're at the point of desperation. The damage from the oil spill was minor compared to the damage the Sanchez administration has brought with this virtual boycott of new permits."

Sally Winston nodded. "We certainly don't have as large a stake in oil production in Mississippi," she said. "But it still accounts for a serious number of jobs along our coast."

"I know we're the newcomers to the oil business," Charles Freeman said, "but oil was at the top of my list for job growth. Now that's gone up in smoke."

Steele passed out folders of notes to each governor.

"We agree we have a serious problem. The next question is, what are we going to do about it?" Steele flipped his folder open. "As you can see, there have been only two deep-water permits issued in the eighteen months since the moratorium was officially lifted, and those both went to Petro Energy Resources. The majority shareholder of PER is Dimitri Borsky. Does that name sound familiar?"

"Borsky is the money guy behind TruthandLies.org, the organization that ran endless campaign ads in support of Sanchez and Lewis," Freeman said. "They're the same group that bankrolled the '99 Percent' protests leading up to the election."

"Welcome to politics Carlos Emilio Sanchez style," Steele said. "He remembers who is with him and he destroys whoever is against him. Borsky is operating without competition when it comes to new exploration in the Gulf."

"And it goes farther than that," Winston said. "Right at this moment, new platforms are being erected just outside U.S. territorial waters by Mexican oil companies. Each one of them is in partnership with Borsky and PER."

"And here we sit," LaPierre said, "four conservative Republican governors from four red states wondering why we can't get permits approved by the federal government. Now that the Sanchez has a replacement as President who is seemingly under his total control and no longer has to worry about reelection and has both houses of Congress, he has no reason to worry about the people in our states."

Steele looked from one governor to the next.

"We really have only two options," he said. "We can continue to futilely beg for relief from the Feds and plead for more permits. Or we can issue permits ourselves and claim that the power to issue drilling permits rests with the states."

"We don't have that authority," Winston objected.

"I disagree," Steele said. "I believe we don't *not* have the authority. There are still some questions about the federal prohibition against each state regulating its own territorial waters. Although the United States claims and ostensibly regulates the waters two hundred miles from its shore, the international treaty that grants this legal right — called the Exclusive Economic Zone, or EEZ — was signed, but never ratified. As my attorney general sees it, the federal government cannot legally regulate territory it does not have legal jurisdiction over."

"Wasn't there a Supreme Court ruling on this in the sixties?" Sally Winston asked.

"Yes," Steele answered. "*United States v. California*. 1965. The Court decided that the rights to the undersea land beyond the three-mile limit off the California coast belong to the United States and not to California. But keep in mind that this decision was based on the assumption that the United States actually had the rights to the territory in the first place. There have been no challenges that dispute that assumption. Our argument will be that the United States is not a legal participant in the EEZ and therefore has no authority over the coastal territory. That opens the way for the individual states to lay claim to it."

"But what about the Department of Energy and the EPA?" Winston asked.

"We, the coastal states, have gradually relinquished our authority over our territorial waters to the federal government one regulation at a time," Steele said. "It has led us to this dilemma. We have been backed to the edge of the cliff. It's time to seize back our sovereign authority or lose it forever."

"You're proposing we violate federal regulations?" Freeman asked.

"It's only a violation if the regulation is legal," Steele answered. "I'm proposing we declare those regulations illegal and the territory was improperly claimed by the federal government. We declare it to be an over-reaching of their constitutional authority. And then we begin to regulate off-shore drilling ourselves and throw the federal government out."

"They'll fight like a bulldog with a soup bone," LaPierre said.

"It could drag on in court for years," Sally Winston agreed. "By the time it's resolved, Lewis's first term, and maybe her second, God forbid, will likely be over. Meanwhile, we can get our oil production going again." She smiled. "We'll be fighting back using their own tactics."

"Governors, the time has come to make this official," Steele said. "I move that we adopt a resolution to issue state permits for off-shore drilling with appropriate environmental protections and safety oversight. We simultaneously agree to mutual legal defense against any challenges from the federal government. Do I have a second?"

CHAPTER 21

"In a time of universal deceit,
telling the truth is a revolutionary act."
- George Orwell -

"I DON'T KNOW WHY you bother listening to this crap," Past President Sanchez said to his former chief-of-staff Tony Delgado over the sound of Whit Horsnby's voice on the radio. Delgado's new title was Special Assistant to the Chief of Staff.

"Good to keep tabs on what the nutbags on the other side are saying," Delgado shrugged.

The conservative radio host was, as usual, railing against the administration. "President Theresa Lewis believes this country was founded for the express purpose of benefiting rich white men at the expense of the majority of the common people," Hornsby was saying. "He believes most people can't be self-reliant. What President Lewis believes, like Carlos Sanchez believed before her, is in socialism, pure and simple. She won't call it that. But that is exactly what it is. She believes if you have been successful and have money, the only way you got it was by cheating and stealing. You got your money at the expense of others."

Sanchez shook his head. "Unbelievable," he scoffed.

"I like it," Dimitri Borsky said, chuckling. "Is very funny — and maybe a little of the truth?"

Sanchez glared at him.

"I joke!" Borsky protested, chuckling again.

"You Russians have a strange sense of humor," Sanchez muttered.

"Okay," Hornsby's voice said. "I told you at the top of the hour we had a shocking sound bite from Past President Sanchez."

"Now what?" asked Sanchez, rolling his eyes.

"During his campaign for his first term," Hornsby continued, "Sanchez was in a meeting with several staffers at the Capitol Hotel in Albany, New York. Apparently one of his staffers was secretly recording these sessions on his cell phone. Our sources say he was discovered and fired. Most of his recordings were found and destroyed, but not all of them. On one campaign trip, this rogue staffer mistakenly took his wife's cell phone with him instead of his own. The recordings on that phone from that trip were never discovered by the Sanchez brownshirts. Now, these are hard to hear, so listen closely."

The muffled but recognizable voice of Carlos Sanchez could be heard above the clatter of coffee cups. "We have a perfect model for building a following," Sanchez said. "The person I'm talking about was a man who started with no money and no followers. Today he has a following of over two billion. Jesus Christ showed us how to build a following. He did it by promising the poor and lowly, the outcasts and slaves of the ancient world, a better life. He promised the poor would inherit the kingdom. He promised food to the hungry. He promised the rich would be humbled. He promised hope. He promised to fulfill the dreams of the people who only had dreams. But there was a catch. Jesus only promised to give people these things when they died. In the meantime, they had to trust him to deliver it all later while they were suffering at the hands of the powerful.

"I can do Jesus one better. I can promise all things he did and with me, you don't have to die to get them. I can take money from the rich and give it to the poor. I can take food from the well fed and give it to the hungry. I can take power away from the powerful and give it to the weak. I can turn society around.

"From his own lips, folks," Hornsby said. "Sanchez believes he is better than Jesus Christ.

"You might think we're beyond the regime of Carlos Sanchez and things can return to normal. But he's not really gone. He still lurks the corridors of the White House. He is Theresa Lewis's Chief of Staff in title only. But don't doubt me on this. Carlos Sanchez is still pulling the strings. Theresa Lewis's first term in office is ostensibly Carlos Sanchez's third term."

"Better than Jesus. That is good one!" laughed Borsky as Sanchez switched off the radio.

"Yeah, real good," Sanchez sighed. "Tony, how the hell did we miss that?"

"It doesn't really matter," Delgado replied. He un-muted the TV and changed the channel. "You've got bigger problems to deal with."

"Good evening," Warren Tufts said as the KBS logo flashed behind him. "In our top story tonight, just days after the sudden death of Chief Justice Louis Weinstein, President Lewis has announced her nominee to fill the vacant Supreme Court seat: Salvador Reyes. Mr. Reyes is well known as the driving force behind the Great American Boycott in California two decades ago, which aimed to gain legal residency status for migrant farm workers. The protest crippled the food industry for two months.

"Republican members of the Senate Judiciary Committee oppose Reyes's nomination, pointing to this radical past as well as his lack of judicial experience and reputation as a litigator for some of the most liberal organizations and their challenges to government policy. However, if the confirmation votes fall along party lines, Reyes will be confirmed by the end of the month.

"Cases that are expected to be heard by the Supreme Court in late spring include the Wellness Security Act and the Wireless Information Neutrality Act. With the confirmation of Mr. Reyes, the balance in the court will tilt to the left and the court is expected to uphold both measures."

"Where's the problem there?" Sanchez asked as the show cut to a commercial for adult diapers. "I couldn't care less what the Republicans think about Reyes. He's going to be confirmed."

"Just wait," Delgado said.

A new commercial started, showing senior citizens on a park bench with children playing on a playground in the background. An attractive senior woman spoke into the camera.

"I love taking my grandkids to the park. But if I want to keep up with those little bundles of energy, I have to stay healthy and eat right. And that can be a real challenge. That's where food stamp benefits come in. They help me eat right when money's tight."

"Come on, Grandma!" the grandchildren could be heard calling from a distance.

Two other senior citizens sat on a park bench next to the playground.

"Would you look at Margie?" one said. "She looks amazing."

"Yes, she sure does," her friend answered.

"I wonder how she stays so fit. What's her secret?"

"Well, she told me that food stamp benefits help her eat right, and she stays active, too."

"Oh. I didn't know they helped people our age."

"Oh, food stamps help lots of people. People you know."

"Wait. You, too?"

"Yes, me, too."

The announcer said, "Find out how you can live better and be healthier through food stamps. This public service message brought to you by the U.S. Department of Nutrition and Wellness."

"That's a damn good ad they put together," Sanchez said. "Almost makes me want to go on food stamps!" He laughed at the ridiculousness of the idea.

Warren Tufts returned to the screen as a map of the Gulf of Mexico popped up behind him. "Drilling in the Gulf of Mexico is still a contentious topic in the oil producing states," Tufts said. "Just moments ago, in an unorthodox and possibly illegal move, the states of Louisiana, Mississippi, Alabama, and Texas have released a group statement declaring the federal authority over their territorial waters invalid and void. The statement was issued on the letterhead of the Gulf States Governors Council, a newly formed alliance of states with a common interest in issues affecting the Gulf of Mexico. Texas governor Brewster Steele has acted immediately, issuing a deepwater permit to energy giant Texoil."

Delgado turned off the television and raised his eyebrows at Sanchez.

"Can they do that?" Sanchez snapped at Delgado.

"The AG and I were discussing this last week," Delgado answered. "The legal answer is maybe. We've got a team on it already. We caught wind of this possibly happening. No one suspected they would act on it so fast."

"You have rogue state on your hands, Carlos," Borsky said. "You going to have to teach them about compromise, like we do in Russia."

"I know about your Russian compromises, Dimitri. I can't just send in the army and blow things up. Unfortunately, here I've got laws I have to follow," Sanchez said.

"It only must appear legal and worked out through courts," Borsky answered with his Russian accent. "We both know that. The longer you let this go on, the harder it will be to stop. It's time for some pressure, my friend, or you will have same problem Soviet Union had in eighties."

Sanchez nodded in agreement. "Tony, you got the list?" he asked. Delgado handed him a legal pad with handwritten notes.

"This is a list of restrictions, embargoes, and controls we plan on implementing to squeeze Texas," Sanchez said, showing it to Borsky. "We'll regulate them until it hurts. I figure if we apply enough pain to the average citizen, Steele will fold like a cheap lawn chair."

"They will defy you," Borsky said. "The harder you push them the stronger they will become. You could see what happened to my country if you need an example."

The phone rang and Delgado picked it up.

"It's President Lewis, boss," he said.

"Tell her hold on," Delgado told him and turned back to Borsky.

"So, what — I just let Steele defy me? Is that what you're suggesting?" Sanchez asked.

"No, my friend," Borsky said. "I am saying that it would be easier to convince the people to turn away from Steele."

"Let me remind you, Dimitri — I only got thirty-two percent of the votes in Texas in the last election and Lewis didn't do any better. Neither one of us is a Texas hero."

"Yes, yes. You forget I absorb numbers and never forget them. And I realize we could never get Texans to like you. That is much too big job. Instead, I think about how you could make them not like this Brewster Steele. Do you have some information about his past you could use?"

"The guy's a regular Roy Rogers," Sanchez said. "Even if we plant something, it won't stick."

"I do not know this 'Roy Rogers.' But if Steele is too good for people to believe bad things about him, then you have to make people dislike what he is doing to them. These regulations are a good way to do that. But you need to make people's life more expensive. Figure out what would cause a protest if price goes up. Those things are your targets."

"As oil goes, so goes Texas," Sanchez said.

"Then that is the jugular vein," Borsky said. "If you want to kill your opponent, you cut jugular."

Part 3

The "Third" Term

CHAPTER 22

*"We would like to live as we once lived,
but history will not permit it."*

- John F. Kennedy -

THE RAYS OF MORNING sun fanned out above the El Cielo Mountains, brightening the little town of Sunrise, New Mexico. The shadows of the ragged peaks silently withdrew from the desert floor. The sun hit the body of Sheriff Eugene Sanderling like a spotlight as it hung from the overpass of Interstate 10. A Mexican flag, pinned to his shirt with his sheriff's badge, fluttered in the early morning breeze.

A crowd of people stood in a semi-circle watching the volunteer emergency medical team consider whether to retrieve the body or wait for the State Bureau of Investigation.

The sheriff had gone missing two days earlier. Speculation was that one of the rival drug cartels had kidnapped him for ransom. Now it appeared the cartel's intent was to send an unmistakable message. There was no proof; no witnesses came forward. No one was brave enough or foolish enough to make themselves the next target for the cartel. But recent history was proof enough that this gruesome violence was the result of cartel activity.

Drug trafficking had reached epidemic proportions in southern New Mexico. Two years prior, the Senate Committee on Energy and Natural Resources had designated 241,400 acres of public land as wilderness, over the objections of the state of New Mexico and the United States Department of Homeland Security. This designation only allowed entry on foot, and only in designated areas, severely restricting vehicular and human traffic and prohibiting border patrol entry to much of the region. The unintended consequence was that these lands now provided protection for the drug cartels. Many conspiracy theorists called these the intended consequences.

With the intensified border security in Arizona, drug traffic and illegal alien smuggling efforts had moved east and were now firmly established in New Mexico. The sparsely populated desert and the network of highways and roads in the southern part of the state made New Mexico ideal for these illegal activities. The new wilderness designation only made matters worse.

Sheriff Sanderling was an outspoken critic of the wilderness designation, pointing out that his town of Sunrise sat at the edge of the battle line. Just the week before, against the federal authority and regulations, Sanderling initiated his own patrols of the wilderness area. The federal government had been seeking an injunction to stop him, but while the district court was considering the matter, Sanderling launched his nightly patrols. Now it appeared the cartels had struck back.

A reporter from the Albuquerque KBS was moving among the crowd. She picked a weathered rancher for her first interview.

"Sir, did you know Sheriff Sanderling?" she asked.

"Oh yeah. Is a small town," he said with a Mexican accent. "Everybody know everybody."

"What did the citizens of Sunrise think when Sheriff Sanderling started his patrols?"

"We thought he crazy. The cartel warn him. They tell him to look the other way. But he was a tough man and he say he would protect us any way he could. It is a sad day for us. Que Dios lo tenga en su Gloria," the rancher said, crossing himself.

Within the hour, New Mexico Governor Walt Grainger faced the camera himself, excoriating the failure of the federal government in stemming the tide of illegal activity entering the country from Mexico.

"In recent years, the level of illegal alien smuggling and drug traffic has multiplied to levels unimaginable," Grainger said, "and the federal government has done little to help. In fact, while one arm of the government has promised more agents and resources, another arm of the government has created an ideal safety zone for the cartels through the idiotic wilderness designation of federal lands.

"This has to stop. It is time to take our safety into our own hands."

Grainger had been paying close attention to the actions of Brewster Steele and the Gulf States Governors Council. He knew that if he took a stand for his state's rights in this matter, he wouldn't be alone. It had only taken a few phone calls to gain the support he needed.

"Today, I am urging the New Mexico legislature to reclaim all undeveloped federal lands in the state and return them to the jurisdiction of the state of New Mexico," Grainger announced. "I am declaring a state of emergency. The governors of Texas and Arizona are at this moment declaring similar states of emergency. In addition, New Mexico, Arizona, and Texas have initiated a Border States Security Coalition. This coalition will be made up of police officers from all three states. They will have interstate legal authority, meaning they will be able to cross state lines in carrying out their duties.

"Until further notice, a buffer zone is ordered extending from the Mexican border to a second line ten miles north and parallel to the border. Unauthorized personnel will not be permitted within this zone. And no warnings will be issued. Cities, towns, and private ranches will be exempt and appropriate identification is being issued to those residents. The Border States Security Coalition personnel patrolling this zone will be heavily armed, they will be backed up by National Guard air assets, and they will have the authority to shoot on sight.

"I ask the cooperation of all New Mexicans in this effort. Together, we will reclaim our state for our law abiding citizens."

CHAPTER 23

"I believe there are more instances of the abridgement of the freedom of the people by the gradual and silent encroachment of those in power, than by violent and sudden usurpation."

- James Madison -

BREWSTER STEELE RUBBED his eyes and yawned. It was an important meeting he was heading into, but he had had a restless night. He was still feeling sick about the gruesome news from New Mexico. Although he was glad to have New Mexico governor Walt Grainger, a moderate Democrat, join him in taking a stand for state's rights, he wished it had come about under better circumstances.

But what had really kept Steele up all night was President Theresa Lewis's first State of the Union address the previous evening. The address focused on the growing trend of individual states claiming back jurisdiction from the federal government.

"We are a nation of fifty states that have chosen to bind themselves to each other for the common good," she proclaimed. "Under no circumstances will I accept rogue behavior from individual states. Those states that have challenged the authority and legal jurisdiction of the federal government risk the loss of federal funding."

Money was the federal government's nuclear weapon. Pull the plug on the flow of dollars from Washington and the lights go out in the state that does not toe the federal line. Lewis made clear that those fighting for state sovereignty certainly had their work cut out for them. With both Houses and the Supreme Court now on her side, President Lewis wasted no time proposing the legislation that had been overturned under a Republican House. In the State of the Union address, she proposed no fewer than four "new" acts.

First was MEFRA, the Marriage Equality and Family Rights Act, which overruled and trumped all state laws banning gay marriage. Next was WINA, the Wireless Information Neutrality Act, which would place all web-based communication under the control of the FCC, and open the floodgates for claims on equal time. Under this legislation, it would be possible to require a person who wished to express their political opinion on a blog or website to provide opposing opinions as well.

Then came FROCA, the Federal Roadway Consolidation Act, which would place control of all toll roads and bridges under the auspices of the Department of Transportation. Toll revenues would go to Washington, despite the fact that the bulk of operating and maintenance costs would remain the responsibility of the states.

Finally, there was MAGRA, the Madsen Guaranteed Retirement Account, which required Americans to invest twenty-five percent of their retirement savings in a new kind of investment called a FORA, or Federal Obligation Retirement Annuity. She claimed that investing in the stock market is too risky for the uninformed average citizen. The federal government needed to do something to secure their retirement money. So she created FORAs.

"Each Federal Obligation Retirement Annuity will be guaranteed by the full faith and credit of the United States of America," she said with obvious pride. "This investment will gain interest over time and most importantly, it will be there when you need it most."

Lewis touted all these acts as ways to make life better for all Americans. But it was clear to Steele that the President was taking the country much further into the uncharted and dangerous waters of socialism.

As happened more and more frequently these days, Whit Hornsby voiced Steele's feelings perfectly. "By the end of the year, half of all retirement funds will cease to exist," Hornsby warned. "Your money will be replaced by millions of these worthless pieces of paper, IOUs actually, called FORAs. And trust me, folks. Lewis doesn't plan on investing your money anywhere. She will use it to manage her mammoth deficits. To pay the interest on past debts that are already smothering economy. Your money will disappear into the general budget accounting, just like social security does. It's out of your hands and into theirs leaving you with a weak promise. When you die, your children lose all of it. It's not your money, anymore. It's theirs.

"Today, President Lewis is only taking a quarter of your account. But the next year we have a declining stock market or another Bernie Madoff Ponzi scheme is discovered, Lewis will claim she needs to broaden her social safety net and increase the percentage. In no time they'll have it all.

"In one evening, President Lewis has snatched away one more piece of state's sovereignty with MEFRA, totally disregarding the Constitution; throttled the Internet, freedom of speech's last stand, with WINA; commandeered the highway system and all of the revenue from tolls with FROCA; and stolen a quarter, and soon to be all, of your retirement account with MAGRA."

As if all of those acts weren't enough, Lewis had heaped praise on the EPA for instituting new regulations banning lead

149

bullets. The EPA claimed lead bullets were an environmental hazard. As an extension of the ban on lead in paint, lead bullets could no longer be manufactured or purchased in the United States.

What the regulation effectively did was to ban bullets entirely. Bullets made of other metals were already categorized as "armor piercing," and had been outlawed for years. Now with a ban on lead bullets, a citizen could still have their gun, in accordance with the Second Amendment, and to the constant distress of all liberals, but they wouldn't be able to buy any ammo for it.

What made this bit so sickening was that Lewis didn't even mention the violence taking place in New Mexico, or the death of Sherriff Sanderling. She made no mention of how the law-abiding people of places like New Mexico were supposed to protect themselves and their families without access to bullets.

Steele had been up all night thinking about what these new acts and regulations would mean. He knew for sure it meant a great deal more hard work for him and his allies in their fight to regain state sovereignty. Not that they had been slacking: along with issuing permits to drill in the Gulf of Mexico and helping initiate the Border States Security Coalition, the Texas governor was also spearheading an effort to get around the Lewis administration's blocking of the TransCan oil pipeline. The pipeline was supposed to bring oil from Canada and the oil fields in North Dakota to the port of Houston — and along with that oil, bring hundreds of thousands of desperately needed jobs to Midwestern states.

Despite the obvious benefits of the pipeline, the Sanchez administration had rejected it and the new Lewis administration was refusing to budge on reversing Sanchez's decision. The pipeline died under oppressive requirements for more and more environmental studies. When it was clear they were being stonewalled by Washington, the states involved — Texas, Oklahoma, Kansas, Nebraska, South Dakota, and North Dakota

— decided to take matters into their own hands. They claimed that the federal government only had jurisdiction over interstate commerce, and not intrastate commerce. The plan was to build portions of the pipeline in their own states in the locations already selected. The pipes would then stop just short of the border to the next state. At the end of the pipeline in one state, the oil would be loaded onto trucks. The trucks would then drive across the state line as they always did. This method of transporting oil was already under the interstate trucking laws and regulations. On the other side of the state line, the trucks would unload their oil into that state's pipeline, where it would then get pumped to the next border. This process would be repeated until the oil arrived at the oil tankers or refineries in Houston.

Brewster Steele couldn't have been happier with this plan. With the Gulf states, the border states, and now the oil transporting states putting up the challenge, the administration would have multiple battles to fight on the states' home turf. And Steele was about to plant another flag.

Steele entered the conference room and sat down between Texas treasurer Chase Bretton and the Texas attorney general, Fred Cameron. Across from them CEOs from four Fortune 100 companies waited expectantly. The room had an aura of secrecy and conspiracy. When heads of corporations were called to a governor's office, it usually meant arduous and expensive new regulations were about to be handed down. All four companies were headquartered out of state, two in New York, one in Chicago, and one in California.

"I know your time is valuable so I'll get right to the point," Steele said. "The folders in front of you contain our road map for making Texas the business mecca of the country. We intend to out-compete all of the other states, as well as the rest of the world." Steele looked at each of the CEOs. "And we want you to plant both feet in Texas.

"Mr. Cresci," Steele continued, looking at one of the CEOs, "I understand your company has one hundred percent of your manufacturing facilities overseas. You've been quoted as saying that it would cost you a billion dollars more to build and start up a facility manufacturing computer chips in the United States than it costs you to do the same thing in Indonesia, and that the majority of the cost is a result of regulation, permitting, and taxes. Am I right?"

"Correct. Most people think we manufacture our chips overseas because the labor cost is lower. It is lower, but that's offset by travel costs for management personnel, shipping costs to get our products back to the U.S., etcetera. We don't have our factories halfway around the world because we like it. It is necessary to remain cost competitive."

"I heard you say you would manufacture your products here if the additional costs could be reduced or removed. Is that correct?" Steele asked.

"In a heartbeat," Cresci said. "But I wouldn't want to commit to that without a complete analysis."

"Fair enough. Is this the case with you, too?" Steele said looking at the other CEOs.

Three nods of agreement.

"It's not going to get any better," Catherine Trent said. "We used to make our fabrics in North Carolina. Now those towns struggle to stay on the map. The textile industry can't compete with Asia — not with new regulations every week."

"We hear you," Steele said. "The Texas treasurer, our state attorney general, and I are preparing to propose dramatic changes affecting how Texas does business. Our belief is that unless we do something to save ourselves, Texas is going to sink into a hopeless economic depression with the rest of the country.

"Our position is that the country was originally founded as a union of sovereign states wherein the states managed their own affairs and governed according to the wishes of the people of those states. The federal government had very limited powers. Regulation of trade between the states and mutual defense were pretty much it. But since Roosevelt's New Deal, the sovereignty of the states has eroded at an increasingly fast rate.

"We intend to opt out of most federal programs, including the federal retirement mandate. We will create our own voluntary, self-directed retirement system. Texas will claim regulatory power over all land, persons, or business located within the territory of the state through the passage and enactment of a State Sovereignty Bill. Our attorney general is prepared and funded to defend this in court, all the way up to the Supreme Court. The sovereignty of an individual state has never been claimed and tested at this level since the Civil War, so we cannot guarantee the outcome. However, I can assure you we intend to fight for our sovereignty with the same zeal as if we had been invaded.

"Texas will drop the corporate tax rate to zero. Our aim is to attract businesses that can no longer tolerate the confiscatory taxation in other states. The revenue benefit to Texas will come from a significantly increased tax base due to massive growth in jobs plus the increased revenues from sales taxes on a substantially more robust economy. We expect to lower tax rates to stimulate the Texas economy and actually take in more tax dollars. It will be a lower tax rate applied to many more dollars. It's the kind of simple math Washington does not seem to understand. Our studies show that every dollar earned and spent within the state will multiply six-fold."

"If I may," Cresci interrupted. "How do we fit in?"

"We want you to commit to building manufacturing facilities in Texas. Frankly, if this plan is to succeed, we need to be sure the jobs will come here."

"You want us to defy the Feds and ignore their regulations?" Trent asked.

"That is precisely what we are asking. Our pledge to you is we will fight the battle for you and with you," Steele said.

There was a momentary silence as the four CEOs considered what Steele was proposing. Finally, Catherine Trent spoke up.

"I made my career by taking calculated risks," she said. "You've got steel cajones, Governor, and I'm damned tired of getting led around by the nose by Washington. We've been looking for an excuse to bring our manufacturing home. I'll join in your revolution."

"I do have one request," Steele said. "It's not a law or regulation, it's a suggestion. People like yourselves work long days under extreme pressure. You have unique and valuable talents. You deserve to be compensated in proportion to the value you bring to your companies. It's no different than professional athletes and top entertainers who deserve to be paid according to the value of their performances. However, when executive salaries grow out of proportion to the wages and salaries of the employees who produce the products, the average working man or woman comes to resent the huge paychecks at the top of the ladder. They don't see the rewards of their own hard work, the very work that makes the company profitable, finding its way into their pockets. The executives are seen as exploiting the employees. I am urging you all to maintain some equity in pay throughout your organizations. Fair wages for a job well done will negate any need for unions. It is ultimately good for all of us."

"You're looking for utopia, Governor," Cresci said.

"No, Mr. Cresci," Steele replied. "I'm looking for America."

CHAPTER 24

"The people will save their government,
if the government itself will allow them."
- Abraham Lincoln -

IT HAD BEEN A LONG morning, and Trexell knew if he spent too many more Saturdays in the Bureau, someone might get suspicious. But he was convinced he was doing his patriotic duty by helping the President rid Congress of the stooges of corporate America. If he, computer geek Robbie Trexell, could help right the wrongs of American history, then he was all in. Plus, the extra money that surreptitiously showed up in his bank account each month gave him plenty of cash to keep up with the latest video games. But deep down, Trexell knew it was the orgasmic rush he got from hacking that was his true motivation.

Today's list of targets was not the usual list of Republicans. Most of the names were Democrat congressmen and senators. Trexell's contact claimed this was the list of those who had been disloyal. These were the sellouts who put their own interests above the best interest of the country. Trexell had started to ask more questions, but when his contact mentioned doubling his fee, Trexell made the business decision to leave it at that.

After entering and altering a dozen files, Trexell needed a break. He grabbed his skateboard and swiped his ID card at the security portal. The midday sun was strong, and the shock to his computer weary eyes made him squint. He dropped his board on the sidewalk and headed to Starbucks mostly by feel. As he pushed off, he slammed into Arthur Campbell, who had stepped from the shadows. Campbell snatched Trexell off his board, temporarily knocking the wind out of him.

"No worries, little buddy," Campbell said as he set Trexell down and kicked his board back to him. "This is no mugging. I just want to buy you a latte and have a nice chat."

"Hey, dude. You scared the crap outta me," Trexell said. "Just who the hell are you?"

Campbell stuffed a twenty in Trexell's plaid flannel pocket.

"Just go over and get yourself your usual, that cinnamon dolce latte with extra whipped cream, and join me on that park bench across the street," Campbell said with a nod across Pennsylvania Avenue.

"I don't think so, pal," Trexell spat. "And how do you know what my 'usual' is? You a cop?"

"Let's just say I'm retired from law enforcement. And I know a lot more about you than what high caffeine sugar shock drink you like every afternoon. I know what you've been doing."

"I haven't been doin' anything," Trexell said, trying to pull away.

"Au contraire, mon ami," Campbell said. "Remember Senator Wes Roberson?"

The name sent a jolt through Robbie Trexell's wiry frame. He nodded. Campbell let him go. Trexell paused for a moment, as if considering his options, and then made a beeline for Starbucks. Five minutes later he and Campbell were sitting next to each other like two old chums in the park on a spring afternoon.

"You say you know what I've been doin'," Trexell said, now a bit more composed and quite a bit more defiant. "And just what do you think you know, Mr. ex-cop?"

"I know what you do in that big building over there."

"Big whoop. Everybody knows what I do in there. It says in my job description. I enter data and manage records. You don't need to be Sherlock Holmes to figure that out."

"You're pretty dedicated, working so many weekends," Campbell said.

"I'm one helluva hard-working civil servant, dude," Trexell said with a smirk.

"I also know you like to make some extra money altering records."

"No, you don't," Trexell shot back.

"A child pornography charge against Senator Roberson a week before the election was pretty nasty, Robbie," Campbell said in a fatherly tone, as if he were reprimanding Trexell for forgetting to feed the dog.

"It's not my fault the guy's a pervert."

Campbell pulled a folded paper from his jacket pocket.

"I've got your bank account here, Robbie. And I've cross-referenced it with certain revelations that appeared in the news that shipwrecked the election hopes of a dozen representatives. There is a surprising correlation. Your account shows a significant deposit just days before each revelation. And then there's this $10,000 deposit the day before Senator Roberson's record was made public. Looks like that was your big score."

Campbell spread the pages out on the bench.

"You know, Robbie," Campbell said, "it turned out those child pornography charges were totally bogus. Of course, that revelation made page seven of the *Post*, just below the half page ad for pushup bras, where no one would find it. The Bureau of Identity Protection said the information was 'keyed in wrong.' You guys are supposed to be so good in there, protecting us and all. How does something like this get keyed in wrong, Robbie?"

Trexell shrugged. He took a sip of his latte and windshield-wipered the whipped cream from his upper lip with his tongue.

"And you know, Robbie, I like the way you talk to your dog when you come home. It's sweet."

"How do you know that?"

"Your dog just can't keep a secret," Campbell said, expressionless. "He told me all about how you write fiction in identity records. He told me that's what you did to Senator Roberson."

"You're full of bull crap," Trexell said between sips of latte. "You're an ex-cop that talks to animals. Did they bounce you off the force when you became delusional?"

"No delusions, Robbie. I have recordings. Your dog was bugged. And I don't mean fleas," Campbell said.

Trexell crumpled his empty Starbucks cup. "That's illegal," he said.

"So's accessing and falsifying personal identification records, Robbie."

"That would be inadmissible evidence. You bugged my freakin' dog. You're a cop. I don't need to tell you that."

"Won't matter. It'll set the bloodhounds on your trail, and they'll find plenty of admissible evidence. You're a pretty good geek, but you're no James Bond. Your trail is as easy to follow as I-95."

"So why are we sitting here, dude? Why don't you just turn me in?" Trexell asked.

"I could say I like you, but that would be a lie," Campbell said. "I want you to do something for me. I want you to hack Romeo Costa's smartphone. He's the head of security for President Lewis's Secret Service detail."

"No shit," Trexell laughed. "Hack the phone of the President's top Secret Service guy? Can't be done. That sucker's probably triple encrypted."

"Between these dates," Campbell said handing him a note. "I can give you forty-eight hours."

"No freakin' way, dude."

"You'll find a way, dude," Campbell shot back. "Do I need to remind you that geeks don't do too well in prison, Robbie?"

In CONGRESS, July 4, 1776.

The unanimous Declaration of the thirteen united States of America,

CHAPTER 25

"The tree of liberty must be refreshed from time to time,
with the blood of patriots and tyrants.
It is its natural manure."

- Thomas Jefferson -

BEYOND THE PORT Bolivar-Galveston ferry, a string of tankers stretched like a serpent out into the Gulf of Mexico. A fifty percent increase in oil production since the Gulf States Alliance chose to defy the federal government by issuing new deepwater drilling permits made the port one of the busiest in the country. Tankers often waited days for an open berth to either discharge or load cargo. Refining output skyrocketed, sending net exports to new highs. Traffic in and out of the port had come to look like Sunday afternoon at a Cowboys game.

Lawsuits against the state-issued permits brought by the Sanchez administration were crawling at a snail's pace through the courts. Each time the United States attorney general's office successfully removed one legal roadblock, the combined resources of the attorneys general of the Gulf States Alliance

161

managed to find another obstacle to throw in the federal government's path and stall a legal resolution. The latest estimates were that the case would not make it to the Supreme Court for at least another two years. The clock was ticking and every oil company was scrambling to extract as much oil as possible before that happened.

Lieutenant Powacki's eighty-seven-foot coastal patrol boat was making twenty knots through Galveston Bay heading for Morgan's Point. He had to reread his orders several times before he let himself believe them. Blockading the port of Houston was not standard operating procedure for the Coast Guard. The last line on his orders said no ships in and no ships out until further notice. Powacki had radioed the Port Authority and ordered all ships' movement stopped from the E Loop Freeway Bridge to the Gulf.

When Port Director Al Jennings heard what the Coast Guard was up to, he couldn't believe it, either. Only four months on the job and Jennings had the crisis of the century on his hands. He knew he would be fighting Washington, but he never dreamed he'd face a naval blockade.

"Get me the governor," Jennings called to his assistant. A moment later, his phone chirped and he picked up.

"Howdy, neighbor," said the familiar voice of Brewster Steele. "You enjoying that quiet retirement job over there in Houston?"

Jennings had been half-volunteered and half-coerced into taking the job. His background as a "take no crap" army general made him ideal for Steele's push for state sovereignty. The fact that Jennings' horse ranch was adjacent to Steele's and they were friendly but tough competing horse breeders led them to forge a bond of mutual respect. When Steele needed to draw a line in the sand in his dealings with Washington, he knew Jennings was his man.

"Brewster, we got a harbor full of hot water over here," Jennings said. "I'm lookin' at a pretty white gunship with a red slash across the hull making lazy circles in my shipping lane. They're callin' your bluff, Brew."

"It was no bluff, Al," Steele said. "Texas is following legal procedure to the letter and contesting the port tax through the courts. We're withholding payments until a decision is handed down. In the meantime, we're in full operating mode. Washington has no authority to interfere."

"You're making the President look bad, Brew. You know that. She may not have the authority," Jennings said, "but she has the firepower to clog up our channel. They're claiming it's because of 'environmental concerns.' On top of that, I've got three news helicopters chattering above my head, too."

"You don't need to say anything to the media, Al. I've got a press conference scheduled in an hour. If they ask you for a comment, just give them that scowl that made you infamous."

"I'm scowling now, Brew," Jennings said.

"I've got a vivid mental picture of it, Al."

"What do I tell all the folks who can't do their jobs? Should I tell them the governor couldn't pay his taxes?"

"Cute, Al," Steele said. "I'm sure you'll figure something out. You might remind them of another important tax protest. That one in Boston two and a half centuries ago. Ports and taxes are critically connected to freedom in America."

"So this is the Houston Petroleum Party," Jennings said.

"It doesn't exactly roll off the tongue. But if it makes you happy, go with it, Al."

Less than an hour later, Steele stood in front of dozens of reporters and bloggers. He read from a prepared statement.

"Today, the government of the United States has illegally blockaded the port of Houston, violating the sovereignty of the state of Texas and jeopardizing the livelihood of thousands of hardworking Americans. The United States attorney general ordered this action based upon the claim that Texas has not paid the recently imposed port tax. Texas has objected to the new port tax as being unfair, confiscatory, and unconstitutional.

"I have directed Texas Attorney General Cameron to petition the U.S. District Court to issue an injunction to lift the blockade. We are awaiting the judge's decision. However, it is clear that President Lewis cares little about the rule of law. She has chosen not to allow the legal process to play out and let our differences be resolved through the courts. Instead, she has chosen the path of confrontation and provocation.

"The state of Texas demands the removal of the blockade. We demand that the President remove the Coast Guard vessels from the shipping channel and return them to their routine duties. If this blockade is not lifted within forty-eight hours, the state of Texas will consider this to be an aggressive military action. Never in American history, including the Civil War, has the federal government taken military action against law abiding citizens. Military incursions have been limited to quelling riots and suppressing insurrections. In the port of Houston, we have neither."

Steele acknowledged a question from the Houston KBS correspondent.

"Governor, are you issuing an ultimatum to President Lewis, and are you calling the Coast Guard blockade an act of war?"

"Those are your words, not mine," Steele said. "When armed vessels from our own government interfere with civilian commercial commerce, I'm not sure what to call it."

"What do you plan to do if the blockade is not removed?"

"We are already assembling an emergency session of the legislature to review our options."

"Would one of those options involve force?" the reporter asked.

"We are reviewing our options," Steele repeated, signaling for no further questions.

Steele knew his ambiguous answer would just infuriate Washington further. But he would not back down. He knew the administration would try to argue that since the port of Houston was important to much more of the country than just Texas, it should be under federal jurisdiction as covered by the commerce clause. But in Steele's opinion, far too much of the overreaching regulation that had come from Washington had been rationalized under the commerce clause.

The federal government was supposed to have checks and balances to ensure it never got out of control, but clearly those checks and balances weren't working. The Supreme Court was no longer the arbiter of constitutionality. Too often, it acted politically, which it was never supposed to do, and deemed laws to be constitutional that were clearly unconstitutional by any reading of the founding document. Now with Justice Reyes on the Court, the tide had turned in favor of centralized power. He knew the Court would eventually uphold any liberal law and absolutely crush any remaining state's powers. The Court was the lap dog of the Lewis administration. The Congress had also lost any backbone it may have had. When the President proposed a new law, Congress automatically approved it. The minority of senators and representatives who disagreed with the direction Lewis was taking the country was too small to make any difference.

The federal government had become a tyrant, exactly the kind of tyrant King George was in 1776. All Steele was doing was fighting back through legal challenges. The Constitution explicitly prohibited unequal taxing of ports. No unequal tariffs could be imposed — but that was exactly what Washington was doing to Houston, New Orleans, and the other ports in the states that were a part of the Gulf States Governors Council. Other states were exempted. They are being targeted.

The TV networks had barely reported on the intensification of regulations in Texas during the past weeks. Steele knew it was retribution for their defiance of the Lewis administration. There had been raids of businesses on trumped-up allegations. The EPA raided a guitar manufacturer in Dallas for supposed possession of illegal tropical wood, wood they had purchased legally through reputable sources. They padlocked the doors, and the employees lost their jobs. In Midland, they staged a surprise test of emissions from oil derricks. Half of the wells were shut down for violations. The Texas government tested those wells the very next day and they all complied. The tests were rigged. The EPA had become a kangaroo court.

Meanwhile, the Transportation Security Administration had intensified scrutiny in the Dallas airport. They claimed they had credible threats, but in fact, they were intentionally slowing air traffic. They staged random screenings of passengers who were simply travelling through on connecting flights. These people had already been screened where they got on the first leg of their flight. Why did they need to be screened again? Dallas was one of the largest hubs in the country. The slowdown of traffic was clearly meant to drive business out of Dallas and through other airports, like Chicago or St. Louis.

Texas was losing jobs because of President Lewis. Lewis was using federal regulation as a punishment. She was trying to turn Texans against Steele's movement to get out from under the thumb of Washington. And this new blockade of Houston was the most outrageous act of oppression from Washington yet. The legal challenge to the blockade would slowly work its way through the courts, but in the meantime, jobs would be lost by the thousands and gas prices would skyrocket.

Steele knew the blockade had to be removed one way or another. His hope was it would be removed peacefully, but he was prepared to do what needed to be done.

CHAPTER 26

"All animals are equal,
but some animals are more equal than others."
- George Orwell -
Animal Farm

DIMITRI BORSKY WATCHED the captain deftly handle the wheel as he maneuvered the forty-eight-foot shrimp boat past the mud flats of Sawdust Bend Bayou. The ride was slow and the tide had to be timed perfectly to guarantee passage through the shallow water.

The shrimp boat was taking more draft than usual. On the deck, hidden within the drapery of limp drag nets, sat a one ton remote-operated submersible vehicle. The computer-generated camouflage pattern painted on the hull of the ROV made it nearly impossible to see from the shore or from the air. Two hydraulic cranes had been installed on the deck that looked remarkably like the original net arms they replaced, complete with peeling red paint.

The smooth ride turned rough at the mouth of the estuary. The trawler pitched and rolled as it plowed its way through the turbulent waters where the Gulf waves crashed into the quiet bayou waters. Borsky steadied himself. Although he owned hundreds of vessels through Petro Energy Resources, Borsky never gained his sea legs. He was hoping the transdermal patch and two elastic wrist bands would save him from the ignominy of hanging over the rail. His ego would not tolerate that. But the risk was worth the rush of witnessing the operation. At his age, and with his wealth, there was little he had not experienced in life. Today would be unique.

The shrimp boat captain and owner had demanded a year's income to allow Borsky to refit his trawler. His boat was out of service for nearly a month. And now he was heading deep into the Gulf on a mission that was certainly illegal. His license and livelihood were at risk. Ultimately, he accepted six months' income and a guarantee from Borsky that if they got caught, he would cover any legal costs and put him on the Petro Energy Resources payroll for life. The semi-maniacal billionaire did not seem to realize that his guarantee might serve as an incentive for the skipper to allow them to be caught. If it wasn't for the risk of spending the rest of his life in jail, the captain might have been tempted. But the risk of jail-time was real, and it also ensured silence.

Two hours of work by the trawler's twin diesels brought the boat within sight of the deep water rig. The early morning sun lit the rig's four optic-yellow leg cylinders. Four cranes and a towering mast made it look like a skeletal dinosaur of steel. Still a mile from the rig, the trawler slowed and dropped its nets. They approached the platform from the east, keeping the rising sun at their backs, making them difficult to see clearly from the oil platform. Their course would take them within five hundred feet of the rig where shrimp often lingered. Borsky gave the nod to launch the submersible ROV.

The sub's operator was Borsky's man, a seasoned technician with over twenty years of seniority at Petro Energy Resources. The ROV held its payload like a loaf of bread in two crablike mechanical arms. The operator jiggled a joystick and the ROV levitated inches above the deck. The hydraulic cranes swung the sub over the side and lowered it gently. With another flick of a toggle, the sub was set free, letting the Gulf of Mexico quietly swallow it up.

The operator lowered the crane arms and turned to a computer screen. Cameras inside the ROV gave the operator both a normal and fish-eyed view of the path ahead of the sub. Numeric readouts flanking the images displayed depth, speed, pressure, attitude, tilt, global position, and vital details of the ROV's mechanical health. The operator pressed the throttle forward commanding the audio-shielded props to push the sub ahead at five knots. It descended as it went. At five hundred feet, he switched on the sub's headlamps. The ROV kept diving.

The shrimp boat cruised ahead at normal trawling speed, approximately following the ROV, but keeping a steady course to bypass the drilling rig. The skipper knew they would be watched carefully by the rig's radar man, always wary of collisions, whether unintended or intended. Environmental activists had tried just such an assault off the Alaskan coast several years before.

"I've got the wellhead in sight, sir," the ROV operator announced.

Borsky felt his heart jump.

"Proceed with the operation," Borsky ordered.

The operator maneuvered the ROV and turned its nose into the current. Moving the craft like it was an extension of his body, the operator hovered the sub inches above the wellhead. He extended the mechanical arms and placed the sub's payload next to the blowout preventer stack beneath the BOP hydraulic control lines. Satisfied with the placement, the operator reversed the ROV and initiated its ascent.

By now, the shrimper had moved beyond the oil rig and was separating itself from the behemoth just as it did any other day of normal shrimping. The operator brought the ROV up to a depth of one hundred feet, leveled it, and allowed it to drag invisibly behind the trawler. He dropped a small canister over the stern and reeled out five miles of control wire. The motion of the trawler let the audio emitter drag a dozen feet below the surface.

As the shrimp nets filled with an unintended sizeable catch, the captain raised the drag nets and helped his crew dump the shrimp into the hold.

"Only five hundred more feet of wire, sir," the operator told Borsky.

Borsky nodded. The trawler was over six miles from the oil rig and a mere speck on the horizon. Borsky pressed the red button he had been caressing since the canister drop.

From the emitter, an ultralow frequency audio command echoed through the deep Gulf waters. Obediently, the bomblet at the blowout preventer detonated, shattering the housing and ripping the hydraulic control lines to shreds. The muffled concussion could have been mistaken for a pressure rupture at the wellhead. Forensics at three thousand feet would be next to impossible. There would be no way to determine the cause of the rupture.

The impact of the explosion initially sent the oil back into the well. But a moment later, the intense pressure of the subterranean reservoir prevailed, and sweet red crude oil began spurting into the pristine waters of the Gulf of Mexico.

CHAPTER 27

"America will never be destroyed from the outside.
If we falter and lose our freedoms,
it will be because we destroyed ourselves."

- Abraham Lincoln -

EVERY NEWS CHANNEL showed the same flyover footage of the most recent deepwater wellhead leak and oil spill in the Gulf of Mexico. An irregular ring of floating orange booms corralled the shimmering iridescent layer of crude oil that floated on the surface.

President Lewis blamed the Gulf States Governors Council for irresponsible and inept permitting and inspections. To reinforce her case, Lewis pointed out that this particular rig was one her predecessor, Carlos Sanchez, had shut down several years ago in the aftermath of the largest spill in the history of Gulf coast drilling. Sanchez had said that despite the fact this wellhead had never leaked, he intended to keep this rig idle due to numerous violations and the brazen disregard for federal safety and environmental regulations. Lewis continued the policy, worried about backlash from the environmental groups if she did otherwise.

"It's just fortunate no one was injured or killed in this accident," was Lewis's sound-bite quote.

The oil spill only served to fuel the already outrageous protests growing in cities like Chicago. A story on TruthandLies.org, Dimitri Borsky's left-wing website, reported that for the third straight week, protesters had staged flash mob roadblocks at random points along the interstate highways that led in and out of downtown Chicago. Drivers in cars with covered license plates were dropping off passengers along the roadside and driving away so they couldn't be identified. Once the flash mob was large enough, they would walk right out in the highway and lie down. The timing was always around morning or evening rush hour, with no pattern or schedule. The protesters received a text message with the time and place and simply showed up. Traffic backups had been enormous. Police couldn't stop it from happening because the places and times were so random.

The protesters said they were exercising their first amendment right of freedom of speech and demonstrating against big oil. They said they were disrupting commuters to show how fragile the automobile-based transportation system is that the United States depends on. However, Whit Hornsby had his own take, one that Brewster Steele couldn't help but agree with.

"My guess is the police aren't really trying to stop this from happening," Hornsby said. "What really reeks of conspiracy with these flash mobs is the fact that no arrests are ever made. Police stand by and wait for the mob to disperse on its own. Are the police getting paid off to leave the flash mobs alone? Are they worried about somebody getting hurt and claiming police brutality or racism? The dirty little secret is that Dimitri Borsky is funding these mobs. People are getting paid fifty dollars per appearance, if you could call it that. Oh, sure. There are some protesters who simply show up because they enjoy protesting. It's their hobby. But most of them are otherwise unemployed or taking sick days from their day jobs or simply vagrants who are used to lying down in streets."

Chicago wasn't the only place with protestors. In Houston, a thousand oil workers were already picketing the Coast Guard station. Steele had deployed Texas Rangers to keep things from overheating, but each day things got more intense.

Thankfully, Steele had good news to counteract the bad news of the oil spill and the continued blockade. More and more states were rallying to the cause of state sovereignty. West Virginia had just passed a bill allowing the mining of coal for use within the state for the generation of electricity without approval from the Environmental Protection Agency. In another strike for state's rights, West Virginia governor Gordon Wexler claimed that mining for coal that would not be sold to other states is exempt from the EPA requirements because it does not involve interstate commerce.

Additionally, Steele's plan to bring business back to Texas was gaining momentum. An article in the *Times* reported that the rate of business relocation from California to states that were more tax friendly had doubled. The majority of those businesses had moved to Texas on the heels of the new policies instituted by the Steele administration.

The pullback on taxes and regulations had been a bonanza for Texas and a catastrophe for California. In fact, the only increase in new business licenses in California had been in Hispanic-owned businesses. Steele suspected this was because California would never ask for verification of status as a legal resident before issuing a permit, since that would be "racist profiling" and "discriminatory."

The loss of business wasn't the only bad news coming out of California. Hidden on page A14 in the *Post*, right after the Virginia spelling bee results, Steele had found a headline that read, "SoCal Feels Brunt of Border Crossings."

The number of illegal border crossings in Southern California had increased dramatically, by the Lewis administration's own admission. According to the article, drug traffic, home invasions, and kidnappings had tripled in the current year alone. Increased arrests had overwhelmed the courts. This had led California to take measures to reduce prison overcrowding. Judges were becoming more lenient because they had no place to put felons. Convicted felons were being released on their own recognizance and disappearing.

Officials were apparently puzzled as to why this recent surge in illegal activity had occurred. Only in paragraph five did the reporter mention that drug traffic and related crimes were down by huge margins in Arizona, New Mexico, and Texas. Instead of connecting the dots and realizing those three states had cracked down on illegal aliens and drug smuggling, the reporter speculated that this was merely a change in tactics by smugglers.

Steele knew the reason for this shift in drug and illegal immigration traffic was absolutely because of what the Border States Governors Council has been doing. Their joint Border Patrol using their National Guard units had been a roaring success. The border fence was three-quarters complete. Aerial surveillance was actually being done and was not simply promised.

California had refused to join the Council. Steele had tried to explain to them that if you're building a dam across a river and you only build it partway across, you will stop the flow of water where the dam is, but all of the water will surge through the gap. California was the gap. It was the only easy way into the United States — and Steele knew the Border Patrol was making sure the drug smugglers were learning that the hard way.

CHAPTER 28

"People sleep peaceably in their beds at night only because rough men stand ready to do violence on their behalf."

- George Orwell -

TWENTY-FIVE MILES from the nearest habitable building and twice as far from anything that could be called a town, Sergeant Kneiss peered down the bank of the Rio Grande and scanned the muddy flats on the river's edge. Construction of the border fence was ahead of schedule. After New Mexico, Arizona, and Texas jointly activated their National Guard forces and placed them under the command of the Border Guard, completing the fence and maintaining it with around-the-clock patrols was top priority.

During the presidential campaign, President Lewis had declared the fence between Mexico and the United States virtually complete, even though a mere five percent was actually built. It sounded good in speeches, especially to audiences living a thousand miles from the border where border problems were simply sound bites on the news. Most Americans saw the swelling Mexican-American population as simply the next wave of

175

hardworking immigrants who wanted a better life for themselves and their children. Supporters of amnesty for illegal immigrants argued that the Mexicans filled jobs Americans didn't want and wouldn't do. Amnesty supporters easily turned the outcry against illegal immigration into a racial hatred of immigrants, completely ignoring the meaning of the word "illegal."

The horrific consequences of the unpatrolled, open border had little immediate effect on most Americans in most states. And the media was cocooned in New York and Washington, insulated from the dangers. The war between drug cartels and the headless and dismembered casualties were compelling video. But just like most wars, these events, even those as gruesome as the death of Sherriff Sanderling, stirred momentary revulsion and nothing more. Politicians would take the opportunity to claim sponsorship of new enforcement initiatives and propose new immigration rules and paths to citizenship, but none of it ever amounted to anything more than rhetoric. Real results never materialized. Thousands of non-citizens drained the resources of hospitals, welfare systems, and schools. And drug cartels crept closer and grew more brazen.

Kneiss and his crew of three set up laser transits. Their job was to survey and mark the location for the high-tech fence. The construction crew was ten miles behind them. Against the directives of the federal government, the Border States Governors Council, having grown weary of waiting for Washington, decided to build the fence themselves. Funding came from the sale of confiscated drug vehicles and property and from large packages of cash confiscated in drug-related arrests. Instead of holding the property until trial, the state and local courts allowed documentation and photographs as admissible evidence. In the extremely rare instance when the accused was found innocent, the state replaced the property in kind. New "no tolerance" laws, passed by the states and under appeal by the U.S. attorney general, essentially eliminated findings of innocence when drug traffickers were caught red-handed.

"We want to hug the ridge," Kneiss told his crew. "Even though the river is technically the border, if we put the fence down there it will wash out every spring. We'll follow the high water line."

Kneiss had been given authority to use his best judgment on the location of the fence. With the establishment of the ten mile, "no go, no warning," buffer zone that prohibited access by any unauthorized personnel, Kneiss could work in relative safety. Unfortunately, they had to work the old-fashioned way, with transits and lasers; the military had denied all requests for satellite assistance.

The craggy, arid terrain and the need to cross arroyo and cliffs made the going slow. Not much lived out here except rattlesnakes and scorpions. Despite that, the EPA had managed to find auger fleas, determine the fleas were critical to the well-being of the planetary environment, and classify them as endangered. Taxpayer funded studies concluded the fleas only flourished in this location and quickly designated the fifty-thousand-acre tract Kneiss was halfway across as an environmentally sensitive area. Fines were being imposed by the EPA against the border states, and the dollar amount was rising fast, creating another legal log jam between the states and Washington. Kneiss had no idea how his fence would impact a flea, but nobody asked his opinion. On orders from the governor, he pressed ahead with his mission.

"Drive a locator pin here and then we'll scout ahead before picking an angle to the next point," Kneiss said.

A straight line fence was impractical. Kneiss was looking for the path of least resistance through the difficult terrain. They drove their Humvee east to the lip of a ravine. Although carved by water, the ground was as hard as concrete and as dry as Mars.

"We'll cross on foot and look at this from the other side," Kneiss said. "We'll figure out how to get the vehicle across after we pick a line. Juarez, you stay with the vehicle and set up the instrument. I'll radio back when we're ready with the reflector."

Kneiss tethered his safety harness to Private Glover, his rod man, and slung the laser reflector target over his shoulder. They started picking their way through the cacti and rocks. With each step, loose stones gave way sending a natural avalanche tumbling down the slope. With his free hand, Kneiss repeatedly planted a hiking pole to brace himself. Halfway down, a smooth stone ledge created a clearing, making progress easier. The sun was brutal and the men stopped for water. As Kneiss turned, the sun caught the reflector and sent a flash of light across the gully like a signal flare. A volley of semiautomatic gunfire bounced back. Rock fragments erupted from the sandstone ledge. The two National Guard surveyors dove for cover.

"Shit. Where the hell did that come from?" Kneiss asked.

Another volley and the survey crew hit the ground. Kneiss toggled his two-way radio.

"Juarez," Kneiss said, "We're taking fire. We must have stumbled on another cartel outpost. We're pinned behind a rock."

"Roger that, Sergeant," Juarez answered. "I'm on the ridge, but I can't spot the bad guys. Can you draw more fire and maybe I can paint them?"

"Love to, Sammy. Do you have a suggestion on how we do that without ending up looking like Swiss cheese?"

"Hey, how would John Wayne have done it? Put your hat on a stick and hold it up."

"Great idea. How 'bout you come on down and show us how?"

"Okay, Sarge," Juarez said. "I've called in our request and help is on the way. I got our new toy set. Get me some burns."

Juarez had set the GPS link heat scanner, a gift from the good taxpayers of Texas, to make rapid hundred and eighty degree sweeps of the ravine. Unless the instrument's infrared line of sight was blocked by rocks, any muzzle flash would display a "burn" on the screen. The internal processor would instantly triangulate the burn position and send it to the Condor.

From behind his sandstone shield, Sergeant Kneiss readied his mini grenade launcher. The low-tech device catapulted four incendiaries not much larger than cherry bombs in the general direction of the incoming fire. Four pops threw up small bursts of sand and gravel. On reflex, a couple of dozen rounds from the smugglers plastered the desert floor around the small decoy blasts.

"Thank you, señor," Juarez said to the invisible shooter.

The scanner processed the positions and transmitted it by cell phone to Border Guard Central Command. Satellites would have been simpler, but Washington was in a snit about the border states taking the initiative on the fence and patrols.

"Sit tight, gentlemen," Juarez said into his radio. "The Condor is on its way."

Minutes later, Juarez spotted the outline of a tiny plane flying less than a hundred feet above the river, following its twists and turns in near silence. Through his binoculars, Juarez could read the emblem of the Texas National Guard on the tail of the drone. The unmanned aircraft, remotely operated by a "virtual" pilot hundreds of miles away through a keyboard, joystick, and a forty-two-inch flat screen monitor, slowed and turned into the gully. The drone was one of a dozen the army deployed around the country for surveillance in the War on Terror. But the governor of Texas, through executive order of questionable validity, amended the drone's mission to include enforcement of environmental protection regulations. On the official authorization paperwork, the drone was protecting the habitat of the precious auger flea, southwest Texas's newest endangered species.

"I've got your men on visual," the drone's virtual pilot said through Juarez's headphones. "And now I've got your bad guys. Cactus doesn't give them much cover from my angle."

"Roger," Juarez answered.

Juarez clicked on his mike in the Humvee and read a warning and demand for surrender over the loudspeaker in English and Spanish. He repeated it a minute later.

"Sarge," Juarez radioed to his crew chief. "We've done our legal duty. We have gotten no response. Subjects are not surrendering. Everyone ready?"

"You are authorized to proceed," Kneiss answered.

An air to surface missile shot from the drone, pulverizing the ground. The drone circled until the dust cleared then flew a search pattern over the impact site.

"We're clear, gentlemen," the drone's pilot radioed.

"What's your recon?" Kneiss asked.

"Four dead drug runners and a stash of weapons that would make Pancho Villa jealous."

"That it?" Kneiss asked.

"No auger fleas were injured," the pilot deadpanned. "The fleas' habitat is secure."

CHAPTER 29

*"Government is not reason; it is not eloquence. It is force.
And force, like fire, is a dangerous servant and a fearful
master."*

- George Washington -

NEARLY TWO-THOUSAND miles away, Arthur Campbell sipped his diet Coke and kept an eye on the entrance to the Bureau of Personal Identity Protection, while wondering why so many nonconformists looked alike. Trexell was late, but that was normal. Rushing out the door would make him look suspicious, and that was exactly the opposite of how Campbell wanted him to appear. Robbie Trexell had been working his own little game for long enough to know the drill.

When Trexell did appear, he dropped his skateboard and headed east for the Starbucks. Campbell got up, walked to a bench on the far side of the park and fed the pigeons. Several minutes later the pigeons became agitated. A growl of skateboard wheels approached from behind. Then came a screech and a thud as Trexell vaulted over the bench from behind and landed hard in the space next to Campbell.

"The Russian judge deducted a point for the landing," Campbell said.

Trexell had no idea what Campbell meant, so he ignored him. He unzipped his backpack and dug out a smashed sandwich, a battered apple, and a tan envelope. He tossed the envelope to Campbell.

"Were you able to get in?" Campbell asked.

Trexell looked at him like he had two heads.

"I put the rootkit in the system in the first place, man. They paid me to get access and I keep it secret. Of course I got in," Trexell said with pride. "That puppy's sick, dude. It feints breaches to send the bots scurrying. But they can never find the real hole. It's my own baby."

"Puppy?"

"The rootkit, dude. That's my hole. That's how I get in," Trexell said. "Do you even own a computer?"

"And may I ask what you found?"

"It's in the packet, man," Trexell said, taking a bite out of his sandwich.

Campbell slit open the manila envelope with a pocket knife and found a surprisingly concise summary on the first page. A wad of pages followed, all neatly collated and stapled.

"Romeo Costa was in on the assassination attempt with Samson?" Campbell asked.

Trexell nodded as he stuffed half the sandwich in his mouth.

"He set it up," Trexell mumbled, spitting a bit of lettuce at Campbell. "He even got him the gun."

"But Costa was the Secret Service agent who killed Samson."

"Precisely, dude." Trexell said. "Kinda shakes your faith in your fellow man, doesn't it?"

"I supposed that was his plan. Get Samson to be the shooter and then kill the only witness and be a hero in the process," Campbell speculated. "And why would Romeo Costa want to assassinate the President?"

"Not so fast. There's more."

Campbell flipped through the pages.

"You won't find it there, man. The rest was outside the scope of our agreement," Trexell said.

"I agreed to pay you to hack Romeo Costa's cell phone. You owe me all the information you found."

"You got it right there, so we're square, dude," Trexell said. "But I got a little carried away and I tried to hack the President's smartphone. Man, that one was tough. Some smart geeks write his security. Took me three days."

"And you got in?" Campbell asked.

Campbell got the two heads look again.

"Okay," Campbell said. "So where's that stuff?"

"We gotta talk about what it's worth, dude."

"I'm keeping you out of jail," Campbell said. "That's worth a lot."

"That was our first deal. I did what you asked me. We're done with that."

Campbell had to agree. That was the original deal. Trexell chugged his bottle of vitamin water.

"And I've been thinking that now we're kinda in the same boat," Trexell said.

Campbell raised an eyebrow.

"Duh," Trexell said. "Don't you think there might be someone out there who would love to know you blackmailed me into hacking Costa's phone? The way I see it, we're now partners in crime."

"Okay," Campbell said shooting him a glare. "What's your price?"

"Hundred grand."

"No way. I can't get that kind of money," Campbell said.

"I can get a million from any of the networks. This is good stuff."

"A million won't do you much good in jail, Robbie."

"I can buy a great defense lawyer with the money," Trexell answered with an impertinent grin.

"For that kind of money, I need to see it first."

"Fair 'nough," Trexell said.

He ripped open a Velcro tab on the side of his backpack and withdrew another thick tan envelope. He opened it up and pulled out the top sheet. It was another neatly typed summary of the envelope's contents. He passed it to Campbell.

Campbell's jaw slackened as he read.

"Holy sh..."

CHAPTER 30

"The Tenth Amendment is the foundation of the Constitution."

- Thomas Jefferson -

THE MOB SURROUNDED the security gate of the Houston Coast Guard Station. For over a week, the United States Coast Guard had maintained the blockade of the port. Early in the morning, hundreds had assembled outside the Port Authority building and made the mile-long march from the Port Authority to the Coast Guard Station in an obvious protest of the blockade.

There had not yet been any reports of violence, but it was clearly an angry crowd chanting loudly for the reopening of the port. Protestors held signs that read "Don't Hold Our Jobs Hostage" and "Texas First."

Although no permits were applied for or issued, the protest was clearly organized, but no one would say by whom. This technically made it an illegal assembly. The Texas Rangers had been called to the scene and flanked the crowd, as if to monitor what was going on, but no move had been made to stop the march or disperse the crowd.

The port itself, meanwhile, which was usually one of the busiest in the country, had been eerily quiet since the blockade. An ever-growing line of ships, primarily tankers, meandered endlessly out in the Gulf of Mexico, waiting to enter. Inside the port, nothing had been moving other than the Coast Guard coastal patrol boats and law enforcement special purpose craft.

Today was different. As the crowd mobbed the Coast Guard station on land, one of the big tankers left the pier at Greyport Refinery. It was followed by more tankers departing from four other piers, despite the fact that the blockade was still in full force, and the Coast Guard remained on patrol.

Above the Coast Guard station, news helicopters jockeyed for position like hummingbirds around a feeder as a Coast Guard vehicle tried to exit the gate and make its way through the swelling crowd. The protestors — mostly oilmen wearing their work clothes and hardhats — did not back off. Although they did not carry traditional weapons, many carried the large wrenches they used on the oil platforms.

The crowd was beginning to rock the vehicle violently as it attempted to exit the security gate. Men were jumping on its roof. Others battered the hood and trunk with wrenches. With a spray of glass, the windshield and side windows shattered. Someone in the crowd reached in and unlocked the door, dragging the driver and passenger out and pushing them back through the security gate. The driver and passenger remained unharmed; within minutes, the car was virtually scrap metal.

Meanwhile, the tanker that left Greyport Refinery headed southeast through the shipping lane at a slow but steady speed, now joined by the four other ships in a "V" formation.

From the bridge of his coastal patrol boat, Lieutenant Powacki watched the oncoming array of tankers through binoculars.

"Radio them to stop," he ordered the first mate as he gauged the speed and distance. He estimated the tankers would be on him in ten minutes.

"No reply, sir. I tried all channels."

"They're ignoring us. It's a direct challenge," Powacki said. "Deploy the RHI. Head up the channel and paint their path with flares."

In minutes the rigid-hulled inflatable boat was speeding toward the tankers. A mile out, they launched orange signal flares, sending them arching gracefully through the sky. The only response they got was the blare of the tankers' air horns. The RHI was no match for the enormous tanker and swerved to the shallows to avoid being mashed.

"Skipper," the first mate said, "I've got a radio signal from the lead tanker. They say, 'Get the hell out of our way or we will flatten you.' Sorry, sir. That's verbatim."

Ahead of the tankers, almost invisible in the froth of the bow wake, several small pleasure boats led the armada. Like remora attending to a shark, the skiffs darted from side to side. As the tankers drew nearer, the skiffs sped up and gained on the CP boat.

"Fire across their bow," Powacki ordered.

A string of miniature geysers erupted a hundred yards from the skiffs as the machine gun shells bit into the brown water. The skiffs swerved around the CP boat's bow. Powacki weighed his options. His orders were to blockade the port, but he'd been given no specific rules of engagement. No engagement was expected. His vessel sat directly in line of the oncoming tankers. The CP boat's missile launcher could rip a hole in one of the tankers, but it wouldn't stop it. And there was no time to hit them all. In under a minute, his boat would be split and flattened by one of the giant double-hulled ships.

"All engines full. Hard to starboard," he ordered, afraid that he may have waited too long. To his relief, the lead tanker slipped dangerously close to, but past, his stern. The black hull towered above him like a ten-story building. One of the skiffs swerved back, intent on harassing the CP boat. The skiff cut in front of the CP boat, oblivious to the power of the tanker's wake. The bulbous bow of the tanker pushed a ten-foot wall of water under the CP boat's stern, lifting it and pushing the Coast Guard boat to the side. Suddenly, the skiff made another quick turn and again swerved across the bow of the CP boat. Like a surfer on a wave, the CP boat gained speed unexpectedly, and the rush of water made steering impossible. The Coast Guard boat lurched forward just as the skiff approached. With a sickening crunch, the CP boat sliced through the defenseless skiff.

CHAPTER 31

"Any people anywhere being inclined and having the power have the right to rise up and shake off the existing government, and form a new one which suits them better."

- Abraham Lincoln -
January 12, 1848

THE CHYRON GRAPHIC behind Warren Tufts said it all. "Three Dead in Houston."

"In a confrontation between port workers and the U.S. Coast Guard this morning, three men were tragically killed," Tufts reported. "Three brothers, Brent, Jesse, and Bobby Wagner, were killed when their skiff was smashed by a Coast Guard CP boat in the port of Houston. The incident occurred near Morgan's Point at the entrance to Galveston Bay. The Coast Guard vessel confronted a quintet of oil tankers attempting to break the two-week old blockade when the incident occurred."

Tufts read through the story of the morning's tragedy with a somber tone. Scenes showed the crushed skiff and debris floating within yards of the Atkinson Island Wildlife Management Area. Video shot by news helicopters followed the recovery of the bodies from the brown water.

"The Coast Guard has issued a statement expressing regret over the loss of life," Tufts continued. "Lieutenant Alan Powacki was in command of the Coast Guard vessel and has been placed on paid administrative leave. No charges have been filed. The Coast Guard has initiated an internal investigation. Families of the victims have called for Powacki's arrest, claiming he acted recklessly and without provocation. President Lewis expressed her condolences to the families of the victims of the accident. President Lewis went on to say that it is regrettable that when laws are not respected, irrational action can lead to tragedy."

In the days following the confrontation, posters, hats, and tee shirts with images of the Wagner brothers, the Alamo, and the slogan, "Remember the Wagners," were the hottest items in shops and on street corners in Houston and throughout Texas. The phrase quickly became the chant along with "Texas Lives Free" at protest marches from Houston to Amarillo.

Candlelight vigils in memory of the three dead oil rig roughnecks continued days after the accident. Demonstrators surrounded the Coast Guard station around the clock while carrying signs calling for the conviction of Lieutenant Powacki. Demands for the flag above the Coast Guard station to be flown at half mast were rebuffed by the Coast Guard on orders from the White House, further angering the crowd.

"The tradition of flying the flag at half staff is reserved for fallen heroes and patriots. What happened in Houston was an unlawful act of insurrection," White House spokesman Todd Furley said. "While we regret the loss of life and send our sympathies to the family of Brent, Jesse, and Bobby Wagner, the tragic accident was a result of their decision to challenge the Coast Guard and interfere with its fulfillment of its duties."

A mile out in the Gulf, just east of Brazosport, the calm seas let Ensign Harper keep his engines running full. The stealth gunboat was making fifty knots and cutting smoothly through the small waves. The boat carried five static mounted M240 light machine guns, a pair of Barrett .50 sniper rifles, and an arsenal of rifles, submachine guns, and grenade launchers. No one ever accused the Texas Rangers of not being prepared.

Harper wasn't sure if he would need all the armaments for his new assignment. He and his boat were being repositioned from the Falcon Reservoir to take up station at the port of Houston. His boat and two others were charged with continuously patrolling the channel from Galveston Bay all the way up to the Coast Guard station and to keep it open to all traffic. Since the Wagner brothers' incident, the Coast Guard had backed off and reopened the harbor. Harper's mission was hopefully just for show. It was a symbolic demonstration of force to secure free shipping, or so he hoped. Harper never thought his duties would include an armed encounter with the United States Coast Guard. He was supposed to be on the same side as them. But lately, Harper wondered if that was still true.

Following the confrontation at the port and the death of the Wagners, enlistments in the Texas State Guard overwhelmed recruiters. Retired veterans from the conflicts in Iraq and Afghanistan signed on and were placed in charge of training. Three new brigades were added with the prospect of adding an additional brigade per week for the next month. With the recently announced influx of businesses, relocation plans for industries that operated overseas, and a resurgence of oil revenues, funding was not a problem.

The fervor of resistance against the will of Washington and the "Don't Mess with Texas" attitude was bubbling up in virtually every county and town in the state. Billboards paid for by citizen groups flashed the "Texas Lives Free" and "Remember the Wagners." Email blasts urging voters to send their opinions to Congress were broadcast daily. Peaceful protest marches were becoming a regular event. Governor Steele hoped to keep them that way. Three accidental fatalities were more than enough. In a show of forceful resistance to the influence of Washington, Steele directed the Texas State Guard to set up monitoring stations at the entrance to all federal military installations with the exception of the Brooke Army Medical Center. Steele hoped to keep the facility that specialized in rehabilitation of wounded veterans out of the argument. Those men and women had earned their right to peace and quiet.

The purpose of the monitoring stations was twofold. First, they were to prevent any demonstrations against the military and the prospect of tempers raging out of control. The second purpose was to keep an eye on what the military was doing. Vehicles coming and going had to run the gauntlet of Texas soldiers who cordoned off the roads from through traffic and forced arriving vehicles to stop for an inspection of their credentials.

Throughout Texas, gas stations were hurriedly changing the prices at their pumps. The latest oil spill was spreading fast. It was the second oil spill in as many weeks. Wellhead 332-12 off the coast of Louisiana had ruptured and was spewing upwards of 50,000 gallons of oil a day, according to estimates from the Borsky Institute of Oceanic Sustainability.

"FEMA is dragging its feet," Brewster Steele complained "They're allowing this accident to swell into an environmental catastrophe. Every day they procrastinate, the oil spreads farther and farther. It's drifting toward the Texas coast. And because of that, the federal government is less interested in stopping it than if it were flowing any other direction."

Today, Steele was addressing the Texas Tea Party. He chose to accept the invitation for the express reason that they had the network he needed to reach. They had the email list of the core group of smaller government advocates.

Steele had his speech prepared, and he knew it would be the start of something big — so big his nerves were jangling. He pulled out his cell phone and hit the speed dial.

"Hi, honey," Mary Ketterling-Steele's voice answered.

"I miss you, darlin'. You coming home from Philly this weekend?" Steele asked.

"I'd love to. You know that. But I've got way too much to do. You heard I was appointed to the Joint Congressional Committee for Equitable Housing. I told you, didn't I? I'm running around so much, I lose track of who I told what."

"You did," Steele answered with a slight groan. "What's your budget and what's your goal?"

"It's a fifty-billion-dollar program," Ketterling-Steele said. "Our goal is to help people who are in foreclosure and eliminate subpar housing."

"That sounds noble. Where's the fifty billion coming from? Did you folks extend yourself another line of credit? You're already running a one and a half-trillion dollar deficit."

"We can't let people get kicked out of their homes, Brew," she said with a huff.

"Mary, you know they should never have bought homes in the first place. People who can't qualify for mortgages the old-fashioned way should be renters."

"Owning a home is the American dream, Brew. We can't let that dream evaporate."

"You know, Mary, if you looked at all those billions of dollars of government money as taxpayers' money and not the government's money, I think you would make different and better decisions with it."

"This from the man who is stonewalling Washington and attacking the Coast Guard," Ketterling-Steele said.

"I had nothing to do with the tankers that ran the blockade."

"The President doesn't think so," she said.

"I don't much care what the President thinks," Steele retorted. "I've had just about enough of her."

Although he said it partly out of annoyance, it was true. Just hours ago, President Lewis had crossed an unthinkable line: she had pronounced the Constitution unfair. "The principles of the founders are noble and correct in the Declaration of Independence," Lewis had said. "However, the Constitution does not reflect the pretense of the Declaration. The high virtues and moral integrity of the Declaration of Independence were compromised by those men in power and the wealthy, white, property and business owners by the time the Constitution was written and ratified."

Even more than Lewis's outrageous declaration, the enormous problem, the one for which there was no easy solution, was the ticking time bomb of the rapidly growing national debt. The federal government was dragging the whole nation into the abyss of financial ruin. The credit rating of the United States had already been downgraded, and would continue to decline. Eventually, and inevitably, the U.S. dollar would lose its privileged position as the world's reserve currency. When that happened, the United States would no longer be able to print more money. Its credit card would be maxed out, and the country would have few options left.

Steele did not plan on sitting by and watching that happen. He did not plan on watching Texas go down with the ship.

"I've got to go, darlin'," he said to Mary. "I've got this speech to make." He paused for a moment, not wanting to end the conversation on a sour note. "I love you," he said, meaning it with all his heart.

Mary sighed, and he could hear the anger leaving her voice. "I love you, too," she said. "Knock 'em dead."

Steele hung up, gathered his papers, and walked into the ballroom. He stepped up to the podium and looked out at the crowd.

"Let me read to you a portion of a letter I received from the Lewis administration this morning," he began. "It's on the letterhead of the Department of Transportation."

Steele held up the page to attest to its authenticity.

"Dear Governor Steele," he read. "The recent oil spill in the Gulf of Mexico is a direct result of lax and incompetent regulation of off-shore drilling. The state of Texas, in defiance of the federal government has illegally issued drilling permits without federal approval and against the demands of the President of the United States. It is our position that Texas holds all responsibility for these spills and for the cost of cleanup and beach and marsh remediation. Effective immediately, the U.S. Department of Transportation is levying an additional gasoline tax of two dollars per gallon on all gasoline sold within the state of Texas. The added tax will fund the cleanup operation and pay compensation to private individuals and businesses for losses that may have been incurred."

Steele held up the letter for all to see and tore it in half.

"My dear ladies and gentlemen," Steele said. "This is unacceptable. When Texas took back the authority to issue drilling permits, we maintained all of the safety requirements the federal government had applied all along. Nothing changed. The only regulations that were relaxed were the tedious and arcane requirements for documentation and fees as well as the nearly stagnant process of obtaining permits.

"I am happy to report that the spills have now been contained through the efforts of the oil companies and the state emergency response teams. FEMA has been no help and has, at times, actually obstructed the cleanup work.

"The oil spill is simply an excuse to tighten Washington's control on Texas. This new tax is blatant oppression. It is the action of dictators. This singles out Texas for punishment simply because we have chosen to stand up to this administration.

"My question to you good people here today is this: will you help me deliver a response to President Lewis?"

"Yes," the crowd roared.

Steele nodded. It was time to make the ultimate stand for his state's rights.

Part 4

Secession

CHAPTER 32

"My dream is of a place and a time where America will once again
be seen as the last best hope of earth."
- Abraham Lincoln -

THE SUFFOCATING San Antonio humidity overwhelmed Senator Nate Cummings as he stepped through the automatic doors from the airport baggage claim. He dropped his bag and loosened his tie as he tried to inhale enough of the thick air to keep from passing out. Would he prefer the low humidity and high taxes in California or the low taxes and high humidity of Texas? At the moment, he would have chosen to endure the taxes in exchange for a good lungful of smog-filled air.

Stu Timmerly spotted him and steered his SUV to the curb, nearly getting clipped by a rental car courtesy bus in the process. He hopped out and waved a long arm to get Cummings' attention.

"Welcome to Texas, Senator. I see you're enjoying a bite of our moist air."

"How do you survive this humidity, Mr. Timmerly?" Cummings asked.

"Oh, it's not that bad. We have four seasons in San Antonio. We have spring, summer, still summer, and Christmas. And it's 'Stu,' please. We're not much for formality in Texas."

"Suits me fine, Stu. Nate is what my friends call me."

"I'm a Republican," the Texas attorney general said as he was loading Cummings' bag into the backseat. "So I may not qualify as a friend."

"Right now we have a common interest, Stu. So party affiliation doesn't matter. I've been called intense and driven. I've fought for what I've believed was best for the country and best for even our most disadvantaged citizens. But there is a line between driven and maniacal. Recently, I've found myself teetering on the edge of the abyss of ruthlessness. In a perverse way, President Lewis saved me from falling in with her. She and Sanchez did me a big favor without realizing it."

"The Lewis administration is a joke in these parts, Nate," Timmerly said. "There is a rising tide against them and that tide might just drown them."

"I've seen it developing, Stu. And it would be more accurate to call it the Sanchez administration 3.0. He's the guy pulling the strings. Lewis is just following orders. They like to make it look like Sanchez is just helping out in the background and managing his pet project, the Wellness Security Act. But it runs much deeper. Sanchez is in on every cabinet meeting. He's right there whenever President Lewis meets with congressional leaders. Lewis does the public appearances with heads of state, and such. But if there is business to be discussed, he's there."

"A shadow president?" Timmerly asked.

"The term would fit. Just like in Russia when Putin was officially out but still ran everything. They named him premier, but everyone knew he called the shots. In Sanchez's case, they call him chief-of-staff."

"And President Lewis is okay with that?"

"Rumor has it she has no choice," Cummings explained. "They say it's blackmail. They say Sanchez holds the key to a jail cell for Lewis. He has the evidence that would guarantee a conviction."

"For her national security blunders?"

"That and more," Cummings said. "There are loud whispers that she's got multiple illegal campaign irregularities. Big donors wanting favors. Money laundered through her so-called charitable foundation. It would be massive. It would make Watergate look like a ticket for jaywalking by comparison.

"But that's not the reason I'm here. I have what Paul Harvey would call the rest of the story."

"Can't wait to hear your story. We need to be discreet, Nate," Timmerly said. "I'm driving you up to my hunting cabin, well away from cameras and microphones. Later, you'll meet with Mary. Now that you and she are working together on that joint congressional committee, it makes perfect sense for you to be meeting. Keep in mind that she thinks you're here only to discuss committee business with her on your way through from D.C. to California. She knows nothing about the information you have. She'll be driving you back to the airport."

Timmerly cranked up the air conditioning. When they exited the airport, he took the second ramp to the interstate and headed northwest. An hour later, Timmerly left the highway and took a winding country road that followed a meandering stream. At the end of a long dirt drive, a one-room cabin sat nestled among the cottonwoods. Unpainted cedar boards clad the exterior, and a weathered tin roof shaped a simple gable and covered a porch across the front. A ten-year-old Ford F-150 was parked alongside the cabin.

"Brew's here. That's his truck," Timmerly said.

They pulled to a stop and waited for the dust cloud to clear before opening the doors. Brewster Steele stepped from the porch to greet them.

"Nate," Timmerly said, "this is Brew Steele, best quarterback the Aggies ever had."

"Pleasure, Brew," Cummings said.

"Howdy, Nate," Steele said. "Thanks for coming all this way. Let's get you inside and put a cold one in your hands."

The cabin was surprisingly cool considering the heat outside. A gentle breeze stirred the curtains.

"Let's get to it so you can catch your flight out this evening. What do you have that required all this secrecy?" Steele asked.

"From your point of view, Brew, you might think I have finally come to my senses," Cummings said. "I'm sure you think I'm one of the ringleaders in the huge overspending. And I can't say I'm not. I've engineered some of the biggest social programs in American history. Try to believe me when I say that I honestly did that out of sympathy for the common man. I was a flower-child in my college years. I went to Woodstock. In fact, you can see me in the movie. I'm one of the long-haired guys flopping around in the mud and fooling myself into thinking I was changing the world. I came from a privileged background and I felt guilty about it. Not guilty enough to give up the comforts of wealth, mind you. But guilty enough to devote my life to making things better for the disadvantaged."

"Sounds like my wife," Steele said. "Her greatest regret is she was too young to have experienced Woodstock."

"You can tell her the stories are better than the reality. And most of us were too stoned to remember much of it. I was one of the few who realized change can really only happen within the system. So I entered politics. I believed in Lyndon Johnson's Great Society. I truly believed that it just needed more government support and more funding to become what I hoped it could be. I would ask myself how this country could be the wealthiest and most prosperous nation on earth and still have poor people with no prospects for bettering their circumstances."

"It sounds like you're about to tell us your thinking has changed," Timmerly said.

"Exactly. It was gradual at first. As a Democrat, and as I became one of the leaders, I found myself giving the knee jerk reaction to anything the Republicans wanted or suggested.

I really believed in what we were doing. I saw the goal of stamping out poverty to be worth any cost, and I believed America was rich enough to pay for it.

"Maybe it was a slow maturing process. I don't know, and I'm not much for psychoanalysis. I do know that as time went by, I saw through the pretense of more and more of my friends and my fellow Democrats. I saw them as they really were. They are mere opportunists. They could talk the talk, but none of them actually walked the walk. They were happy to tax away everyone else's money for their favorite causes, but they hardly put in a nickel of their own. Worse than that, they did these things to gain political points with their constituents. Government handouts are the currency of elections. Democrats bribe the voters with other peoples' money, tax money."

"We have plenty of Republicans like that, too," Steele said.

"Well, I realize that. It seems to be the norm with politicians. It's all a game of pandering and destruction of your opponents. Show me a politician with a working moral compass and I'll show you an election loser. President Sanchez managed to bring Washington to new lows and President Lewis is keeping us heading down that same path. Either that or my eyes are now open like never before."

Nate Cummings swallowed hard and wiped his forehead with the back of his hand. He knew he was sweating more from anxiety than from the heat and humidity.

"So here's part of what I came to tell you. I'm resigning from the Senate," Cummings said.

"Why? And more to the point, why did you come all the way to Texas, and covertly at that, to tell a couple of Republicans you're resigning?" Steele asked.

"Oh, I'll tell everyone soon enough," Cummings said.

He turned and spoke directly to Steele.

"I came here because you can see what's happening to this country and you're trying to do something about it, Brew. You're holding onto the spirit of America. I don't need to tell you that

Sanchez and Lewis are out of control. They're turning America into what the Soviet Union only hoped to be. Only you and a few of your fellow governors are offering any resistance."

"Why don't you stop them?" Timmerly asked. "You're the Senate majority leader. You're one of the most influential men in Washington."

"I can't," Cummings said. "I'm in too far. It's got to be done by someone on the outside. After the Reyes confirmation, I fell into a depression. I even considered suicide."

"But you led the way on his confirmation," Steele said. "And now you have buyer's remorse. I don't mean to be blunt, but you're just as responsible for Reyes as Sanchez and Lewis. That horse has left the barn."

"I know I was responsible, too. I should have fought back, but I had no choice," Cummings said, shaking his head. "Sanchez has me by the balls. I didn't know how at the time, but Sanchez managed to concoct a charge of election fraud against me, and he got it buried into my personal identity record. He linked me to a radical environmental group and to a plan to disqualify absentee ballots."

"I remember when that happened. You were involved in that?" Timmerly asked.

"Hell, no. But now my file says I was. The way it's been done, I end up looking like I directed the whole thing. It's all false, of course. But the falsified record even includes my wife. If it comes out, our lives would be ruined. Sanchez showed me all of this when Lewis nominated Reyes. Reyes was Sanchez's man, not Lewis. She's his puppet and does whatever he tells her to do. He blackmailed me into confirming Reyes with this phony allegation."

"You are only one vote. Couldn't the other committee members block the confirmation?" Steele asked.

"Sanchez threatened to bring out the charge if I failed to get the Reyes nomination through. The Republicans voted against him, of course. But they are a small minority. They have no influence. And surprisingly, I didn't get much pushback from the Democrats on the committee. They either sold out for some paybacks from Sanchez and Lewis or they'd found or created some trash in the committee members' files. Christ, I wish we'd never passed that idiotic Personal Identity Protection Act."

"You said on the ride out here you had something you wanted to show us," Timmerly said.

"Yes, that's the main reason I came."

Cummings took a long draw on his beer. He pulled the packet of papers Arthur Campbell had given him out of his briefcase, along with a flash drive containing the same files.

"When I started the background check on Reyes, I asked my man to dig into Romeo Costa and see what he could find. The Lewis assassination attempt in Miami never rang true with me. When Lewis and Sanchez nominated Reyes and blackmailed me, they gave me the motivation to dig in and see what I could find. I got vindictive. I'm not going to spin it any other way. I wanted to get even with the bastards."

"And that's what brings you here?" Steele asked.

"Exactly. What I found goes way beyond Costa and way beyond that day in Miami. You and Texas are in a battle with Sanchez, Lewis, and Washington. And I'm here to tell you I'm with you. It took me a while to come to terms with the implications of all of this. You're looking at a reformed man, a man who wants to return to the principles and dreams that first energized me to make a difference in this country.

"There will be no public statement of my change of heart. I can be more helpful to you in my present position. You'll hear me say things in public that may make you doubt my sincerity. But I'll need to be seen as still loyal to Lewis and Sanchez so I can know what's going on inside the White House.

"Sanchez is coming after you. And you need ammunition to fight him off." Cummings dropped the packet of papers and flash drive on the coffee table.

"Think of me as your weapons dealer."

CHAPTER 33

*"The principle of spending money to be paid by posterity,
under the name of funding, is but swindling futurity on a large
scale."*

- Thomas Jefferson -

THE TEXAS ECONOMIC Summit began on time. The state treasurer called the meeting to order. He stood before the assembly knowing what he was about to say could be a pivotal point in the history of Texas and possibly the history of America. He hoped to turn things upside down.

"Ladies and gentlemen," Chase Bretton said, "let me remind you that what transpires here is strictly confidential. This is not official state business and is not a position or policy statement. We are here to discuss the problems we face and examine a potential solution."

Bretton tapped his remote, and a chart appeared on the large screen behind him.

"The red line you see is the annual state budget. The blue line is our annual state tax revenues. Up until President Sanchez took office, we had run a surplus. Then the Great Recession hit and every state in the union was faced with massive, unforeseen deficits. The effect of deficit spending on Washington is much less than on states. They have the luxury of printing money. We do not. When we're out of money, we're broke.

"Texas has fared much better than nearly every other state. By reducing the corporate tax rates, we have attracted new businesses that have increased our tax base. More businesses have relocated to Texas in the past eight years than to any other state. This is proof our strategy is working. And we plan on doubling our efforts. This country is teeming with businesses that are drowning under the weight of incredible tax burdens and smothering regulations. Our objective is to give those businesses a friendly home."

Bretton tapped the remote again. Up came a colorful banner with the single star state flag fluttering above the Alamo. The slogan "Texas Lives Free" spread across the banner. Below it, in a smaller font, were the words "Life, Liberty and the Pursuit of Happiness."

"We are at a crossroads. Washington has gradually siphoned off the independence of the states. Texas has allowed itself to be dragged down the path of dependency along with the other states. Our citizens send their tax money to Washington to fund the operation of the federal government. We only get a fraction of that money back, and every dollar that comes from Washington has strings attached. Our funding for education, transportation, housing, environmental protection, workplace safety, energy consumption, and nearly everything else comes from Washington with a mountain of rules and regulations. The states have been emasculated to the point where it seems the sovereignty of the individual states has evaporated into thin air.

"We have made projections of the costs Texas would have if Texas were to provide the same services and benefits to the citizens as the federal government does. It includes welfare checks, defense, bank deposit insurance, a phased-in version of Social Security, anything you can think of. Hypothetically, Texas could replace the federal government. Our projections show that if we were to somehow keep the federal tax revenue in Texas and never send it to Washington, we could run our government at a surplus and no one would be negatively affected.

"Any questions so far? Yes, Carl," Bretton said, acknowledging the president of Fort Worth Trust, the state's largest bank.

"I don't mean to jump ahead, Chase," Carl Ingerstein said. "But this is wildly hypothetical. Why even worry about what gets sent to Washington and having the state replace federal services? Isn't this an exercise of fantasy?"

"We feel it is an exercise of necessity, Carl. Every year, the Federal Reserve adds billions of dollars to the money supply. The creation of the Federal Reserve on that fateful day on Jekyll Island was the moment our dollar began to die. It was slowly detached from the only real tangible money, gold and silver. The Federal Reserve can't make more gold to prop up failing banks or manipulate interest rates. But they can easily print more dollars. These days they don't even have to print them. They simply credit member banks with the funds they need. Presto. More money is in circulation. When Nixon took the dollar completely off the gold standard, our money was no longer solid. The Federal Reserve, and our government, could play with it all they wanted."

"That's the way the game is played, Chase," Ingerstein said. "We don't make the rules. Washington does. All we can do is play the game as best we can."

"That's why we called you all here, Carl," Bretton said. "We intend to change a few rules."

Bretton hit the remote. An image appeared of several coins that looked like shiny copper doughnuts with a gold or silver disk where the hole should be. A single large star had been imprinted from rim to rim.

"We are proposing that the state of Texas issue its own coins. These coins would contain pure gold and pure silver. Denominations are still being determined based on sizing. We will establish a floating exchange rate that adjusts with the diminishing value of the U.S. dollar and other world currencies. Our new coinage is called the Lone Star. It will be legal tender within the state of Texas, and banks will be free to exchange them for U.S. dollars at the customer's request. But our expectation is that most folks will hold their money in Lone Stars instead of dollars because of the stability they will offer. We can defend ourselves against inflation with our money."

Bretton looked around the rooms and saw the puzzled expressions he expected.

"Is this constitutional?" Ingerstein asked.

"Absolutely," Breton said. "The Constitution expressly permits states to mint gold and silver coinage."

"This is going to really piss off the Federal Reserve," Ingerstein said.

"Let it," Bretton said. "We need to save ourselves. We cannot stop Congress and the President from expanding the deficit as they have. But we can protect ourselves and our heirs from them. We can reject all of what Washington is doing to us.

"If Texas detaches itself from the United States, it can detach itself from the debts Washington has given us that can never be repaid. We have the right as free people to determine our own future."

CHAPTER 34

"Iacta alea est, (the die has been cast)."
- Julius Caesar —
49 BC

HE THOUGHT OF HIS high school Latin translations of Suetonius, when Julius Caesar crossed the Rubicon to retake Rome and defeat Pompey. Today, Brewster Steele would cast his own die. The outcome was unknown, and the decision was irreversible.

Lieutenant Governor Marshall Flynn sat behind Steele on the dais. Flynn had made the rounds and confirmed potential support in the Senate. The groundwork had been laid. Chase Bretton had assured Steele that the banks were on his side. And thanks to Nate Cummings, Steele knew he had the ammunition to fight President Lewis, should it come to that. But this speech would be the deciding factor, and it was anything but certain. Steele needed to make an eloquent and convincing case. If he failed, tonight would be political suicide.

A hundred and forty-four members of the house, thirty-one senators, and four special delegates filled the House chamber of the Texas capitol building. But this was not a normal session of the legislature. Each regular member of the House and Senate had been elected for this extraordinary convention through a popular vote the week before. Four representatives declined to serve as delegates in protest. Their places were taken by the specially elected delegates. Only one question was on the agenda. There were no absentees. Even eighty-three-year-old Senator Evan Collier III was in attendance, having demanded to be wheeled in despite being tethered to an IV drip following his fourth bypass surgery, so he could witness the historic event.

The balcony was crammed to overflowing with spectators. Extra security measures were taken to prevent demonstrations within the chamber. Outside, protesters and supporters battled it out with verbal volleys and chants. Word of what Steele was about to propose could not be contained. It was just too big for that.

"My fellow Texans," Steele began. "We have faced many adversaries in the past. From the Texas War of Independence through two World Wars, Korea, Viet Nam, the Cold War, to this present day, Texans have courageously paid the price required of them to keep us safe and free. We have prevailed with heroism, strength, and courage. Every outside threat has been defeated.

"Today, we are being threatened by an enemy within. Our enemy is ourselves. We, as Americans, are eroding and dismantling the core of our American way of life. With every act of Congress, with every regulation from the President, with every new tax, our freedoms are being lost.

"In the name of compassion, the hard-earned wealth of Americans and Texans is being forcibly seized and redistributed by a federal government that believes it knows how you should live your life better than you do yourself. Our government is building a debt larger than any ever seen on earth. The responsibility for repaying that enormous weight of debt will fall to the states and all of the citizens of America.

"We have crossed a critical line. Every government program removes a stone from the foundation of the country and places it as an added burden on top of the foundation they have just weakened. Lincoln said, 'A house divided cannot stand.' But I say to you that a house can crumble under its own weight. The United States will sink under the weight of its massive debt, and it will drag Texas down with it. Our house is doomed to collapse — and we cannot let that happen."

The audience stood and cheered. The chant of "Texas Lives Free" came from the balcony.

"Our only salvation is to seize back our independence. We must detach ourselves from the clutches of the national debt. We must free ourselves from the oppressive government of the Lewis administration. We must build a future for our children. We must preserve the ideals of America."

Steele paused as the applause drowned him out. He scanned his audience. All but a few Democrats were now standing and cheering.

"America is more than a place. Our founding fathers fought for more than mere real estate. They fought for an idea. They fought for the natural rights of mankind. They fought for the belief that men and women of all classes were free and equal in the eyes of God. They fought for the idea that a free society was the birthplace of great things.

"Destiny has granted us the opportunity to rescue what our forefathers cherished and fought for. History will record what we do today. We must hold the torch of freedom high and carry on the idea of America. Texas must declare its independence and become a sovereign nation unto itself."

CHAPTER 35

"A man may die, nations may rise and fall,
but an idea lives on."
- John F. Kennedy -

THE TEXAS DECLARATION of Independence read as follows:

The free people of the state of Texas, in order to preserve and protect the liberties and opportunities that our forefathers fought and died for, and to preserve and protect those liberties and opportunities for the generations who will follow us, resolve, that the state of Texas is, and of right, ought to be, a free and independent state, that they are absolved from all allegiance to the United States of America, and that all political connection between them and the United States of America is, and ought to be, totally dissolved.

When in the Course of human events it becomes necessary for one people to dissolve the political bands which have connected them with another, and to assume among the powers of the earth, the separate and equal

215

station to which the Laws of Nature and of Nature's God entitle them, a decent respect to the opinions of mankind requires that they should declare the causes which impel them to the separation.

We hold these truths to be self-evident, that all men are created equal, that they are endowed by their Creator with certain unalienable Rights, that among these are Life, Liberty, and the pursuit of Happiness. That to secure and protect these rights, Governments are instituted among the Citizenry, deriving their just powers from the consent of the governed. That whenever any Form of Government becomes destructive of these ends, it is the Right and Duty of the People to alter or to abolish it, and to institute new Government, laying its foundation on such principles and organizing its powers in such form, as to them shall seem most likely to affect their Safety and Happiness. Prudence, indeed, will dictate that Governments long established should not be changed for light and transient causes; and accordingly all experience hath shown, that mankind are more disposed to suffer, while evils are sufferable, than to right themselves by abolishing the forms to which they are accustomed. But when a long train of abuses and usurpations, removes such liberties and transforms a government to absolute Despotism and effective Tyranny, it is their right and their duty, to throw off such Government, and to provide new Guards for their future security.

Such has been the patient sufferance of the state of Texas; and such is now the necessity which constrains them to alter their former Systems of Government. The history of the present Federal Government of the United States of America is a history of repeated injuries and usurpations, all having in direct object the establishment of an absolute Tyranny over this state. To prove this, let Facts be submitted to a candid world.

The Federal Government has:

Seized powers and jurisdictions that are protected and preserved to the states by the United States Constitution;

Abdicated its fiduciary responsibility, permitted and abetted exorbitant borrowing and spending, and thus depleted the wealth of this nation and assumed extreme, unsustainable, and unserviceable debt;

Failed to protect the value and integrity of the currency of this nation;

Imposed confiscatory taxation for the sole purpose of redistribution of wealth;

Repeatedly imposed laws and regulations beyond the powers permitted by the Constitution;

Blatantly manipulated the judicial system rendering it no longer a free and independent branch of government;

Failed to properly protect and secure the borders of the country and the state of Texas and ignored the safety and dangers of invasion from without and convulsions from within;

Seized lands without justification under the pretense of protecting the environment;

Restricted and prevented exploration and recovery of natural energy and mineral resources that are the rightful property of the state of Texas;

Established a multitude of new offices, departments, and agencies and sent hither swarms of Officers and Regulators to harass our people and impede their pursuit of happiness and property;

Granted the rights, benefits, and privileges of legal citizens to illegal aliens and non-citizens;

Forcibly attempted to restrict free trade and access to our ports, highways, and airports;

Plundered our businesses through excessive taxation, fees, and regulations.

We have petitioned the Federal Government in the most humble terms for redress of these grievances. Our petitions have been answered in only repeated injury. A Government thus marked by every act which may be defined a tyrannical government under the guise of a democratic government, is a Tyrant just the same and is unfit for governance of a free people.

We, therefore, the Representatives of the state of Texas, in General Congress, Assembled, appealing to the Supreme Judge of the world for the rectitude of our intentions, do, in the Name, and by Authority of the good People of Texas, solemnly publish and declare, That they are of Right ought to be a Free and Independent State; that they are Absolved from all Allegiance to the United States of America, and that all political connection between them and the United States of America, is and ought to be totally dissolved; and that as a Free and Independent State, they have full Power to levy War, conclude Peace, contract Alliances, establish Commerce, and to do all other Acts and Things which Independent States may of right do. And for the support of this Declaration, with a firm reliance on the protection of divine Providence, we mutually pledge to each other our Lives, our Fortunes and our sacred Honor.

On the fourth of December, the congressional delegation from Texas sat patiently in the Cabinet Room of the West Wing waiting for the President to arrive. Senator Vance Garlan occupied the center seat opposite the President's chair. By a flip of a coin, he got the nod over his counterpart, Senator Glen Dunn, to lead the delegation. A dozen Texas congressmen and congresswomen filled the remaining chairs. The meeting was scheduled for ten. Garlan's watch read ten-thirty.

A door opened and Vice President Charles Stafford stepped through. He set his "Dreams Can Be...Reality" coffee mug on the long conference table in front of the chair next to the President's.

"Vance, Glen," he said, reaching across to shake the senators' hands. Stafford worked his way around the table giving each congressman his best two-handed campaign handshake. "I never thought we would meet under these circumstances."

"Neither did we, Lou," Garlan said.

At 2:30 P.M., President Lewis arrived. She offered a greeting to no one, but simply took the center seat and gave Senator Garlan a stone-faced stare.

"State your business, Senator," the president said.

"Ms. President," Garlan began, "We represent the state of Texas and our purpose in coming here today is to present this document to you. With your permission, I will read it aloud."

Sanchez nodded. "Please get on with it, Senator."

Garlan opened a thin, leather-bound document and began to read. Lewis glowered at him, steely-eyed, unmoving, as Garlan read through the text of the Declaration.

"This Declaration shall have the full effect of law on the first day of the next year," Garlan said after he finished. "The signatures of a super majority of the Texas legislature, the governor, lieutenant governor, and the Texas attorney general attend this document."

Garlan folded the Declaration into its leather folio and passed it across the table to the president amid a flurry of camera flashes. Lewis picked up the document without comment, turned on her heel, and left the room.

CHAPTER
36

"If any state in the Union will declare that it prefers separation...to a continuance in union... I have no hesitation in saying, 'let us separate.'"

- Thomas Jefferson -

NEWS OF THE SECESSION of Texas sent shockwaves through the country. The only political and historical precedent for this event had led to a bloody civil war with seven-hundred-thousand casualties. Everyone wanted to know what Texas was planning.

With so many legal, financial, and social ties between Texas and the United States federal government, the process of secession would be difficult and complicated. The separation was scheduled to go into effect on January first, which left only a month to get everything in order. But Brewster Steele and his new administration had not been slacking.

The state already had a fully functional government in place, not to mention its already existent constitution — after all, Texas had been a republic before it was a state. A skeletal structure of a state department and other agencies had already been planned. Treaties and trade agreements were in the works, patterned after existing treaties. Texas had already issued its own gold and silver backed coinage. From there, it was a small step to create a currency and wean the state off any dependency on the U.S. dollar.

Before January rolled around, there would be a period of time during which people could choose their citizenship. Those who wished to remain American citizens could do so. As long as the United States recognized those individuals as American citizens, they would be considered non-Texans who were in Texas as guests, and would be issued the proper documents.

Additionally, Texas would set up a relocation program so anyone who wanted to leave and live in the remainder of the United States could do so easily. For a period of one year from the commencement of the Independent Republic of Texas, anyone on welfare who wished to leave would be provided with free transportation to any town within three hundred miles of the Texas border, and would be given a modest sum for relocation costs. By the Texas treasurer's calculations, it would be less costly for Texas citizens to pay for this relocation than to continue to pay people to not work.

On January first, the payroll withholding taxes and other funds employers had been sending to the IRS would start going to Texas. Large amounts of money would flow to the state treasury instead of flowing to Washington. The Texas treasurer calculated that the state would easily be able to replace all federal benefits to individuals with equal benefits from the state. No school lunch programs would be interrupted. No welfare checks would be skipped. And no one would miss a Social Security check. The plan was that Social Security payments would still come from the U.S. government. American citizens who lived in other countries in their retirement years still collected; it should be the same if they lived in the country of Texas. For those people approaching retirement, Texas was planning a supplemental retirement account to fill in any gaps if an individual's benefit was diminished because of the secession. Continuity of benefits was a key element in getting public support for secession.

However, continuity of benefits did not mean falling into the same money-splurging trap the United States had. The treasurer had run the numbers on the amount of each tax dollar Washington skimmed off to pay for federal bureaucracy, along with the dollars lost to government inefficiency and waste. Texas would not have the same loss of funds as the federal government did. Moreover, they would initiate an aggressive effort to rid the system of improper payments. Proof of citizenship would be required for all citizens in order to collect any financial benefit or service from the government. The deletion of the costly layer of federal bureaucracy and the inefficiency in Washington would allow more tax dollars to go where they were intended. The house cleaning of the welfare and assistance rolls would reduce costs dramatically. By the treasurer's calculations, they would have plenty of money to keep everyone happy.

The second phase of Steele's plan was to implement reforms of most of these programs in what Steele described as a "gradual and compassionate way to return the role of government to peacekeeping and regulation of trade." Social engineering would no longer be an objective of government. Charity would be left to charities.

Of course, it would take some time to collect enough money from the payroll taxes and other funds to pay for these programs. In the meantime, Texas would have to float government bonds and borrow the money.

Steele knew that on the surface, this would appear hypocritical. After all, it was exactly the kind of behavior Steele had decried in the U.S. government. However, there were several major differences between Texas and the U.S. First of all, Texas was not already in a gigantic financial hole like the United States. Their budget was usually in the black, especially now that oil revenues had returned. Second, Texas would repay the bonds in Lone Stars. This currency would be much less prone to inflation than the U.S. Federal Reserve notes. Third, Texas would be writing a balanced budget amendment into their Constitution. It would require that no annual budget could exceed the amount of the average budgets of the previous three fiscal years without a referendum vote of the people. Of course, in the first three years, Texas would be unable to refer to previous years, but this anticipated limitation alone would make their securities highly prized by conservative investors. And the fourth major difference between Texas bonds and U.S. bonds was that they would be promissory notes against a growing and thriving economy — not a rapidly sinking one.

Then there was the matter of the federal property within Texas — military bases, parks and recreation properties, federally funded highways. Steele and his administration had an answer for that as well, although Steele knew the U.S. wouldn't like it. Texas would not demand its fair share of the gold in Fort Knox, or its fair share of the national park system outside of Texas, or its share of other natural resources owned by the citizens of the United States but which were located in other states. Texas waived any claim to those valuable assets. At the same time, Texas would honor no claim by the United States upon any federal lands, including highways, within the Republic of Texas. Texas also rejected any responsibility for the repayment of a prorated portion of the national debt. Steele's position was that the cost of the Texas portion of the national debt, while large, was dwarfed by the value of the gold, the natural resources, and Texas's portion of the federal lands they were relinquishing to the remaining states and federal government. Steele was calling it square.

Of course, the greatest question on everyone's mind was whether this secession was legal. Many scholars said the U.S. Constitution did not provide a vehicle for separation of a state from the Union, and therefore it was unconstitutional. There were others who claimed the right to secede was retained by the states on the basis that the Constitution does not explicitly prohibit it. Steele's view was that secession was probably illegal only because the North won the Civil War. If the South had won, it would be another matter.

The truth was, it did not actually matter if secession was constitutional or not. Once a state declared itself to no longer be a part of the Union and declared all legal bonds severed, they would no longer be bound by the laws of the United States or the Constitution. Texas could say, "What Constitution? We're not part of your country anymore." The question of constitutionality didn't matter. And even if it did, where would the United States take the legal dispute? What court would settle it? If the U.S. Supreme Court ruled that the secession was illegal and unconstitutional, Texas could simply say, "We are no longer subject to the decisions of your Supreme Court. We have our own Supreme Court." The argument was moot, since there was no longer a jurisdiction that both parties honored.

The only way to keep a state from separating was by force, and Steele was pretty sure the majority of Americans wouldn't want that. Some informal polling done by KBS news showed that more than fifty-one percent of the people asked said Texas had the legal right to secede. Thirty-seven percent thought the United States would be better off without Texas anyway. And twelve percent thought the Union should be preserved at all costs, including taking military action. In other words, eighty-eight percent of the people asked favored Texas seceding in one form or another. When KBS asked specifically about the use of force to keep Texas in the Union, the vast majority opposed it.

However, Steele knew well that President Lewis was not bound by what the majority of American citizens thought or felt. President Lewis was only bound by what her chief of staff and immediate past president, Carlos Sanchez, thought and felt — and what exactly that was remained to be seen.

CHAPTER 37

*"Any people that would give up liberty for a little temporary
safety
deserves neither liberty nor safety."*

- Benjamin Franklin -

IN AUSTIN TEXAS the protesters had gathered. Hundreds were clogging North Congress Avenue to demonstrate their opposition to the secession. The crowd, which consisted primarily of students and university professors, started their march on the campus of the University of Texas, with the goal of reaching the state capitol building. They had been blocking traffic for hours as they slowly meandered south, often stopping, usually in front of news cameras, to chant slogans.

Upon reaching the capitol grounds, the protestors were greeted by rows of riot police, mounted Texas Rangers, jersey barriers, and steel fencing. Also greeting them were many more hundreds, if not thousands, of secession supporters. The chants of "America First, Texas Last" and "Fuck You Brew" from the protestors were countered, then overwhelmed by the chanted motto of the secession movement: "Texas Lives Free."

The protestors, however, were not there merely to chant. The media reporters watched as march organizers, dressed in white wigs and colonial garb, displayed copies of the Texas Declaration of Independence to the crowd, then proceeded to tear them to pieces and burn the remains. The secession-supporting bystanders hurled chants and jeers at the protesters, but it only seemed to egg them on.

A group of several dozen protesters broke away from the main crowd. Before anyone could stop them, they stormed the police line at the gates to the capitol building, trying to tackle the police to the ground and get inside. The police had no choice but to break out their billy clubs and start beating the protesters away.

By the time things had calmed down, several protesters had been taken by ambulance to the hospital. Two head injuries were reported, leaving one protester in serious but stable condition.

Austin police chief Henry Lunden looked shaken and saddened as he faced the news cameras early the next morning. "The Austin police regret having to use force in what started as a peaceful protest," he said. "Unfortunately, the protesters left our officers no choice. Three officers were injured, one with a stab wound to the arm. A total of thirty-one arrests have been made."

President Lewis muted Henry Lunden on the television in Air Force One.

"Have you been able to hold the crowd together?" she asked Tony Delgado, her campaign manager and new special advisor.

When the Texas delegation had first come to her with their ridiculous Declaration of Independence, Lewis had been pissed — to put it mildly. After a few glasses had been shattered against the wall, Tony Delgado had managed to calm her down by reminding her that they might be able to turn this in their favor. All they had to do was cook up a way to blame Texas and Brewster Steele for all the troubles the country had.

Sanchez agreed. He knew he could turn this into something President Lewis could cheer about. They could say the country was better off without the reddest of the red states. They could say Texas had stood in the way of the social reform they were trying to enact. Lewis could call them out as the bigots they were. She'd point out that if it weren't for Texas, her plans and Sanchez's before hers would have fixed the broken economy and pulled people out of poverty by now. Sanchez knew Lewis's diehard supporters would believe her. They just needed to get the word out.

"I want to have a good audience in place," Sanchez emphasized to Delgado.

"Borsky's people are there with free food, free beer, and tents," Delgado replied. "That should keep the crowd around. Porta-johns are on the way. News images of kids taking a crap on the street corner won't do our message any good. Hopefully we can keep things more civil this time around. There's a band scheduled for tonight. The street's blocked off for two blocks in all directions. It's turned into a party. The crowd is actually growing. And the government employees' union has sent in extras. They won't be charging the police line now that they know it's dangerous and the police are willing to use force."

"Are your troops moving into position?" Sanchez asked Steven Hamm, the secretary of defense.

"General Ostermann is coordinating the troops across Texas," Hamm answered. "There will be patrols in the major cities 24/7. We have soldiers on foot patrol and armed rubber tire vehicles cruising the streets. If large crowds won't disperse when ordered, they will be confronted with tanks. All personnel are prohibited from firing weapons, except in self-defense if confronted. However, they are ordered to hold their ground at all times."

"Good. I want this to look like an occupation. We need to make Texas look like a conquered country. The rest of the country doesn't have the stomach for an actual war. But I can't let Texas simply walk away," Sanchez said. "The president wants this to show she won't stand by and allow this kind of insurrection. Right Ms. President?"

Theresa Lewis nodded, looking more like a deer in the headlights than the leader of the free world.

"An information campaign is ready to go," Tony Delgado said. "We're going to plaster the networks with anti-secession messages. They'll be labeled as public service messages. But the purpose is to scare people into reversing the secession."

"Christ," Theresa Lewis said, finally finding her voice. "We should have thought of that before their secession convention. Then we wouldn't have had this mess. I'll be remembered as the President who lost America."

"Our polling showed only thirty-six percent of the population was even a little bit in favor of secession. Nobody, not even the most highly-regarded polls, thought this would actually happen," Delgado argued.

"I'm not an American history expert, Delgado," Sanchez said. "But I got curious and looked it up. It turns out less than half of Americans favored independence from England when the Declaration of Independence was signed. Hard to believe. So it clearly does not require a majority to make something like this happen. We call it a revolution, but that was, in fact, secession. Just like the Civil War, the Revolutionary War wasn't caused by the act of secession; it was caused by the country that didn't want to allow the secession trying to stop it. That's where we sit today with the question of whether we let them leave or force them to stay. I sure as hell don't want a war. Too messy. Nobody wins. But we have the power to intimidate the citizens. Let's see how devoted they are to the great Brewster Steele."

President Lewis looked out of the window as the plane began its descent into Austin-Bergstrom International Airport. Two hours earlier, an unmarked jetliner had landed, without fanfare, carrying the President's advanced security team. As Air Force One approached, all vehicles and aircraft were ordered to hold their positions and remain stationary.

A pair of Air Force fighters roared across the field less than two hundred feet above the runway. A moment later, an Air Force Boeing 747 landed alone and taxied to a non-descript gray hangar across the tarmac from the commercial terminal. Immediately behind it, Air Force One touched down, causing a minor stampede toward the tall glass windows that lined the commercial terminal as delayed passengers strained to get a glimpse of the President's plane.

Security vehicles circled Air Force One like covered wagons. Sanchez steered Lewis out of the far side of the plane and hustled her into a Marine helicopter that sat with its rotor turning at idle speed. The door was abruptly pulled closed and the chopper took off.

Ten minutes later, the helicopter settled softly on the grassy rooftop terrace of the underground Texas capitol extension. The President's surprise visit had been radioed ahead to the Austin police and the Texas Rangers only a few minutes before she landed, about the same time fifty-two Secret Service agents began combing through the crowd, randomly wanding protesters with handheld magnetometers, confiscating bags, and swabbing clothing for explosives. Agents were ordered to ignore drug possession since apprehending so many people would take too much time and greatly diminish the crowd.

As President Lewis walked behind Sanchez toward the mobile podium her staff had hastily assembled, news crews that had been given more advance notice of the President's impromptu appearance than the Texas authorities, pushed their satellite broadcasting vans through the throngs of protesters, claiming the best vantage points by sheer force. By now, word of the President's arrival swept through the ever-growing crowd. The dead weight of the mob pressing toward the podium was a more potent force against the police line than the surge of angry protesters had been the day before. Officers struggled to hold their ground.

"Let's keep it orderly out there," Chief of Staff Sanchez said through the PA system. "We don't need any more injuries. Our purpose here is not to hurt people and destroy things. Our purpose is to prevent people from being injured and prevent lives from being destroyed by the irresponsible and illegal acts of the Texas governor and the Texas legislature."

A smattering of cheers came from the crowd. A group of students standing among a carpet of empty Solo cups chanted, "America First, Texas Last."

Sanchez turned the microphone over to President Lewis. She opened her prepared notes and flattened them on the podium.

"It saddens me," she read, "to come here today to denounce the treasonous action taken by the government of Texas. Never has a body of elected officials acted so heartlessly. When Texas chose to illegally declare itself an independent nation, it disenfranchised millions of Americans with utter disregard for their welfare. If Texas is allowed to secede, the people who depend on government assistance, the people who think of themselves as Americans first and Texans last, will become people without a country.

"I will not stand by and let that happen. I will not let them steal the future from innocent children. I will not let them steal citizenship from you. This attempt to break one state from the Union is a simple act of terrorism. And I pledge to you that I will do everything in my power as the President of the United States to hold Texas in the Union.

"As of this moment, I am declaring a national emergency. The ports and airports of Texas will be closed at midnight tonight. I have ordered federal marshals to seize and secure this capitol building complex and to limit entry to only those with authorization from the United States attorney general. United States Army troops will be stationed throughout the state for the purpose of peacekeeping and protection of law-abiding citizens. Members of the Texas legislature will be required to sign a statement of allegiance to the United States of America within forty-eight hours or face arrest for treason.

"And I have issued an order for the immediate arrest of Brewster Steele."

CHAPTER 38

*"On account of being a democracy and run by people,
we are the only nation in the world that has to keep a
government for four years, no matter what it does."*

- Will Rogers -

RIDING GAVE BREWSTER STEELE a chance to clear his mind and order his thoughts. His ranch in the rolling Texas hill country was that mythical place far, far away, and he got too few opportunities to enjoy the serenity of the saddle. Today the air was clear and calm, giving the blue sky an iridescent glow. It was the kind of day when Reagan, Steele's favorite appaloosa, loved to run. Steele gave him his head. They rode to the top of Rattlesnake Ridge, the highest point on the ranch. Looking across a wide meadow of bluebonnets, he could see the swirls of dust following two Crown Victoria police cruisers as they made their way from the road to the house. His cell phone chirped. The caller ID said it was Stu Timmerly, his chief of staff.

"Brew, Lewis and Sanchez have done just what you predicted. There's a federal warrant out for your arrest."

"And that's why the Rangers just pulled up?"

"Right. The state attorney general's office has filed a motion in the U.S. District Court to void the arrest warrant. Fred says it won't stand up because there are no grounds to uphold it."

"Unless Lewis has her thumb on that judge," Steele said. "We both know she's got enough control over judicial to make anything happen she wants."

"True enough," Timmerly acknowledged. "But this is Judge Carver. He's been my source for constitutional law opinions since we first considered the secession option. He's the guy who insists every state has the right to leave. I'm confident he'll tangle up the Feds' case against you until January first. Then we're declared a free nation, and all constitutional claims are off. That's when the court of public opinion will support our claim that the laws of the United States no longer apply to Texas or Texans."

"And in the meantime, what do you suggest?"

"My personal opinion is that Lewis only called for your arrest to get a good sound bite to make her look tough to her supporters. My guess is she would have liked to throw Texas out of the country, but we decided to leave first. Why the hell would she want us around? We only give her opposition."

"We've got oil and gas she needs, even though she and Sanchez have pledged to put carbon-based energy out of business. And she needs us for her legacy. No President, especially the first woman president, wants to be remembered as the person who was at the helm when the United States broke apart. She sure as hell doesn't want to be America's Nero."

"So I sent the Rangers to keep the hounds away in case Lewis sends the FBI after you."

"Let 'em come," Steele said.

"You want them to arrest you?" Timmerly asked, a bit incredulous.

"More than want, Stu. I'll turn myself in. Is President Lewis still in the state?"

"She's here for the night," Timmerly said. "She's making a big show of how she's hunting you down single-handedly. Mano a mano, sort of. There's a morning event scheduled for tomorrow in Austin for legislators to step up and sign a statement of allegiance to the United States. She laid down that gauntlet today, threatening arrest of the legislators if they don't sign. The members who voted for independence are holding their ground and refusing to sign. The Democrats who opposed the Declaration are lining up for this mock show of patriotism. That move's got Sanchez's fingerprints all over it."

"Where and when?" Steele asked.

"Capitol steps at nine." Timmerly said. "What are you thinking, Brew? You've got that sound in your voice that makes me worry."

"I can't hide, Stu. That's what Lewis and Sanchez want. If I hide, it's an admission that secession is illegal. It also could bring a charge of being a fugitive and resisting arrest. And you know me too well to think hiding's gonna happen."

Steele leaned forward and patted Reagan on the side of the neck. The horse answered with a head nod and a soft snort.

"The President wants a photo op," Steele said. "I'll do my best to give her one."

The next morning, as members of the Texas legislature's Democrat minority lined up to sign the allegiance document, President Lewis sat in the morning sun looking like a conquering Cleopatra presiding over a surrendering army. A string of satellite uplink antennae stood at an angle above the crowd. Media outnumbered everyone else four to one. Network and cable news channels were broadcasting live and without commercials.

Beyond the allée of trees that linked the capitol building's south façade and the south gate at 11th Street, a squadron of police motorcycles rumbled up, escorting an eighteen wheeler. The brakes hissed as the big rig groaned to a stop. Secret Service agents closed ranks around the President, but she waved off their attempts to shield her. Agents pushed open the oversized doors to the capitol building in case a safe haven was needed quickly.

President Lewis's eyes stared down the long rows of trees as every camera swiveled to capture the commotion. Two trailing motorcycle cops jumped off their machines, flung open the trailer doors, and dragged out a metal ramp.

Three horses with riders appeared. On the two lead chestnut stallions rode Texas Rangers. Behind them, Reagan, the governor's unmistakably beautiful appaloosa, stepped easily down the ramp, carrying the governor. Lewis had no trouble spotting Steele's tan Stetson from the capitol steps.

The horseback trio walked in formation along the allée with Steele in the center lead. There was no haste in their movements. They walked as if in control of time itself. A calm authority seemed to wrap itself around them like an aura. The crowd was silent. Governor Steele had been named an outlaw by the President. He was wanted for treason, yet there he was, sitting tall in the saddle. The throng of reporters parted like the Red Sea to let the riders through. Even the Secret Service agents seemed mesmerized by the grand entrance.

Steele stopped when he reached the capitol steps.

"President Lewis," Steele said. "I hear you're looking for me."

Lewis paused. This wasn't what she had expected. Outlaws run and hide. That's what Sanchez told her Steele would do. Lewis never dreamt he would turn himself in. Lewis regrouped and began to ad-lib.

"Thank you for saving taxpayers the expense of a manhunt, Governor Steele," she quipped.

Lewis looked around her for a federal law officer. She wondered whether the Secret Service could arrest someone.

"Ms. President," Steele said. "Let me help you with procedure. I believe I should be read my rights and I should be informed of the charges against me. What is my crime?"

"Treason," Sanchez answered, stepping in front of Lewis at the microphone.

"There's been no treason here. I thought you were a constitutional law professor once, Mr. President," Steele mocked.

"The Constitution specifically defines treason only as levying war against the United States or giving aid to their enemies. I don't believe those conditions exist here. You're going to have trouble making that charge stand up. But I'm happy to play your game."

Sanchez bristled at being upstaged by Steele. He turned to Romeo Costa.

"Arrest this man."

WILLIAM HIRSCH

240

CHAPTER 39

"Loyalty to the country always.
Loyalty to the government when it deserves it."

- Mark Twain -

"I SAW YOU ON TV."

"Was I more entertaining than *American Idol*?"

"You always have to be the smart-ass, don't you, Brew?" Mary Ketterling-Steele was in no mood for jokes. "Now you pull this stunt."

"I was hoping the single phone call they gave me from prison might get me a bit more sympathy," Steele said.

"Look somewhere else for that, buddy boy. And I'm not coming to your rescue."

"It wasn't a stunt, Mary. And I didn't initiate it. Lewis did. She's got no basis for arresting me or any members of the legislature. No crimes were committed. The last thing Lewis wanted was for me or anyone else to actually be arrested," Steele explained. "When I showed up on live national television right in front of her, I forced her hand."

"This isn't poker, Brew," Ketterling-Steele said. "You're playing with the lives and futures of millions of people. You don't seem to realize the impact this will have on everyday citizens. You can't take this so lightly."

"I'm not taking anything lightly, my dear," Steele said. "I'm dead serious. And I'm fully aware of how this affects people's lives. That is exactly why we are doing this. Texas is standing up for what America means, or more accurately what it meant before Sanchez and Lewis got their hands on it.

"The government is dead broke now. You in Congress sold your souls to the devil to get elected and stay in office. The devil paid you in taxpayers' money. Now the devil wants his due. I've got news for you, darlin'. I'll be damned if I'm going to let Washington take the good people of Texas down with it. That's the reason I'm doing the stunts I'm doing. I'm trying to rescue my country. And if I can't rescue all of it, I'll rescue the part I can. The American idea is the greatest gift from God to mankind. I've been given the opportunity to protect it. I'll sacrifice anything to accomplish that."

"Would you sacrifice our marriage if it came to that?" Ketterling-Steele asked, her voice quiet.

"I'd give my life for you, darlin'. You know that," Steele said. "I love you, Mary. I always will. But right now I have to do this. When you can see what's really happening, when you can see the edge of the earth the United States is heading for, when you can see how you've been used, call me. I'll come rescue you, too."

CHAPTER 40

"Here in America we are descended in blood and in spirit from
revolutionists and rebels – men and women
who dare to dissent from accepted doctrine. As their heirs,
may we never confuse honest dissent with disloyal subversion."

- Dwight Eisenhower -

AS BREWSTER STEELE SAT a hundred miles away in the prison in Fort Hood, Stu Timmerly, his chief of staff, sat in a conference room across the table from the Japanese delegation.

The secession of Texas had been getting attention outside of the country as well as in the United States. Already, the new country was appearing on international maps. If Texas managed to successfully open diplomatic relations with Japan, it would be a true sign that they were being acknowledged as an independent nation.

The negotiations had been going well, but they were not without tension.

"President Lewis has threatened to levy trade sanctions against Japan if we acknowledge Texas as a sovereign nation," Daisuke Saito said.

"We are aware of this," Timmerly replied. "But we believe the oil in Texas can be greatly beneficial to the Japanese economy. As an independent nation, we would like to establish a trade deal with Japan."

Saito looked over the papers in front of him. He looked back at Timmerly. "We would like that as well," he said.

"What about President Lewis's threat?"

"The United States is not the only country that can make threats." Saito said. "If President Lewis levies trade sanctions against us, we will put tariffs on American imports."

Timmmerly smiled. That would stop Lewis in her tracks. She could not deny how important Japan was as a trading partner.

Timmerly extended his hand to Saito. "On behalf of the Independent Republic of Texas, I am honored to establish this diplomatic relationship with the great country of Japan."

Back in the United States, the repercussions of the Texas Declaration of Independence continued to reverberate across the country. The action taken by Texas had caused several other states to reconsider their status as members of the Union.

In New Mexico and Arizona, the states that had joined with Texas to protect the border, special secession conventions were assembled to debate independence resolutions. Polls showed that pro-secession sentiment in those states had risen sharply since the Texas declaration. Arizona governor Jerri Welsch and New Mexico governor Walt Grainger had both sent emails to Brewster Steele's office congratulating Texas on taking the plunge. Charles Freeman, the governor of Alabama, was also emailing Steele's office, expressing his interest in learning about the process Texas used to get the convention and the vote organized.

The rift between the federal government and other individual states had widened as well, with Alaska, Kentucky, West Virginia, and Louisiana also polling in favor of secession. Montana was just jealous they weren't first. They had two counties drafting declarations of independence not just from the

United States, but from Montana, too. The counties were calling themselves "Islands of Independence."

Demonstrations in favor of independence were breaking out in states all through the middle of the country. Texas had clearly broken a psychological barrier.

President Lewis, meanwhile, was claiming that the secession was a sham. She had refused to recognize Texas diplomatically, and had placed sanctions on products manufactured in Texas, as well as partially shutting down the airports. It was hurting business, but at the same time everything she tried to do to hurt Texans galvanized them in favor of independence. Public opinion polls showed nearly two-thirds of average citizens thought the Lewis administration was actually the one that was acting illegally.

Of course, there were people who agreed with Lewis. Every urban area had been hit with new protests. Unions had come in from out of state to rally local members and show support. Teamsters were staging random slow-rolling blockades of the highways. The University of Texas was essentially shut down, as the faculty staged a walkout protest. The president of the university sympathized with their position and refused to dock their pay.

The Welfare and Social Services Administration building was essentially under siege. People were lined up for blocks trying to get their tickets and money for relocation out of Texas and back into the U.S. The program was quite popular. It seemed most folks would rather move out now that the handouts were coming to an end than find work and take care of themselves. However, most were not disabled enough to keep them from throwing bottles and overturning cars. The police had their hands full.

As if that wasn't enough, the federal government had dramatically increased the number of soldiers and supplies in military bases within the state. Convoys of trucks and a stream of cargo planes had been flowing into Fort Hood. Fighter jets made frequent passes over populated areas at low altitudes — a blatant attempt to remind the residents of the authority of the federal government.

Brewster Steele saw these shows of force as a clear provocation and incitement to violence, and said as much in a statement to the press. "My wish was that we could settle our differences peacefully and the sovereign rights of Texas would be honored," he told the reporters as the prison guards looked on. "But if President Lewis chooses war as a solution, Texans will not back down. We are fighting for our freedom, our families, and our future."

A week after Brewster Steele's arrest, an unmarked police cruiser exited the Tank Destroyer Boulevard gate at Fort Hood. It was met with a half-mile long gauntlet of protesters cheering the release of Governor Steele. Within hours of Steele's arrest, the crowd had formed and maintained an around-the-clock vigil, often blocking the gates completely.

After a week of imprisonment, a federal judge released Steele on his own recognizance. The judge issued a statement saying Steele was not deemed a flight risk and that the U.S. attorney general had not presented a convincing case for treason against Steele. By now it was a foregone conclusion that the judge would throw the case out following a hearing next week.

Stu Timmerly was with Steele in the cruiser. Steele was glad of the hour and a half drive to Austin — it would give Timmerly time to catch him up on everything that had been happening while he was in prison.

"You're scheduled for a web conference with the governors of Arizona, New Mexico, Louisiana, Mississippi, and Alabama at four this afternoon to discuss alliance possibilities if they also declare independence," Timmerly told him.

"So we aren't going to be on this path alone," Steele said.

"Doesn't look like it, Brew. But Lewis isn't making it easy for us. The Navy is moving in on the port. It has all the earmarks of a seizure."

Steele started to protest, but Timmerly stopped him. "I know you think Lewis is bluffing, Brew. But when armed men are confronted, all bets are off. I think she needs a victory to keep public sentiment on her side. The longer we stand our ground, the more desperate she'll get. We're making her look weak."

Steele nodded. He knew Timmerly was right. But looking at the cheering crowd outside the car gave him strength and hope.

Steele opened the darkened window and waved to the crowd, initiating a swell of shouts and cheers that followed the car like a tidal wave.

"They love you, Brew," Timmerly said.

"They don't love me, Stu. They love what we're doing," Steele answered. "The pot's been heating up for a long time. It's finally come to a boil."

CHAPTER 41

"Patriotism means to stand by the country. It does NOT mean to stand by the President or any other public official save exactly to the degree in which he himself stands by the country. It is patriotic to support him insofar as he efficiently serves the country. It is unpatriotic not to oppose him to the exact extent that by inefficiency or otherwise he fails in his duty to stand by the country."

- Theodore Roosevelt -

TWO HUNDRED MILES north of Bermuda, tethered to a refueling ship, the USS *Peleliu* was filling its tanks in the open sea for the last time. Commander Lincoln Smith had gotten his orders to bring the last Tarawa class amphibious assault ship in the U.S. Navy to Newport News for four months of training and then decommissioning in February. According to the current administration, the cost of maintaining a fighting ship like the *Peleliu* was outweighed by the need to provide free abortions for any woman who wanted one and other questionable social programs that President Lewis held so dear.

"We are protecting babies and they are killing them," Smith muttered to himself.

The news of the decommissioning had hit Smith hard. Only he and his executive officer knew. In a few months, he would walk off this ship that had taken him around the world and back. He felt like he did when his mother was dying. That frustrating helpless feeling settled into the pit of his stomach and would not leave.

At least his Texas A&M fraternity brother was no longer in jail. Smith and Steele stayed close after graduation, even serving side by side when Steele was on active duty with the Marines. Smith was a lifer, but Steele had bigger plans and noble ambitions. Now those noble ambitions got him plenty of face time on live TV, a few nights in the brig at Fort Hood, and whatever else Lewis might throw at him.

Smith knew he was a Texan first. He knew he had fought to protect the America Steele and Texas said they were determined to preserve. After bringing the *Peleliu* home, Smith figured he'd hang it up and get that little ranch Brew had been trying to convince him to buy near his own spread. By the time the *Peleliu* and he finished the training assignment, Smith was sure to make captain. But the promotion would probably come with a desk job, and a nagging part of him felt there was something more for him to do in this life besides pushing papers.

Commander Smith looked around his cramped quarters. Even on a ship this size, the commanding officer's cabin felt about as big as the back of a bread truck — and these were the luxury quarters. All the same, he loved this ship and its crew.

He couldn't help but think of the men who fought so bravely and the thousands of Marines who died on the island his ship was named for. One of the bloodiest battles in the South Pacific, Peleliu was still a graveyard of rusting tanks and beaches strewn with live munitions. The skeletal remains of brave Americans lay buried in the sand by the shifting tides. There had been no time to retrieve the bodies. To this day, no one seemed to care enough to try. The world had moved on. Seven decades made the heroics at Peleliu an unimportant footnote in modern history books. The island had lacked strategic importance and was never used as a staging point for the invasion of the Philippines as was originally intended. Tragically, the men had died in vain.

And now the island was slowly sinking into the Pacific as the lava and coral beneath it gradually eroded and collapsed. It struck Smith as an apt metaphor for his ship — and his country.

CHAPTER 42

"In the long history of the world, only a few generations have been granted the role of defending freedom in its hour of maximum danger.
I do not shrink from this responsibility. I welcome it."

- John F. Kennedy -

WITHIN THREE WEEKS, more states had seceded from the United States. After only two weeks of debate, Arizona and New Mexico ratified declarations of independence following Texas. In a surprise announcement, Alaska also passed legislation calling for its secession. All three states chose the effective date of independence as January first, to coincide with Texas.

The list of states lining up to file declarations of independence of their own was growing fast. Kentucky, West Virginia, Louisiana, and Oklahoma were scheduled to vote on similar resolutions shortly. Secession conferences were underway in Mississippi, Alabama, Georgia, South Carolina, North Carolina, Tennessee, Kansas, Nebraska, Iowa, South Dakota, North Dakota, and Montana.

That so many states were discussing secession, if not actively moving toward it, complicated the legality question even further. In 1869, during Reconstruction, secession was argued in the Supreme Court case of *Texas v. White*. In the Court's decision, Chief Justice Salmon P. Chase wrote that there was no place for secession "except through revolution or through consent of the States." The court never defined "consent of the States," but experts in constitutional law agreed that a case could easily be made to define it as a majority vote of the states. With four states already declaring independence and fifteen discussing it, if only seven more states joined, they would be a majority, and would be able to vote to allow each other to secede. If twenty-six states voted to secede, all bets would be off.

Meanwhile, in Washington, the Lewis administration continued to struggle with massive budget deficits. Lewis had initiated a one hundred percent tax on personal income above five million dollars, essentially capping personal income at that level. She also mandated a ten percent increase in the required contribution to mandatory Madsen Guaranteed Retirement Accounts through the mandatory purchase of more Federal Obligation Retirement Annuities.

Lewis's spending cuts also included a dramatic cutback in the budget for national parks. Many sites would be closed or consolidated, and park hours limited. One such cutback involved one of the most recognizable symbols of America: the Liberty Bell.

"The Liberty Bell is simply too costly to maintain," White House spokesman Todd Furley said. "Staffing the historic Independence Hall as well as the Liberty Bell Center is not an expense we can afford at the present time."

Prior to the bicentennial, the bell had been on display within Independence Hall. But large crowds and security concerns prompted the National Park Service to construct the glass Liberty Bell Pavilion on Independence Mall, where it was now housed. In 2003, a larger Liberty Bell Center was built adjacent to the pavilion.

"Once the Liberty Bell is moved out of the buildings and replaced by a replica that will not require expensive security and maintenance, the pavilion and the center will be leased out to a private operator for use as a gift shop," Furley explained in his statement.

Brewster Steele switched off the TV. He couldn't believe his ears.

"How does Lewis even think she has the right to do that?" he asked Stu Timmerly. "The Liberty Bell is owned by the State of Pennsylvania, under the custody of the National Park Service."

"You're forgetting," Timmerly replied. "Last year, Sanchez claimed ownership of the bell, through a highly questionable use of condemnation laws. Apparently they're going to 'display it at significant locations, as the budget allows,'" Timmerly said, reading from the press release on the White House website. "God forbid Lewis would reverse anything Sanchez had done.

"So the greatest symbol of freedom in the country is going to sit in storage in Washington, D.C.," Steele said. "If that's not a perfect metaphor, I don't know what is."

CHAPTER

43

"I saw the Statue of Liberty. And I said to myself, '"Lady, you're such a beautiful! [sic] You opened your arms and you get all the foreigners here. Give me a chance to prove that I am worth it, to do something, to be someone in America.' And always that statue was on my mind."

- A Greek immigrant recalling his arrival in America -

THE GOVERNOR OF Alabama was not spending his Labor Day weekend listening to Jimmy Buffett on his iPod and dozing on a Gulf Shore beach. Instead, Charles Freeman was attending marathon sessions of the First Constitutional Convention of New America in White Sulphur Springs, West Virginia.

Now that Oklahoma, Kentucky, Louisiana, Mississippi, North Dakota, and Freeman's own state of Alabama had issued separate but similar declarations of independence from the United States, the group unanimously agreed to convene and discuss the merits and problems with banding together in a new union with a revised Constitution intended to bolster the sovereignty of the individual states and prevent the new federal government from running amok, as was happening in the original United States.

In the first hour of the first day of the Congress, Charles Freeman had been unanimously elected chairman. A tall, lean black man with a splash of gray at his temples, Freeman was blessed with a commanding and distinguished presence, along with an innate humility that made him easy to like.

Freeman suspected that Vermont, a state that had threatened secession for nearly as long as its tenure as a state, would separate before the end of the year, along with Maine. Delegates from those states were in attendance, but only in an unofficial capacity. The two traditionally independence-minded Northeastern states held a long heritage of opposition to the federal government, but they were decidedly liberal. Secession was likely, but odds were not good that they would find enough common ground to join in a union with an alliance of conservatives. The political balance would potentially make them powerless. But an invitation was extended to the two sparsely populated states and they accepted.

South Dakota, Nebraska, and Kansas were non-voting invitees as well, but appeared likely to secede on their own and join the Union of New America. If that happened, the same north/south corridor of states that established an alliance to build a disjointed oil pipeline from the massive oil fields of North Dakota and Canada to the thriving port of Houston would be able to interconnect the TransCan pipeline as originally designed. And even more significantly, if those states were to be admitted to New America, the nascent country would reach from the Gulf of Mexico to the Canadian border in an uninterrupted swath, severing the eastern United States from the Western states completely.

The method of ratification was left to the individual states to decide. If only two states ratified the document, that would be enough to establish New America. On the first day, it had been assumed that several of the states would decline to ratify and become independent republics. But as the merits of a union were discussed, it became clear that the advantages each state would gain by bonding together for defense and regulation of trade were compelling, so long as the dark side of a central government could be contained and restricted.

This Constitutional Convention had a considerable advantage over the one that launched the experiment of self governance in 1787. Those men had only short experience with the Articles of Confederation to draw on. This assembly of men and women had more than two decades of successes and failures of the United States Constitution to analyze and learn from. With the overall goal being to rescue the original concept and intent of America from the monster the United States government had become, it made sense to use the original Constitution as a starting point. For that reason, the process was more of a thorough editing than a writing of a new document.

Along with calling for a mandatory balanced budget, the new Constitution included several mandates regarding members of the new Congress. All laws that applied to citizens of New America would also apply to members of Congress. All congressional, executive, and judicial salaries would be taxed at the rate of the highest tax bracket, regardless of the actual income level. Members of Congress would place all of their assets in blind trusts for the length of their terms in office. Lastly, Congress would only physically assemble in cases of extreme emergency. All members would be required to reside within their own jurisdiction. Congressional sessions would be accomplished through virtual meetings with each member remaining in his or her local office. This would ensure that congressional members remained fully informed as to the mood and opinion of their constituents, and would make it much more difficult for lobbyists to exert undue influence.

The new Constitution also set term limits for all political representatives: two four-year terms for the President and Vice President, two six-year terms for senators, and four two-year terms for representatives. It mandated that only individual states would be allowed to levy taxes, and the states would jointly decide what percentage of tax revenues would be designated to fund the federal government. The national currency would be known as American Eagles, and the Treasury Department would designate its denominations. The currency would remain tied to gold and silver bullion. A national bank would be prohibited, and banking regulations would be established and administered by a Congress of state treasurers.

In today's session, the first item on Charles Freeman's agenda was the question of how to deal with the large numbers of illegal and undocumented immigrants living in the Union of New America.

"Governor Steele has asked for the floor to present a proposal," Freeman told the assembled delegates.

Brewster Steele stepped to the podium. "Thank you, Mr. Chairman," he began. "As you all know, Arizona, New Mexico, and Texas have accomplished what the federal government had failed to do for so many years: we have substantially secured the border with Mexico. That is step number one in dealing with the immigration issue. Step two involves the process of either deporting aliens who are in this country illegally or creating a path to citizenship for them.

"We have already diminished or halted government assistance to non-legal residents, except for public education for the children. The result is that large portions of the illegal population, mostly single men and women, have voluntarily migrated, mostly to California. Most of the remaining illegals have been in the U.S. for five years or longer. They have families here, and they are hardworking, law-abiding people. Their children are in school. No one wants to uproot those families. Deportation is a cold and heartless solution for the problems created by our own neglect in enforcing the immigration laws.

"Our proposal is this. Deportation should only occur for individuals or couples who cannot prove gainful, legal employment for themselves or for their spouses, or who are convicted felons. All others must register as foreign nationals within one year and simultaneously enter a program that will lead to naturalization.

"The second part of our proposal is to firmly establish English as the singular official language of New America. There is no racial bias in this requirement. It applies whether a person immigrates from Mexico, China, Pakistan, or any other country. New America must join all citizens into one culture that is enriched by the influence of many nations and cultures.

"We must be New Americans first."

In CONGRESS, July 4, 1776.

The unanimous Declaration of the thirteen united States of America.

CHAPTER 44

"A good Navy is not a provocation to war.
It is the surest guaranty of peace."

- Theodore Roosevelt -

CAPTAIN LINCOLN SMITH was enjoying two days leave by repairing fences that enclosed the south pasture of his newly acquired Texas hill country ranch, when he heard the clomp of approaching hoofs. He looked up and recognized the man who had talked him into buying the spread.

"Good evening, Mr. President," he said to his new neighbor.

"Howdy, Captain," Brewster Steele called back from the saddle. "Congratulations on your new rank. You remember my good buddy, Reagan."

"Best-looking appaloosa in the state."

"He is that," Steele agreed.

"How's that new title fitting you?"

"It takes some getting used to, Linc. I was hoping the delegates would elect someone else," Steele said. "You know it's only a temporary position, just until the general election in November. I think I got the job because none of the other delegates wanted it."

"Don't be so modest, Brew," Smith said. "We need someone who instills confidence. There aren't many men or women who have that ability. You're the right man at the right time. You'll win in a landslide in November."

"Hope not," Steele said. "There's too much to be done, and I'd really like to spend more time out here riding. When's your hitch in the Navy up?"

"Four more months and I can climb another rung on the retirement pay ladder," Smith said. "The bump to captain helps."

"I've got some neighborly advice for you, Linc. When those retirement checks come in, convert them into American Eagles as fast as you can. Get all your money out of dollars. The buying power of those things is shrinking faster every year. And now that a third of the U.S. is out of the equation, the dollar is going to be dropped as the world's reserve currency. The Federal Reserve won't be able to print more whenever they need it. The bubble's gonna burst, and it'll burst big-time. That's why Texas got out when we could."

"You telling me my retirement pay's in trouble, Brew."

"Oh, they'll pay you the same number of dollars. But the dollars will be worth less each month. If you think we saw inflation under the Carter administration, you're in for a wild ride to the poorhouse this time. The smartest thing you did was to buy this ranch while your money was still good."

"Are you telling me I'm going to need a retirement job? I can't see myself as the greeter at Wal-Mart."

"Your retirement pay won't be enough, soon," Steele said. "And the way Sanchez has Lewis cutting the military budget, it wouldn't surprise me to see him force her to cut the actual amount of pay. Now that he's pulling the ropes from behind the scenes and he's not worried about getting re-elected, there's no telling what he'll do. But we've got a job opening, if you're interested. We need a secretary of the Navy."

"You mean your little coastal patrol?" Smith asked.

"No," Steele chuckled. "We're in need of a serious Navy. We can't hide behind the skirts of the United States military. You know as well as I do they're losing their clout. Training is being cut. Equipment and supplies are being cut. President Lewis is withdrawing from two-thirds of the bases overseas."

"Tell me about it. My training command that was supposed to be one year got sliced to three months. Morale is dangerously low. There's no way the Navy's ready for a conflict."

"Morale always ebbs if you don't give it a kick in the ass from time to time. I've got energized people here just waiting for leaders. If we lag in getting the government and the military strong and functional, we'll lose energy, too. We need you, Linc. I need you to build our Navy. Will you consider the job?"

"There's no considering needed, Mr. President. If you choose to appoint me as the first Union of New America Secretary of the Navy, it will be my honor to accept."

"Excellent," Steele said. "I have your first assignment, if you'd like to end your career in the United States Navy with a flourish and give New America a monstrous moral boost. It's time for a public demonstration of the courage and conviction of New America."

"I'm all in, sir."

CHAPTER 45

*"The federal government did not create the states;
the states created the federal government."*

- Ronald Reagan -

THE NEXT MORNING Lincoln Smith was back in Newport News to complete his tour of duty with the United States Navy. Smith despised shadow-boxing exercises. The more realism he could provide, the more effective the training would be. Today would have an added measure of realism. The crew of the USS *Peleliu* was readying for a stealth material recovery exercise within an urban area. The six-man SEAL team, two stealth Seahawk SH-60 gunships, and a Sea Dragon MH-53E helicopter were on board. In the briefing room, the men scrutinized maps and pored through details of the planned naked mission. There would be no air cover, no GPS tracking, no radio communications, and they would fly under the cover of darkness. Perfect synchronization and execution was the difference between life and death. Despite this being a training mission, the mood was somber and professional. The enemy might be imaginary, but the equipment was not. Accidents kill as often as hostiles do. "Careless" was not in a SEAL team's vocabulary.

At 0800 hours, the USS *Peleliu* slipped past the submarine installation at Fort Story and Cape Henry, the spot where the Jamestown settlers first landed in 1607. Smith loved the history of the place and knew he wouldn't pass this way again. The hulking assault ship entered the waters of the Atlantic Ocean leaving a rich heritage in its wake. Captain Smith ordered radio silence and activated radar-jamming defenses. They could still see every vessel within thirty miles through one-way satellite uplinks. But the eye in the sky could not see them. To other ships and planes, the *Peleliu's* radar signal was blurred. There was no way to hide a ship of its size, but its top secret electronic shield deflected its location effectively enough to make it appear to be several miles from its true position. A mile out to sea, a light fog hung over the water, masking the rising sun. The grey ship vanished into a wall of grey water and sky.

Brewster Steele stepped through the starboard hatch onto the bridge.

"Your briefing over, Mr. President?" Captain Smith asked.

"It is, Captain," Steele answered, complying with Smith's order to use proper titles and rank while on board his ship. "The SEAL team now knows this mission is outside regulations. And they know it's real. We'll go over it all again in six hours and again two hours before the operation."

"And you're still in? It's not just an exercise anymore. Things can get rough. And you never know what wrinkle the commanding officer might throw in the mix to challenge the team."

"It's a rogue incursion if it's just your men. We're making a statement, and the statement is much more powerful if I'm along. And I've never been much for leading from behind, Captain."

"I heard that, Mr. President," Smith said.

"And somebody's got to take the fall if this goes bad," Steele said.

He looked out at the featureless mass of grey fog dissolving into grey water. February was not the best time for a North

Atlantic cruise. The USS *Peleliu* was making twenty-four knots despite a slight headwind.

Steele thought about the email Mary had sent him that morning:

> *My Dearest Brew;*
>
> *You always told me that someday I would "look behind the curtain" and see how the great Oz of liberalism really worked. Well, it's happened. I met with Nate Cummings yesterday, and he pulled back the curtain. I was wrong, and you were right. There, I said it. I saw government and politicians the way I wanted to see them and not the way they really are.*
>
> *Brew, I'm so sorry for the hurtful things I said to you. And I miss you so badly. I resigned my co-chair on the Joint Congressional Committee for Equitable Housing. It looks like a sham now that my eyes are open. And I want to resign from Congress. I'm sitting here in Philly crying my eyes out.*
>
> *I need you, honey. You said when I saw through the pretenders in Washington and finally understood what you were trying to do, I should call you and you would come and rescue me. It's happened, Brew. I can see who the pretenders are. I need you.*
>
> *Come rescue me.*
>
> *With all my love, Mary*

Steele turned to Smith.

"Captain," he said, "I've got an additional mission for our team."

CHAPTER
46

"Failure is not an option."
- Navy SEAL team motto -

TWO STEALTH SEAHAWK SH-60 helicopters, code name Liberty One and Liberty Two, lifted off the flight deck of the USS *Peleliu* at precisely 0700 Zulu, two in the morning, Eastern standard time. The muffled sound of the gunship's engines could barely be heard over the droning of the big ship's steam turbines. Pressure waves from the rotors drummed against the bridge as Captain Lincoln Smith watched the sophisticated machines head north into the starless sky.

A Sea Dragon MH-53E chopper carrying fifteen Marines took off moments later and headed southwest. The machine's non-stealth engines rattled the carrier's antenna masts as it roared past on its way to a scheduled shore landing exercise on Assateague Island National Seashore. The pilot had orders from Captain Smith to fly low and fast past Ocean City, Maryland's string of oceanfront hotels, both coming and going, to their landing site. Even in the dead of winter, Smith was sure the helicopter would shake enough windows and awaken enough people who could later verify the chopper's presence. He would need all the corroboration he could get that the *Peleliu* was running training exercises exactly as planned if he expected to keep his retirement pay and benefits. Other than him and Steele, only the SEAL team members knew their true mission. And they were masters at the art of leaving no fingerprints.

Brewster Steele sat in the rear of Liberty Two and looked across the aisle at his companions for the night. The men wore black camo battle dress uniforms that looked like off-the-shelf Army surplus standards. No insignias or standard U.S. Navy indications of rank were permitted. Each team had identity patches linked to a nickname with a meaning known only to them. Steele wore a silhouette of a stallion, his nickname for the mission. Next to him was the team leader, known as Gator. Steele guessed his rank to be lieutenant, but none of the men ever addressed him by rank. Stealth was the watchword of Navy SEAL teams. Faces were camo painted, making the whites of the men's eyes the only bright spot on them. And those would soon be covered in standard combat goggles. This was an urban mission. Streetlights would blind a man wearing night vision goggles.

Each man carried a single holstered M11 Sig Sauer P-228 handgun, a favorite weapon of the SEALs and Special Boat Teams. Heavily-armed resistance was not anticipated, and the team needed to stay fast and mobile. Several men also carried lightweight tranquilizing dart rifles. Packs and pouches were stuffed with tools, flares, glow-sticks, explosives, ammo, and medical gear. A five-ton capacity winch with a cargo net was mounted above a cargo door in the underside of the fuselage.

There was no chatter among the men. All of the talking had been done in the briefing room before takeoff. The Seahawks nosed down slightly and raced toward the New Jersey coastline at top speed and below the radar. The cold front had lifted, and the night skies cleared. In minutes, the sparkling lights of Atlantic City formed an irregular line in the distance. The two helicopters slipped undetected through the gap of Great Egg Harbor Inlet that separated segments of the barrier island.

They travelled northwest, paralleling the Atlantic City Expressway, but stayed south and over the darkness of mostly empty farmland and marshes. Further inland, a steady stream of commercial planes crossed above them in the tight corridor of the Philadelphia International Airport landing path. The helicopters hugged the ground, slipping well below the jetliners. When they reached the Delaware River, the pilots veered north, expertly skimming just above the inky waters and beneath the elevated roadway of the Walt Whitman Bridge.

Ahead, the battleship *New Jersey* lay quietly at its permanent mooring on the east side of the river. The team turned west and took a route over the low row houses of South Philadelphia and made a straight path for Independence Mall.

Liberty One swooped across the mall and held its position hovering above the Liberty Bell Pavilion. Two men dropped ropes from the cargo hold and rappelled quickly to the roof below. A sharpshooter set up at the open door armed with a tranquilizing dart rifle. He scanned the streets and confirmed they had attracted no attention. The helicopter's muted engines were absorbed in the city noise even in the early morning hours. No one on the ground noticed the intruders yet. The men on the rooftop pulled out laser cutting torches tethered to batteries in their packs and traced crimson lines across the metal roof. In a minute, they began peeling back the terne metal sheets like a sardine can. They double-clicked a signal to Liberty Two that was circling the steeple of Independence Hall monitoring activity on the ground.

On command, Liberty One launched a canvas bag onto Chestnut Street a half block east of the mall. The bag hit the ground behind a panel van near the door of the Ben and Betsy Tavern and exploded, sending a thousand five dollar bills skyward in a swirling mini mushroom cloud. The concussion set off car alarms and brought the late night drinkers out to the street. When the people on the ground realized it was snowing money, a mad scramble to scoop up the windfall turned the street into a frenzied scavenger hunt. The chaos drew the late night street people like moths to a candle. In minutes, police cars converged on the Ben and Betsy from all directions.

At the precise moment the money bag exploded, the men positioned on the pavilion rooftop dropped tear gas grenades through the hole they had cut. Liberty Two landed on the lawn of Independence Mall. The SEALs leaped from the helicopter and fanned out around the pavilion. Steele stayed by the Seahawk per plan and out of the way of this well-oiled team. Even on the ground, the helicopter was nearly invisible. The dull, near-black, radar-deflecting coating that made the skin stealth transformed the big machine into nothing more than a shadow.

Shouting could be heard along with sirens from Chestnut Street. The diversion was working as intended. The tear gas drove the guards from the pavilion gasping for air. The sailors from Liberty Two and the sharpshooter still peering from the cargo hatch of Liberty One efficiently, but mercifully, picked them off with tranquilizer darts. The men and women crumbled in their tracks for an unexpected nap. Contrary to his personality, Steele was relegated to observer.

The rooftop sailors went to work on the roof trusses. They strung high strength braided steel cables between the skeleton of the structure to hold the severed assembly together and keep some or all of it from crashing to the floor below. The sharpshooter onboard Liberty One slipped a foot into the cargo net that hung from the lifting cable and activated the winch. He lowered himself between the mangled roof trusses to the floor below. When motion sensors detected his presence, claxons went off with a deafening blast. The SEALs had only minutes left. The man on the floor slung the cargo net around and under the bell. With a few deft swipes of his laser cutting torch, he sliced through the steel clamps holding the bell's antique wooden yoke to the supporting post. The bell shifted slightly when it broke free, and its weight was caught by the cargo net. He signaled the chopper to lift and hooked a foot and arm through the netting. He and a ton of cast copper and tin rose in tandem through the cold winter air.

Brewster Steele saluted the ascending bell proudly. He knew many people would see this as an act of robbery. But to him, and to the people of New America, the spirit that motivated the brave patriots on this spot in 1776 was being rescued for the millions of people who still knew what it meant to live free and be an American. It was impossible to rescue Valley Forge, Concord Bridge, Yorktown, Mount Vernon, or any of the sacred sites or homes of the founding fathers that held so much meaning and importance to the birth of America. All he could do was hope that maybe someday the true Americans who live in those states would join this "Revolution from Within." The Liberty Bell was a symbol of a people throwing off the yoke of tyranny. And it was portable.

CHAPTER 47

"The course of true love never did run smooth."
- William Shakespeare -

RETRACING THEIR ROUTE would have greatly increased the chance of detection. Liberty One took off and headed west. The exit route would take them over the western suburbs, beyond the airport and its commercial air traffic, south over Delaware, and then southeast across more marshes and hamlets of southern New Jersey. Liberty Two did not follow. It had another stop to make. Brewster Steele and the SEALs hustled on board, and the second helicopter slipped away without a shot being fired, tranquilizing darts notwithstanding.

On the ground, EMS personnel attended to the anesthetized guards. The police were untangling the near riot around the exploded bag of money, and the park police were just realizing that the most cherished relic of the birth of America was on its way to some unknown place taken by unknown intruders.

Liberty Two slipped between the taller buildings along a zigzag course heading generally southeast. The other helicopter was charged with getting the bell out of the country. Liberty Two had a personnel extraction added to its mission at the last minute by Captain Smith. SEALs follow orders and don't ask questions. But this was a hand-selected group of men from states that were now a part of New America. Smith had given each one the opportunity to decline the mission. None had.

Mary Ketterling-Steele could not sleep. She paced her Society Hill condominium begging the clock to move faster. Brew had told her to pack her bag and head down the elevator at three-fifteen in the morning. It seemed he always had a unique surprise for her whenever they had been apart for long periods. Tonight's reunion would come after the first major argument of their marriage, and it had been her fault. Was this her punishment?

When the clock finally flashed the appointed time, Mary rushed out the door. At this hour, the elevator was at her floor almost immediately. When she stepped into the lobby, the doorman gave her a puzzled look.

"Are you okay, Congresswoman?" he asked.

Mary knew she looked unsettled.

"I'm fine, Jeffery. My husband's coming to get me."

"At this hour?" the doorman said. "Are you sure, ma'am?"

"Yes, Jeffery," she answered. "He sometimes does crazy things. I'm not sure what this is all about, but I've learned not to ask a stubborn Texan too many questions when his mind's made up. I'm supposed to meet him out at the fountain."

"It's freezing out there, Congresswoman. Why don't you stay in here until he comes, and I'll come for you?"

"I can't do that, Jeffery. He said if I'm not out where he can see me, he'll keep going. We had a bit of an argument. I think he's worried I'll change my mind and stand him up."

Mary pushed through the revolving door and felt the cold blast of the northeastern February air take her breath away. The fountain was drained for the winter. The three tall towers of the Society Hill Towers loomed around her in the darkness. The air began to swirl and Mary felt a rhythm of low-pitched vibrations in her chest. Like a monstrous bat, the black helicopter settled onto the fountain plaza. One man jumped from the hatch and ran toward her. Instinctively she pulled back and turned for the revolving door. She lost her grip on her bag and fumbled to recover it. Before she could, the man had her in his arms.

"Mary, it's me, Brew."

By the time the Seahawk helicopter landed on the USS *Peleliu* flight deck, Liberty One and its cargo were safely stowed below deck. Mary stepped onto the flight deck a bit wobbly and trembling from the combination of raw February sea air and the adrenaline rush of the night's events. She had never been on a helicopter before, let alone a stealth Seahawk flown at low altitude at breakneck speeds with no lights. Captain Smith met her and escorted her to his quarters. Steele went with the other SEALs for debriefing.

Several minutes later, the Sea Dragon and its sailors returned from their Assateague Island landing exercise. As far as the crew of the *Peleliu* was concerned, this was a night of routine drills. As far as Captain Lincoln Smith was concerned, he was ready to close this chapter and open the next as the first Union of New America Secretary of the Navy. His first mission was already accomplished.

By daybreak, the Liberty Bell would be in a crate labeled as "scrap metal," loaded onto a train, and heading for its new home in the world's newest country and the last best hope for freedom on earth.

CHAPTER 48

"Proclaim LIBERTY throughout all the land unto all the inhabitants thereof."

- Inscription on Liberty Bell -

THE THEFT OF THE Liberty Bell was the top story in every paper and on every channel. The White House had released a statement emphasizing President Lewis's condemnation of the act. "While this bell is a symbol of freedom to some and a symbol of an invasion and oppression by others, the Liberty Bell is an icon of America," Lewis said in the press conference. "It must remain accessible to all so that the mixed history of this country can be remembered. I have asked the FBI to stop at nothing to recover the Liberty Bell."

A day later, a crate labeled "scrap metal" was being offloaded from a boxcar in Dallas, and would continue by truck to its new temporary home in the climate-controlled vault deep below the art museum. Construction had already begun on a travelling display that would travel throughout New America endlessly.

"The Liberty Bell is safe," Brewster Steele announced in a noon press conference. "It has been rescued from those who do not choose to see and appreciate its value. It has been rescued from those who would bury it away in a government warehouse, just the way the current government of the United States has buried the hopes and dreams of most Americans.

"No one can own the Liberty Bell and what it symbolizes. We can only be its faithful guardians. The people of the Union of New America pledge to the people of the United States of American to cherish this icon of freedom."

Carlos Sanchez cursed the television image of Steele.

"That son of a bitch. How the hell did he get his hands on that bell?" Sanchez spat.

"He's already contacted us about a summit," Tony Delgado said. "Steele says he has information we need, and he wants to make a deal."

"So the bell has been kidnapped?" President Lewis asked. "He's holding it for ransom. Is that his game? What's he want?"

"There was no mention of the bell. I didn't get the impression he cares to return it." Delgado said.

"And how the hell did he get it?" Sanchez asked.

"It's looking more and more like some special ops team did it. We don't know who or how. But we got this communiqué from Captain Lincoln Smith, who is in command of the USS *Peleliu*. He says that he's quote, 'Taking his ship home with him.' That would be Texas. He's friends with Steele. He says any members of his crew who do not wish to remain in Texas with him will be free to leave. He is emphatic in his message that the men and women are guests and not hostages. He says since you clearly don't want the ship since you are decommissioning it, he'll take it off your hands and keep it on the job protecting freedom-loving people wherever he finds them."

"So we've got a wise ass Navy captain helping out Steele," Lewis said.

"A former Navy commander. Smith sent along his resignation," Delgado said. "So what's your answer to Steele about a meeting?"

"Bring him in," Sanchez said. "It's time for a showdown."
He did not ask the President's opinion.

CHAPTER 49

"I pray Heaven to bestow the best of blessings on this House, and all that shall hereafter inhabit it. May none but honest and wise men ever rule under this roof."
- John Adams' Blessing for the White House -
in a letter to his wife, Abigail, November 1, 1800

BREWSTER STEELE WAITED patiently as the White House security officer swept him with the wand.

"Everyone gets the same treatment, Governor, or Mr. President, I should say," the officer said, correcting himself. "Please don't take offense."

"None taken, Officer. I like seeing a man take his duty seriously."

They returned Steele's briefcase and his Texas A&M fountain pen with the rattlesnake skin cap. President Lewis's head of security waited to escort him through the building.

"Welcome to the White House," Romeo Costa said as he shook Steele's hand. "Your name's been mentioned a lot around here lately."

"I imagine it has," Steele said.

Costa led him through the central lobby and then a short maze of halls to the Oval Office door. They stepped through. Costa offered Steele a seat on one of the sofas. Costa closed the door behind them. Steele took note of how the door was clad with the same wainscot and plaster as the wall, causing it to nearly disappear into the wall. Another stealth door led to the President's chief of staff's office. Two oversized doors, detailed in the Federal style with closed pediments atop, flanked the room. One with glass led east to the Rose Garden. The other on the west wall clicked open almost as soon as Steele had sat down. The President stepped in, and Steele rose to greet her. Sanchez was right behind her.

Costa began to make introductions, but Sanchez raised his hand to stop him.

"We're well aware of who we are, Mr. Costa," Sanchez growled. "You may leave us."

President Lewis ignored Steele's outstretched hand and took a seat by the fireplace.

"Sit there," Sanchez said, pointing to the matching chair on the opposite side of the hearth.

"I should have you arrested again, Steele," Lewis said.

"You guaranteed safe passage and protection, Ms. President," Steele said, intent on being diplomatic. "Any injury to me would be an international incident."

"Don't make me laugh, Steele. You're nothing more than an outlaw. You're the leader of an illegal nation. The United States and your so-called New America have no diplomatic relationship."

"That's our primary point of discussion here, Ms. President. New America has formally requested diplomatic recognition by the United States, and you continue to withhold it. You have attempted to blockade our ports, harass our citizens, limit entrance to the United States from Texas, and you've imposed trade sanctions on us. You've treated New America worse than you've treated two bit dictators."

"You, Texas, and all of the other states that chose to secede are illegitimate. Secession is illegal. And now you've stolen a cherished piece of American history," Sanchez spat.

"No, Sir. Secession is not illegal. But murder is," Steele said.

Sanchez held his composure and stared straight through Steele.

"Staging a phony assassination attempt, falsifying personal records, and killing a man are illegal, Sanchez," Steele said, now dropping any formality. "I'll grant you it energized your supporters and brought a wave of sympathy. But that still wasn't enough to get your vice president elected. You had to ruin a good man along the way."

Sanchez hid his flinch with a loud laugh. Steele persisted.

"It is illegal to falsify personal records and then defame someone as you did Wes Roberson."

Sanchez leaned forward aggressively from behind the president's chair.

"You are delusional, Steele. Roberson was a pervert. He couldn't keep his past buried. It was better the public knew what kind of scum he was before he managed to get elected."

"I've got proof you made it all up and planted it in his identity file. And I know what caused the death of Chief Justice Weinstein," Steele continued. "Both of your fingerprints are all over that, too."

"A very old man stays out in the January cold and suffers a heart attack. How could my fingerprints or anyone's fingerprints be on that?" Lewis mocked.

"Actually, Ms. President, that was not a simple metaphor. I have your fingerprints on your gloves along with the ricin you used to poison Weinstein," Steele said.

"There is no proof Weinstein was poisoned," Sanchez said. "There was no autopsy. He was cremated the next morning in accordance with Jewish custom."

"Wrong, Sanchez," Steele said. "He requested cremation in his will. You know that because you had his will read secretly a month before his death when you were making your plans to murder him. Weinstein was the only barrier between an honest court and one stacked with your surrogates. But you should have done a bit more homework about Jewish traditions. Cremation is not allowed. Even if the deceased willed cremation, his wishes must be ignored to observe the will of God. If you didn't have such distain for religion you might have known that. Weinstein was exhumed by court order, and an autopsy was performed."

"Don't try to frame me, Steele," Sanchez shot back. "Any gloves you have are cold evidence. Anyone could have dusted them with ricin long after Theresa wore them. You've proved nothing."

"I have a confession from the fellow at the Bureau of Personal Identity Protection who hacked Roberson's file, a Mr. Robbie Trexell. He's living somewhere in the West Virginia mountains right now under witness protection," Steele said. "And I also have your cell phone records that show some interesting conversations you had with Romeo Costa before the assassination attempt."

"My phone's triple encrypted," Sanchez said, starting to pale. "No human or computer can crack it."

"Geeks aren't human, Sanchez," Steele grinned. "Anything can be hacked. I have proof that there were no shots fired at Ms. Lewis in Miami. What people thought were bullets hitting were charges planted in the column and the presidential seal, triggered by a remote signal from the tricked-up rifle Romeo Costa gave Hank Samson to shoot. When Samson pulled the trigger, the charges went off. There was never even a chance you would get shot. You were never in danger at all."

"None of that will hold up in court."

"Do you want to take that risk? I'm certain it will get you run out of office," Steele said. "There are still good Americans in America."

"I told you your fake assassination idea was a piece of crap," Lewis shouted at Sanchez. "You've ruined me."

Sanchez glared at Steele.

"I'm not here to destroy you, Ms. President. You'll do that on your own. I'm here to cut a deal," Steele said as he reached down and pulled his laptop out of his briefcase.

"It's all here," Steele said, pulling up the electronic files that Arthur Campbell had procured and Nate Cummings had handed over. "Care to take a look? Don't worry. I have several copies backed up in Austin in case something happens to me or this computer. My aides have instructions to retrieve it in an emergency. Only a few people know any of this.

"I'm offering to keep it that way in return for you backing off and allowing New America to live peacefully with no intervention or resistance from the United States or from you or your people. That would include Dimitri Borsky. I know all about your ties with him, too. And if other states choose to join us or declare their independence, you will agree to let them go."

"You sonofabitch," Sanchez growled as a sudden rage overwhelmed him. He reached past Steele and grabbed the wrought iron poker by the fireplace. In one motion he swung hard at Steele's head. Steele ducked the blow. The poker bashed the computer, knocking it from his grasp and smashing it down on the stone hearth. Outside the door to the Oval Office, Romeo Costa heard the crash. He threw the door open and dove through launching himself across the carpet. He rolled to a kneeling position and leveled his gun at Steele.

Inside his head, Sanchez heard himself yelling, "Shoot him," but his survival instincts suppressed the urge. Killing Steele would mean the end for himself.

"There's no problem here, Agent Costa. President Steele simply dropped his computer," Sanchez said, sarcastically emphasizing Steele's title.

CHAPTER 50

"These are the times that try men's souls.
The summer soldier and the sunshine patriot will, in this crisis,
shrink from the service of his country; but he that stands it now,
deserves the love and thanks of man and woman."

- Thomas Paine -

"THE UNITED STATES has formally opened diplomatic relations with the Union of New America," Warren Tufts said. "This ends a contentious period of transition and allows trade, travel, and communication agreements between the two countries to be normalized.

"'We are anticipating the sort of friendly neighbor relationship with New America similar to the kind we have had with Canada and Mexico for decades,' President Lewis said in a statement from the White House rose garden," Tufts said.

"The United States has agreed to withdraw all troops from military bases within New America. A lease/purchase agreement is being drafted for the transfer of equipment, vehicles, and other assets to New America. A spokesman for the Lewis administration said, 'The deal will allow the United States to accelerate President Lewis's plan to trim the military and its budget while helping our new neighbor fortify its defenses.'"

While President Lewis was putting a positive spin on the military withdrawal, Brewster Steele knew he held the trump card. This was the President's only option or he would face criminal charges. Steele had agreed to keep his information about Lewis's and Sanchez's role in the ruin of Wes Roberson and the deaths of Chief Justice Weinstein and Hank Samson quiet. But he knew that no such restriction applied to Nate Cummings and the people who discovered the facts for him. It was only a matter of time before Lewis would be impeached and she and Sanchez were tried for their crimes. In the meantime, the leverage helped Steele get the concessions he needed to enable New America to get on its feet without interference from President Lewis or Sanchez.

The division of the United States spurred a mass migration that rivaled any that the country had ever seen. Land rushes, gold rushes, the Dust Bowl disaster, and the connection of the coasts by rail were formative events in the demographics of America. But the Great Separation, as the series of state secessions was being called, would result in more voluntary relocations of individuals and families than all the other migrations combined.

The U.S. dollar continued in a downward path until it was replaced by a basket of currencies as the world's reserve currency. The Texas Lone Star was abandoned in favor of the New America Eagle as the official currency of New America. By constitutional law, the new American Eagle was fixed to a gold and silver standard, and coinage similar in design to the Lone Star was minted. Inflation became a distant memory. U.S. dollars were still accepted, but with a floating exchange rate. And most retailers offered a discount for payment in Eagles.

Major hospitals and world-class doctors led the rush to New America, fleeing the nationalization of health care in the United States. The lucky ones were already located in states that had seceded. Medical travel grew into a major source of revenue for the new country, attracting patients from not only the United

States, but from Canada, England, and other countries where socialized medicine and massive waiting periods, especially for elective procedures, were the norm.

Vermont and Maine took their own course and formed the country of New England along with New Hampshire. They maintained no military and lived peacefully cocooned within the protection of the United States and Canada. With no strategic value, the new country of New England had no natural predators. Government went on as it always had, with town meetings being the method for nearly all public decisions.

Travel from one coast to the other became more difficult now that New America bisected the continent and left the two coasts with no land connection. Tolls for through-passage were imposed by New America on all six major cross-country interstate highways. The new tolls produced significant revenue for the states, and "truck only" express lanes were built from border to border. In-state travelers were exempt from the tolls.

The TransCan pipeline was completed, and the trucking depots to cross state lines and sidestep EPA regulations were never implemented. New America expedited the permits, and all of the involved states agreed to reasonable safety and environmental regulations. The residents of the states now received a yearly dividend from pipeline leases, much the same way Alaska had for years. ANWR, the Alaska National Wildlife Refuge, was ceded back to the state of Alaska. Oil drilling was approved and implemented with stringent controls. The wildlife refuge was the size of the state of South Carolina, while the disturbed area was limited to a desolate segment of flat wasteland the size of the Magic Kingdom at Disney World. Production greatly exceeded projections, and the caribou population doubled.

New America quickly tapped oil, natural gas, and coal to become the largest producer of energy in the world. The energy industry responded to a challenge issued by President Brewster

Steele by developing effective carbon containment technology before the end of the decade.

"Even if the global warming argument is specious, at best," Steele said, "it is in our best business interest to develop a way to let people use our products without fear of doing any harm to anyone or anything. If we were smart enough to put men on the moon, we certainly are smart enough to capture carbon and lock it away for eons, just as it had been locked up before we put it to good use."

Against his polite protestations, Brewster Steele was elected President of New America in the country's first popular vote. He accepted with three stipulations. First, he would serve only one term in consideration of the fact he had already served a transitional term while the country was being assembled. Second, a new capitol city would be authorized and built, and it would be named Concord in honor of the place where patriots first shed blood for the freedom of all mankind. And third, the President's powers would be strictly limited. Whoever occupied the office could be recalled by Congress at any time.

"New America must always be what the founding fathers intended so many years ago in Philadelphia," Steele declared. "This must always be a country of sovereign states, independent and free, that bond together for limited benefits, namely mutual security and defense, regulation of commerce between the states, and the fellowship of mutual respect for the individual citizen's freedom.

"The federal government must remain subservient to the will and power of the union of states."

The End

About the Author

Bill Hirsch is an architect and the author of the Amazon #1 Bestseller *Designing Your Perfect House*. He lives with his wife, Maureen, in North Carolina. They have four children and four grandchildren.

"I was a strong liberal in college and in my early working years," Bill says. "I cheered when Lyndon Johnson announced the Great Society. It made no sense to me that there could be so many poor people in the United States, the land of plenty. But I opened my eyes more and more with each passing year. I saw the blatant hypocrisy of liberalism and the futility of trying to force a social structure on people against their instincts and will. I saw the exploitation of the common man by politicians who really do not care about the welfare of those they represent. They literally only care about keeping themselves in office.

"I worry about the future of America and what it will be for my children and grandchildren. The founding fathers knew that governments need to be overthrown and liberty renewed from time to time. Maybe it's time for a peaceful revolution like the one in this story."

Look for Bill's next book, *Caribbean Ice*, a tropical thriller, coming out soon. Matt Thornton and his wife are on a second honeymoon when they get tangled up with diamond smugglers and a murder. To make matters worse, their friend is wrongly accused of committing the crime. While trying to prove his innocence, they become the next targets, putting themselves in mortal danger. Pristine beaches, fast boats, ruthless villains, and a place called Skeleton Island make this book a perfect escapist read.

A PREVIEW OF

CARIBBEAN ICE

A Novel

A Matt Thornton Thriller

William

Hirsch

CARIBBEAN ICE

1

The west coast of Africa, twenty years ago.

He stood frozen in the smoldering pit mine. Only his eyes moved as he watched the guard drag a chair to the shaded side of the quarry. The guard sat, tipped back against the rock wall, and freed the straining buttons on his sweat-soaked shirt. He laid his rifle across his bulging stomach and settled into his favorite position. Stifling heat and a belly filled with a heavy lunch made a potent sedative and within minutes, the guard struggled to keep his eyes open.

Malleet Bindra stared at the guard as if trying to hypnotize him into a deeper sleep. From beneath Bindra's broom had come the tantalizing, dangerous call of freedom, the signature sound of a rough diamond scraping granite.

The guard's fat eyelids sagged. He hadn't heard the telltale sound. Bindra took a slow, calculated step. He placed his tattered boot beside the diamond and crouched as if reaching for his bootlaces.

The guard's head bobbed. His arms jerked. Bindra froze. Above the din of the machinery, he heard his pulse hammering in his ears like a sledge on an anvil. But the guard's movement was merely the final spasm before sleep. His eyes twitched then fell shut. His head tipped forward until his chin pressed his chest. Bindra took a slow breath and fingered the gem. In one fluid motion, he straightened to his full height and lifted the rough stone to his nose. With a jab, he pressed it deep into his nostril.

Rivulets of sweat streamed from his forehead, stinging his eyes. His hands trembled. He had not been seen, at least not by the guard. If other miners had noticed him, they would tell no one. It was the way. No eye contact, no gestures, no words.

Bindra remained motionless, but he could not stop his mind from racing ahead to the time his shift would end and his heart would again beat hard, to the time he would walk through the x-ray scanner at the security gate, to his moment of reckoning. He imagined his nose glowing as the radiation illuminating the diamond revealed his crime. He imagined the nightmare of the guards seizing him, slapping on handcuffs and dragging him away to a jail from which he would never return. It was a scene he had witnessed many times when others had taken the gamble and lost.

Like every miner, Bindra knew that diamonds glow when bombarded with x-rays, giving the mine owners an effective method for exposing thieves. He also knew the owners could not afford to expose men to daily radiation without gradually killing off their oppressed labor force. The buzzing of the machine was often a decoy, a false scanning meant to terrify miners into honesty. Stealing a diamond was a life or death wager with odds no better than Russian roulette. Despite the odds, desperate men take chances and Bindra was a desperate man.

The cloudless day wore on and the relentless African sun seemed paralyzed in the sky, as if fearing to move westward to the time Bindra would confront his fate. But the hours of trepidation and fear also brought a strange rush of exhilaration, and Bindra felt alive for the first time in his miserable life. When the bell clanged ending the work day, Bindra took his place in the security line.

'Act like it's a day like any other,' he told himself, hoping to calm his adrenaline-charged body as he prepared to walk the gauntlet of guards and x-ray machines, just as he had done every day for six wretched years.

Bindra stepped into the darkened scanning tunnel, heard the usual buzzing sounds, and held his breath. He readied his ears for the first wail of the alarm, waiting for the guards to rush toward him and drag him off to the black hell of his certain punishment.

Silence. He heard nothing. No screaming alarms. No hurried footsteps. No guns. He was through. He breathed, expelling his fear and inhaling an intoxicating rush he had never felt before.

Clutching his battered lunch pail, Bindra left the security gate, and set out to catch the afternoon bus. Even late in the day, heat still rose from the barren land, stirring the dry air into hot, gusty whirlwinds that whipped across the desert, spitting gritty dirt against the weathered buildings of the Haarkenborg Mining Company. Bindra's eyes stung. He pulled the brim of his hat low, leaned forward, and walked against the wind, following the same dirt road he had walked twice a day for as long as he could remember.

The bus was late, as usual, but not yet full. Bindra climbed the steps, bypassed open seats and walked to the rear. Today he needed to keep the other passengers in sight. He felt his nostril throbbing with the pressure of the stolen diamond. No one ever talked on the bus and that suited him well today. He heard only the wind-driven debris sounding like rain pelting the sand-etched windows. But rain rarely came to Namaqualand.

Bindra looked out through hazy glass windows. The chaos of a million scratches fogged his view. He saw the blur of a gnarled tree clinging to the parched, ochre earth, bent by the constant wind, framed by the blue haze of the sky. Only the strong survive, he thought. The tree had no choice but to suffer through the hardships of this unfortunate location where its seed took root. But Bindra was a man. He could choose where his roots would grow. He was not yet twenty and not yet ready to surrender to a life of near slavery in the mines.

Three miles east, along the Diamond Coast, lay Port Nolloth, a city of bland uniformity. Dirty, dilapidated buildings, most little more than shacks, lined a haphazard network of unpaved streets.

Bindra looked out across the undulating rows of rusting corrugated rooftops spread across the land like an endless ocean of poverty and despair. Passengers on this bus looked like those on all the others. Dark, tired, brown faces perched atop drooped shoulders, bobbed in weary regiments as the aged machine bounced its way toward town. Each face held empty eyes peering out from empty lives.

Today, Malleet Bindra's eyes were filled with the anticipation of a new life. His heart still raced, sending blood throbbing into his nose where the key to his future lay secretly embedded. It was only slightly larger than a marble, yet the diamond possessed the power to deliver him from his hellish and hopeless existence.

The bus rattled through Port Nolloth, retracing the morning route, dropping miners as it went. Bindra got off earlier than usual. He knew where he had to go. Stepping out of sight in a dirt alley, Bindra bloodied his nose as he pried the jagged stone from his nostril. He wiped his face with his grimy sleeve and used his dirty shirt tail on the diamond. Grinning, he examined his treasure. He had done it. A twelve carat, uncut jewel was his and he knew where to sell it.

Barely six feet separated the crumbling walls of the buildings framing the alley. Bindra's destination stood at the end of the broken concrete path. A dented, metal Coca-Cola sign hung above the doorway. The doorknob had long since disappeared, replaced by a battered, red-handled Craftsman screwdriver whose rusted, steel shaft had been stuck through the square hole of the lockset. Bindra grabbed the tool and turned it. The warped door sprang opened when the bolt cleared the strike, relieving the tension that held it closed.

"Not open," a voice called out.

"I'm here to see the man they call the Beggar," Malleet said.

"And who are you?" a gravelly voice asked in measured words from behind the bar.

"My name is Malleet. Najim is a friend of ours."

"Najim?"

"I worked with him at the mine."

The man with the rasping voice stood and walked to the far side of the room and retrieved a chair.

"Sit," he said.

Bindra obeyed. His eyes began to adjust to the dim light. He could now see the whites of the man's eyes and the rows of bottles behind him.

"I have something." Bindra hesitated. "Something I want to show the Beggar. Is he here?"

"You found him."

Bindra took an anxious look past the empty tables. It was still early. In an hour or so, miners would wander in, washed up and thirsty following a hard, hot day of labor. From the deep shadows he saw the slow movement of an immense man eclipse the light of a dirty window.

"My partner," the Beggar said.

Bindra nodded, reached into his shirt pocket, withdrawing his diamond, and placed it on the table. The Beggar fingered the stone, cradling it in his calloused hand, assessing the weight. He stood and Bindra lurched forward to stop him. The massive hand of the Beggar's partner pressed Bindra back into his chair, not in anger, but with authority.

Switching on a light behind the bar, the Beggar pressed a jeweler's loupe into his eye socket and examined Bindra's prize. He withdrew a balance scale from a drawer and weighed the stone.

"A pink. And a large one at that," the Beggar said. "Well done, indeed."

Outside, twilight had calmed the evening air, but Bindra felt the oppressive heat of the day still radiating from the concrete walls in the narrow alley. He reached down and caressed the lump of cash bulging in his pocket. It was more money than he would earn in ten years working in the mines.

7

His mind bounced from one thought to another. He had never allowed himself to think about the time that would follow. Before today, he was consumed with how he would do it, how he would steal the diamond, the dangers, the fear. And now it was done.

He thought of his life before today. The fifteen year memory of the accident that killed his parents came flooding back to him. The police said the brakes on the bus failed. In his mind, Bindra could see the narrow mountain road. He could see his father standing in the crowded aisle. He remembered the sensation of weightlessness as the bus slipped over the edge of the ravine. He could still feel the surreal free-fall as the bus plummeted.

When they hit the rocks, he heard the concussion as the bus crushed itself and most of the passengers to death. But he did not see his father smash through the windshield. His head was cushioned against his mother's breasts, cradled as when he was an infant. He felt her warm embrace cushioning him from the impact, protecting him with her body.

When the terrible sounds ended, he remembered how his mother had laid so still, holding him silently. He remembered thinking that everything was going to be all right. Then he felt the warm moistness of her blood wetting his shirt, her skull fractured by the steel frame of the seat in front of them. That was the part he remembered too vividly and too often. Memories of his rescue from the wreckage, his first years in the orphanage, and scattered fragments of the years before the accident lived deep in the mist of a distant thought.

Bindra stopped walking, reached into his pocket, and found his wallet. He slipped the aged photograph from a yellowed, plastic sleeve.

"What would you think of me now, Momma?" he murmured. "Today, I am a rich man."

He never heard the man step from the darkness and slip behind him. He only felt the cool steel knife blade against his throat and the crushing grip twisting his arm up between his shoulder blades.

"Move and you're dead."

Bindra felt hot breath on the back of his ear as the unseen thief snatched his wallet. He heard him pull out three crumpled bills, the remainder of his last payday at the mine. Angry, the thief threw the wallet to the ground.

"I know you got more," he demanded as he fumbled through Bindra's pockets. He jerked out the wad of bills, tearing Bindra's threadbare pants.

"Ah, yes. Thank you for being so generous," the man whispered with mock courtesy.

He punctuated his words with a hard kick that buckled Bindra's legs and sent him to the ground. Rolling over, Bindra looked up in time to see the thief, and his newfound wealth, race into the darkening streets.

Just as the thief was about to turn out of sight, a man stepped from the shadows, extended an arm the size of a tree limb and sent the thief skidding through the dust and gravel.

"That's not yours," the giant said as he retrieved Bindra's money. He grabbed the knife and snapped the blade like a dried twig.

"Go," he said, lifting the thief to his feet and shoving him down the alley.

Bindra watched the big man turn toward him. He had seen him before. He was the Beggar's partner.

"Yours," the man said, handing Bindra the cash.

Bindra nodded his thanks, not understanding why the man did not keep the money for himself.

"Were you following me?" Bindra asked.

"Watchin' you. Street's got eyes you can't see. Gotta be more careful."

The big man's voice was as deep and soothing as a well-played cello.

"Never had nothing worth stealing before."

"Your old life's over."

Bindra heard the truth in what the man said and he was just beginning to comprehend the impact of what he had done this day. The big man helped him brush the road grit from his clothes.

"What you gonna do? You got somewhere? You gotta plan?" the man asked like a concerned grandfather.

Bindra shook his head.

"Can't go back to the mine. You got family?"

"No."

"That thief's not the only one. Lotsa them in the street. They know. Everybody knows you got money now. And they know how to take it."

Bindra stared at him, still high on emotions he never knew before. The twisted mixture of fear and excitement he felt in the mine still lingered like a drug in his bloodstream. The indescribable exhilaration he felt when he cleared the x-ray and first realized the diamond was his would tantalize him for the rest of his life. His psyche would beg for more. Each hit would have to be stronger than the last. And with it came a growing rage against not just this thief who had tried to steal it all from him, but against all others who might dare to try. He took a silent vowed it would never happen again. Next time he would be ready.

"Your old life is dead," the big man said. "I can help you start a new one."

The man had proven himself to be a friend and Bindra chose to trust him.

"How?" Bindra asked.

"Go home, pack what you have, and sleep well tonight. Meet me at pier number three at sunrise."

Bindra knew nothing of what lay ahead, but he did know he would not be riding the old bus tomorrow. He would never see the inside of the mines again. Instead, a trawler waited for him, rising on the tide, its engines idling, poised to disembark for the open ocean.

2

The Present

Skeleton Island lay dead ahead. Matt Thornton steered the Zodiac straight at it. Ann sat in the bow, gazing at the water, wondering how she had let her husband talk her into a diving expedition at the crack of dawn.

He didn't need to check the navigational chart that came with the rented boat. A chart, a map, a floor plan, it didn't matter. To him they were all the same. His architect's eye and his spatial way of thinking let him memorize images easily. He determined that if he held a course toward the island until he reached the halfway point, then veered forty-five degrees left toward the open ocean, he could expect to see the rock formation known as The Bishops in a mile or so. The nimble boat cut a neat slice through the calm waters, leaving a wake that sparkled in the morning sun like a garland of crystals.

Through the clear air Matt caught sight of the tallest of the three rocks even before he reached his imaginary turning point. After again consulting his mental charts to confirm the water's depth, he turned the boat early and made a beeline for the isolated rocks that pierced the blue water a mile out from the nearest land.

As the boat closed on the rocks, the distinct shapes were revealed, the tallest rising seventy feet above the waves. Their shape gave the rocks their name. The monoliths had weathered into the curious shape of the helmet-like, pointed hats worn by bishops with the sides bulging outward and then tapering to a point at the top. Each rock was crowned with a white coating of droppings left by countless seabirds that used the formation as a resting place, safe from the heaving sea. Beyond the rocks, nothing but miles of ocean spread out to the horizon. These extremely dense rocks had withstood the erosion that crumbled the igneous rocks around them. The Bishops clung to the edge of an underwater shelf that formed the foundation of the San Pablos archipelago and marked the spot where the ocean floor plummeted to a depth of a thousand feet.

The submerged cliff was the dwelling place for a dazzling array of sea life, from crustaceans to deadly predators. Yet, despite the underwater scenery, most divers avoided the place because of the persistent rough seas. Only a few weeks each year provided smooth enough waters. And on those days, divers had to start out near dawn to avoid the afternoon winds. Islanders avoided the place not because of the waves, but because of superstition. These rocks sat within the threatening glare of the skull of Skeleton Island.

Matt slowed the boat and maneuvered toward the orange mooring ball floating on the leeward side of the pillars. He tied the boat and killed the motor. Ann looked across at Skeleton Island.

"This is not my idea of a dream vacation," she grumbled.

As sunlight began to highlight the ridges and cast shadows in the recesses of the craggy rock, an unmistakable image of a human skeleton emerged. The figure lay on its side with a portion of its hips and legs beneath the water. The skull, complete with sunken eye sockets, nose crease, and jagged fragments of teeth, lay to the left with the edge of its jaw touching the sea. The figure's shoulders and rib cage were partially submerged, with spotty clumps of vegetation growing from between its rocky, black bones. The skeleton looked as if it was rising from sleep, lifting its head, while glaring across the water.

"How many months did you spend planning this trip?" Ann asked. "And this is where you take me? I can't believe you woke me up before dawn to come out to a creepy place like this?"

"You're going to love it, Honey," Matt said.

"There's a reason nobody comes out here," she said. "James told us the stories. Weren't you listening?"

"Just a silly superstition."

"You can say what you want, but it gives me the chills."

"Don't you think these rocks are impressive?" Matt said, changing the subject. "Look how they rise straight out of the water. They'd be a class five rock climb. Look how smooth they are around the waterline where the waves have polished them. All the sharp corners are up higher. So beautiful, but imposing. There aren't any handholds. You'd have to throw a grappling hook …"

"Now rock climbing? Isn't the cave dive enough?" Ann asked as she stared up at the three stones towering in the brilliant blue sky.

"I was just thinking out loud, is all," he answered.

"Well, think about me once in a while. Matt, you do this to me all the time. Here we are on what was supposed to be a relaxing vacation and now you've talked me into scuba diving in some cave. Who knows what lives in there?"

"Okay, okay. I'm sorry," Matt said as he began to take the diving gear from the cargo locker at the bow of the boat.

"This is too dangerous, Matt. We don't know what's inside. What if the current's too strong?"

"We've been through all of that, Honey," Matt argued. "You don't have to go inside the cave. Just wait outside the entrance, where you can still see me. That's what we agreed to." He was not doing a good job of hiding his annoyance. This vacation was supposed to be something of a second honeymoon and already there was friction.

"We've got our extra tanks and our lights. We're prepared and we're here. I'm not going back to the cottage without seeing that cave," Matt said.

Still unhappy, Ann relented and let him help her with her gear. He tightened her weight belt and guided her over the side of the boat into the clear water. Matt fell in backwards and followed her swirl of bubbles. They swam near the surface while getting reacquainted with breathing through a regulator and giving themselves a chance to visually survey the terrain below the water. The base of The Bishops continued in a near vertical descent from the wave tops to the coral forest that covered the sea floor. Below the waves, the three stone peaks were joined by a shallow saddle filled with roiling surf cresting and falling in a tumult of foam. Dangerous dense growths of razor-sharp coral grew close to the surface, making swimming through the passage unimaginable.

They circled to the ocean side, floating like eagles soaring high above the sheer cliff searching for prey. Matt motioned and they began their descent. Multicolored fish hovered near them, suspended in the rising and falling water. Several large groupers hid beneath overhangs, waiting in the shadows. Matt spotted a green moray. He tugged Ann's arm and pointed to the eel's camouflaged head protruding from a crevice in the coral. Its unblinking eyes stared out while its jaws of razor sharp teeth gaped, warning of danger. A large brain coral bulged out from the rock. Hundreds of tiny fish scoured its wrinkled surface, looking for food. Great antler coral grew from every ledge of the cliff face, with arms reaching upward, creating safe places for small fish to hide from larger predators.

The two divers became creatures of the sea. A dozen translucent cuttlefish floated in formation, like UFOs above the coral. Twenty-four unblinking, saucer eyes stared with transfixed curiosity at the wet-suited swimmers and their own large, googly-eyed masks. They descended for several minutes until they reached the cave opening. Matt motioned and Ann answered with the "okay" sign. He switched on the dive lamp and sent a brilliant beam of light toward the cave floor, lighting up a school of tiny silver fish that shimmered like hundreds of sewing needles. Matt kicked his fins and entered the opening.

He swam forward a couple of body lengths to the point where the tunnel made an abrupt turn. Pausing, he twisted back and coaxed Ann to come in behind him. To his surprise, she did, her confidence growing. She caught up and reached for his hand, but grabbed it hard when something large moved between them. The curious octopus paused, as if to greet them, then jetted gracefully out of the cave, its long tentacles dangling behind.

They moved forward until the cave floor opened beneath them. Matt descended first. He released air from his buoyancy vest and drifted down between the rocks, aiming his dive lamp ahead into the abyss. The brilliant, blue-white beam sliced the inky blackness showing him the way.

Nearing the bottom, he stopped and painted the cave walls with light. To his left, the rocks were only an arm's length away. To his right, the space extended the length of a railroad car. The floor was strewn with jagged protrusions of fallen rocks, countless crevices, and hidden recesses.

When he turned further, his powerful light caught something reflective and it flashed back at him, searing his retinas. He bolted upward and banged his head against Ann, who was trailing close behind. Blinking to regain his vision, he realized he was looking at another man's dive mask less than two feet from his own. He could feel his heart pound as a rush of adrenaline surged through his body. The other diver had surprised him and the shock sent his mind racing. Matt pulled back.

The stranger stayed motionless, holding his stubborn, unblinking stare. Matt gazed back as if hypnotized, frozen in the grip of the other man's stare. The man's bulging red eyes were cold and motionless behind the foggy mask.

Ann saw the man and she clutched Matt's arm. Still, the other diver did not move. Matt struggled to regain control of his senses.

15

His initial shock was subsiding and he began to scrutinize the stranger. The blanched skin on the man's face showed no expression. His jaw was slack. No bubbles rose from the regulator hanging in his mouth. His arms floated up and out to his sides, like a skydiver. Matt raised a hand, giving a tentative wave. No response. He reached out for the man's wrist and checked for a pulse.

There was none.

- End of Preview -

If you enjoyed this preview, please order a copy of *Caribbean Ice* at your favorite ebook seller or online book store.

www.ingramcontent.com/pod-product-compliance
Lightning Source LLC
Chambersburg PA
CBHW071108250626
47159CB00002B/655